Reid Stone: Hard as Stone

J. D. James

This is a work of fiction. Names, characters, organizations, places, events, and incidents are either products of the author's imagination or are used fictitiously. Any resemblance to actual persons, living or dead, or actual events is purely coincidental.

No part of this book may be reproduced, or stored in a retrieval system, or transmitted in any form or by any means, electronic, mechanical, photocopying, recording, or otherwise, without express written permission from the author, except for brief quotations in a book review.

ISBN: 978-1-954763-24-1 (paperback)

Printed in the United States of America
Desert photo by Diego Jimenez
Cover art by SelfPubBookCovers.com/RLSather

Writing as J. D. James

Reid Stone: Hard as Stone

Writing as J. Willis Sanders

The Eliza Gray Series
The Colors of Eliza Gray
The Colors of Denver Andrews and
The Colors of Tess Gray

The Outer Banks of North Carolina Series
The Diary of Carlo Cipriani
If the Sunrise Forgets Tomorrow
Love, Jake

Readers: at the end of this book, please enjoy the first chapter of Reid Stone: Red Rage, coming later in 2022.

Reid Stone: Hard as Stone

1

Slap-slap, slap-slap.

Reid's running shoes struck the sidewalk in a distance-eating jog. Her ponytail bounced a steady rhythm against her back. Sweat ran down her neck.

She passed the familiar telephone pole, studded with rusty thumbtacks that secured tattered posts. A half mile to go.

Her arms pumped in short, piston-like strokes. Her breaths came in quick, explosive bursts. A car passed, leaving bitter exhaust in its wake. The searing south Texas sun beamed down, causing more perspiration to form, trickling down her spine and into the hollow of her back.

She rounded the corner to her street and raised her pace to a sprint. Fifty yards later she entered her driveway. At the front porch, she wiped stinging sweat from her eyes and checked her watch. Not a bad time for ten miles. She scuffed the first step with her shoe. But she normally would've done better.

In the kitchen, she drank ice water, sending a flash of cold down her throat. She rubbed the frigid glass across her forehead, face, and neck, and drank again, crushing ice between her teeth.

The phone rang.

Reid slammed the glass to the counter, sending a chip clattering across the kitchen floor. As she threw the piece of glass in the trash, the answering machine beeped.

"Reid, I need you to come in." A pause. "And I mean right now." Another pause. "Come on, Reid, answer the—" A heavy breath huffed into the phone's mouthpiece. "I guess you're out. Come to my office when you get this." A third pause. "And I mean *directly* to my office." The handset clattered to its holder.

Jeff. Uptight. Worried about losing his job like she was worried about losing hers.

Reid left for the shower. The phone rang again, stopping her.

"Make sure you bring your badge and service weapon."

She started to aim her extended middle finger at the phone. Instead, she went to her bedroom dresser, where the photo of her parents comforted her. Mom would tell her to hold her head high, that she had only been trying to protect women who couldn't protect themselves. Dad would tell her she had nothing to be ashamed of, that he was proud of her for caring about others enough to stop such a tragic thing as human trafficking.

Reid dropped to the bed. What a mess her life was. Forty-years-old, about to lose her job, no love life to speak of, never married, no kids.

She stood. Like Mom and Dad would say if they were alive, time to end the pity party. Life owes you nothing but what you make of it, now go make something of it.

Wearing faded jeans, a white button up men's shirt, and a scuffed pair of black western boots, she holstered her service weapon for the last time, slipped her badge into her pocket, and backed out of the driveway in her dad's pickup.

About halfway into the drive, she passed a pair of motorcycles, the type enthusiasts drove on extended trips, with hard-cover compartments on each side and another behind the two seats resembling easy chairs. She had considered purchasing one for the longest time. She would consider it no more. With no job and no federal pension if they charged her, she could no longer budget 25,000-dollar luxuries.

Twenty minutes later, in the busy halls of U. S. Immigrations and Customs Enforcement in El Paso, agents passed her. How many were aware of what had happened, or was it being kept quiet? Likely the latter. Her superiors wouldn't want this problem getting out, meaning she would likely be made the fall *woman* to keep it hidden.

She knocked on Jeff's door. His muffled voice said to come in. Reid closed the door behind her, something he would certainly want. His eyes met hers. She returned his stare. Sure, he was her boss, and a good boss, which meant he deserved her respect, but she deserved respect too. If she had to pull it from his eyes with her own stare, she damn well would. After all, Mom and Dad would demand it.

"How's this going down? I know I'm losing my job, anything else?"

"I have no choice, Reid. You can't shoot someone regardless of the situation and expect to avoid consequences." Jeff snatched his reading glasses off and dropped them to the desk. "You're getting off easy. I kept it quiet and kept you from being charged."

Reid's heart rate rose a notch. He hadn't even offered her a seat. Make it short, sweet, and final. Might as well have her say and get it over with.

"This is bull and you know it. You're forcing me out after fifteen years because I took a human trafficker out of the criminal food chain. No, let me rephrase that—a piece of *scum* human trafficker out of the criminal food chain. Dammit, what choice did I have? You know he was paying an agent off, or maybe even more than one. We can't get them, but he won't kidnap women and bring them here any—"

Jeff slammed his palm on the desk. "Enough! You don't know that's what was going on and I won't hear it anymore. If something like that got out to the press—"

"You'd lose your job like I'm losing mine. Don't my years of service count as much as yours? I'll lose my pension, so what the hell am I supposed to do for retirement?"

"You must not have heard me say your pension is safe because you're not being charged."

Reid's heart rate slowed. He was right. Her situation could have been worse—a *lot* worse. Best to take what she could while she could, and since her pension was safe, she knew exactly how to do that very thing. She placed her service weapon and badge on his desk and offered her hand. "I'm sure that put you at risk."

Jeff released her hand. "Any idea what you're going to do now?"

She smiled—the first in too long a time. "I know *exactly* what I'm going to do now."

In the locker room, after deciding nothing was worth taking, Reid tore the taped pictures from the inside of her locker door. Pictures of her shaking hands with Jeff while receiving her last three promotions. Pictures of her holding the last shooting trophy she had won by besting all two hundred agents in her division. Pictures of her in a Mixed Martial Arts outfit, green eyes blazing, long auburn hair in twin braids over her shoulders, abs, forearms, and biceps ripped with muscle. She had trained for a year and tried a few bouts just to see if she could, but gave it up when no one wanted to spar with her. Funny how they didn't like knife-edged elbows slashing into their ears, sledge-hammer knees knocking them out, or lightning-fast kicks bruising their thighs and calves. And those were the men who wore protective padding. The women just watched, shaking their heads. Then, in her second bout, when she had splattered the nose of the trash-talking loudmouth with a devastating knee while securing her with a Muay Thai clinch, the resulting plastic surgery had never made the trash talker look quite the same again, leaving Reid with no competitor who wanted to take a chance on ending up in the same condition.

She dumped the photos in the trash and squinted as she entered the sun's heat outside. August in El Paso. What a hell hole. A hell hole she had loved working in for fifteen years. At least one son-of-a-bitch Coyote would never kidnap another woman in Mexico and bring her to Texas to sell for prostitution again.

Reid breathed in the warm air, heavy with the fragrance of several rose bushes planted by the steps leading down to the sidewalk.

Had she smelled them before today? If not, what could that mean? She picked one, trimmed the thorns with her pocketknife, and slid the stem behind her ear. As she strode toward her dad's pickup, boot heels striking a rhythm on the sidewalk, a line from the song *A Yellow Rose in Texas* came to mind.

No, she wasn't going to see Texas because she was already here, but she needed some time away to figure out her life, which would only happen when that new Honda Gold Wing carried her somewhere else, preferably far, far away.

2

Reid burped the flavor of greasy pepperoni. A week on the road and she still hadn't found a decent pizza. They all either had too much or not enough cheese, too much or not enough pepperoni, and so far, they all swam in nasty, red grease. She would be out of Texas soon. Maybe another state would do better.

She took one last swallow of ice water with lemon, left money and a tip on the table at the hole-in-the-wall pizza joint, and went outside, where her Gold Wing sat in the scorching sun. Climbing on the seat gained her an uncomfortably warm rear end. Too hot to ride now.

Rear end off the hot seat and helmet removed, she eyed the sign at a pool hall down the street. The red L flickered between POOL and POO, making her grin. She didn't know whether her quirky sense of humor was a curse or not, but laughter was rarely a bad thing. Why not let the shade gradually easing toward her from the buildings across the street cool the Gold Wing's seat while she tried her hand at cue ball geometry?

Inside, Reid paused to let her eyes adjust to the dim light. A patron never knew who might lurk in these seedy places. A beer-bellied bartender, white T shirt stained with who knew what, nodded her way. Several tables, a few with men tossing back mugs of beer, were scattered about. No peanut shells on the floor, but the stench of sweat and aftershave hung in the air, warmed by testosterone-filled male bodies. To the right, in a space to itself, two unused pool tables beckoned.

Reid inserted quarters in the slot and shoved the chrome mechanism in. Balls left the inner confines of the table and battered their way out. She chose a cue stick from a nearby rack, chalked it, and returned the stick to the rack. The ice water from the pizza place had gone straight through. In the restroom, while drying her hands, the sound of male voices caught her attention. Maybe someone was racking up at the other table. When she opened the door, three guys had racked up the balls at her table, and one, the tallest of the three, picked up the sugar-cubed sized square of blue chalk.

Reid remained in the darkened alcove outside the restrooms.

Tall Guy, with black sideburns to his jaw, could've passed for Elvis, except he was stick-thin, unlike Elvis in his later years. Elvis didn't keep his hair that greasy either, nor did he keep a leather case on his side with a folded knife, one brass end shining in the light over the table. To the left of the table stood a five-five runt with a blond crew-cut, upper arms bared because of his rolled-up sleeves. To the right stood a guy with no distinguishing attributes, except his beady, black eyes that focused on Reid. "Hey, there, Red. How 'bout joinin' us fer a game of strip pool?"

"Damn straight," Runt said. "Think you can handle three against one?"

Elvis finished chalking his cue stick. "Don't mind these bozos. From the looks of a woman like you, you like one man at a time." He grabbed his crotch. "Think you can handle this?"

Reid left the shadows of the alcove, chose a stick, and pointed it at Elvis's crotch. "You can either pay me for my game or lose that miserable excuse for a penis that barely makes a bulge in your jeans."

"It ain't bulging right this minute. When you start doing what I want you to do" —Elvis licked his lips— "it will."

Reid rested the rubber tipped end of the stick at her feet. Leave or not? Hell no. She was a woman of principles, and these jerks needed to have a run-in with a woman of principles. She sidled up to Elvis and leaned near his ear. "When I found out my last boyfriend was an asshole like you, know what I did?"

Elvis took a step back. "How'd you find out he was an asshole? He smack you around like I'm gonna do if you call me asshole again?"

Reid tapped a fingertip to her chin. "If I remember correctly, and I do, he was in no shape to slap anyone with all that blood coming from what was left of his scrawny excuse for a penis I cut off. He should've known better than to go to sleep drunk with a woman of principles waiting for him with a butcher knife."

"Bull. Law woulda hauled you in."

"Don't know 'bout that," Runt said. "If that happened to me, I wouldn't want no one to know, wouldn't you, Mack?"

A snort came from Beady Eyes. "I always thought you was as dumb as you was short. She ain't cut nothin' off no one. She's just actin' like she did."

"Wouldn't put it past her," Runt said. "Wouldn't you, Mack?"

"Both you idiots shut the hell up." Elvis—now Mack—took his cue stick to the other table. "Take your game and be damned." Runt and Beady Eyes left too, not wanting to risk losing their miserable excuses for their manhood either.

Reid found the stick she had chalked earlier and broke the balls. Three dropped, two in the far-left pocket and one in the right-side pocket. Between shots at the other table, the men huddled their heads together. Done with the game, they threw their sticks on their table and went to the bar for beer, where they continued to huddle and watch her.

Reid racked up several more games, keeping an eye on the men until they left. Game after game the balls fell while the bar emptied, until the bartender came over. "Time to close." He pointed at a clock over the bathroom alcove. "You sure must love you some pool."

Reid compared her watch to the clock. Twelve in the morning. Where had the time gone?

Outside, the humid night air, almost like a warm, wet blanket, surrounded her. Here, near Laredo, further south than El Paso, it was even warmer. Being September, why couldn't Texas have a decent fall and cool off a little? She would probably work up a sweat during the walk back to the pizza place, where the Honda Gold Wing's reflectors gleamed under the street lights. At least her greasy burps had ended.

As she strolled down the sidewalk and neared an alley, the sound of a tin can rolling on concrete reverberated from its dark mouth. A cat bulleted from the opening, stopped across the road beside the Gold Wing, and eyed her with yellow, shining eyes. It arched its back, faced the alley to hiss, and streaked down the sidewalk—a dark gray blur against the lighter concrete.

When Reid neared the center of the alley, Mack, Runt, and Beady Eyes materialized from the shadows. Mack walked around her and into the street. "You didn't really think we was through with you, did you?"

Runt and Beady Eyes stood on either side of her. They were boxing her in, attempting to force her into the alley.

Reid said nothing. The three men stepped forward: mistake one. She obliged them by backing into the alley.

Mack pulled the knife from the holster and flicked it open. Four-inch blade at least. Deadly as hell.

Mistake two: bringing a lethal weapon into play. Did they deserve a chance? No, they deserved nothing. Regardless, she would give them that chance.

"Look guys, how about we just chalk up what happened in the bar to experience and head home?" She placed her hands on her hips and hooked her thumb beneath her shirttail, where the Glock 19 waited in its holster. "No need in getting roughed up over a comment at a pool table."

Runt spat and hitched his pants. "Who the hell are you to think about roughing anybody up? You might be tall, but you ain't nothing but a high-headed bitch that don't want to hang with guys like us. Screw you."

"Damn good idea," Beady Eyes said. "Not that I need reminding."

Mack pointed the knife at Reid. "What's it gonna be bitch? Goin' down easy or goin' down hard?"

Mistake three.

Reid drew the Glock. Sixteen rounds, thirteen too many.

Movement from Runt on her left. Something chrome in his hand, shining in the dim streetlight and coming up fast. Instinct took over. She centered the green and glowing tritium front site on his chest and fired—switched targets in time to see Mack lunging forward, knife gleaming. The Glock roared. Movement from Beady Eyes on her right, the gun a black mass in his hand nearly all the way up. She fired and he joined his friends, three piles of trash ruining the alley.

Reid holstered the Glock. Sweat ran down her neck. Gun smoke stung her eyes. She leaned against the alley wall. The adrenaline burned, almost the worst she had ever experienced, and it needed to stop. People would be coming. No way anyone could ignore all that gunfire. Better get her head on straight for the inevitable questions by the police.

Five minutes passed. No shoes pounded the sidewalk. No yells of "Who's shooting out there?" No sirens. She left the alley, knees slightly weak. The street was as quiet as a trail coming across the U.S.-Mexico border at dawn, minus the occasional armadillo rustling in the brush or coyote yipping in the distance. She checked her cell phone and cursed under her breath. One of those signal-less anomalies. She cursed again. She wasn't about to wait here all night. The bar, was it still open? She strode across the street to the Honda for a better look. The bar's neon CLOSED sign shone in the window, the D flickering off and on. The D went out altogether, a blackened and dead D. CLOSE? Damn straight, a good reason to be armed, especially for a woman. Maybe the bartender went out a back way and missed all the excitement.

Reid took a seat on the Honda and considered the three bodies lying half-in and half-out of the alley. With her recent law enforcement troubles, she would like to avoid more if possible. If not for the bullets, the only evidence connecting her to the shooting, she could —

She ran across the street and checked the backs of each man. The nine-millimeter hollow point bullets had left gaping exit holes in the shirts of Mack and Beady Eyes, who were rail-thin. The bullet even exited the short and squat Runt, leaving a particularly bloody mess beneath him on the concrete. The bullets couldn't be used as evidence against — Yes, they could, if the cops found them.

She took her shooter's stance at about where she had stood before and sighted behind where each corpse lay. First, she walked in line with Runt's body, on a path toward a fire hydrant on this side of the street, directly under a street light. She stopped and snatched the bullet from the sidewalk. It was mushroomed and dented, as if it had nicked a rib. She dropped it into her jeans pocket.

Time for Beady Eyes. She found the fully mushroomed bullet on the sidewalk beside a sign post. Must have gone straight through the heart and lungs and hit the post. Talk about lucky.

She checked the path that lined up with Mack's body and walked a line between him and the Gold Wing. No bullet appeared. She walked it again, this time stooping over. No matter how hard she looked, she couldn't find the bullet. Ricochet maybe, but that would mean—

At the motorcycle, she checked the entire side facing Jake's body and found nothing there either, meaning it hadn't hit the bike and fallen to the asphalt. The reasonable theory? If *she* couldn't find it, the police couldn't find it, and since the police couldn't find it, she was gone.

Leather jacket on, hair tucked in the collar to avoid tangles, Reid donned the helmet and cranked the Honda, only to curse and immediately kill the engine. Better find the three spent casings ejected from the Glock. She put on her riding gloves and found the shining brass cylinders. After verifying Runt and Beady Eyes' pistol calibers as 9mm, she wiped the casings in case of fingerprints, pressed them into each man's thumb and index fingers to add their fingerprints, and dropped two beside one body and one beside the other. There was no telling how many crimes the three men had committed, likely victimizing untold numbers of women like they had almost victimized her. They damn well wouldn't victimize any more, like they would if they hadn't run into someone who was willing to stop them.

Bullets in her pocket and safe from prosecution, Reid set off down the two-lane, the soft rumble of the Honda Gold Wing echoing back from the buildings. Sure, some people would criticize a former law enforcement officer for planting evidence, but those people hadn't almost been raped. Too few people, her dad had said, possessed the perspective to judge a situation they weren't in, and this was one of them. She'd be glad to trade boots with any of those people and let them live her life, with all of its trials, all of its tragedies, and see how they might handle it. Many would give up at her first challenge as a teenager, the evidence still on her back. She *never* would give up, regardless of what life threw at her.

A few miles later, she downshifted the Honda and pulled into the quiet hotel parking lot, where the low growl of the engine reverberated among the few cars. She parked in a spot outside her room, removed the warm helmet, and covered the bike in case of rain.

The room wasn't much, basic accommodations. Thank goodness for the air-conditioning and a shower with enough pressure to scour the stink of the road from her body. She hung the jacket on a chair and tossed her keys and slim wallet onto the dresser, added the Glock and its holster to the pile and threw her clothes on the bed.

In the cracked bathroom mirror, she touched a reddened cheek. Got to stop forgetting sunscreen while on the road. Still, not a wrinkle in sight. During her last relationship, the guy had initially thought she was thirty. He should have known better. Her last stop in a library, she had read how a woman's sex drive peaked at her age, and she had smiled in agreement. That last guy would have too, and did, even after he had learned her age. Jackass wanted to call her by her first name though. Pamela was okay, but she preferred her middle name. Reid had a flair to it, sleek and sophisticated, while Pamela was just— Well, Pamela was just Pamela.

She turned the shower on as hot as she could stand and let it stream down her back and shoulders. Steam filled the tiny stall. The tiny bar of soap, what a joke, slipped from her hand. She managed to grab it before it hit the rusty drain. When she had first trained for ICE more than fifteen years ago, her instructor at the Brunswick, Georgia, gun range told her she possessed the quickest reflexes of anyone he had ever worked with. She had nodded, unsure, but considering how quickly she had disposed of those three men, including her numerous shooting trophies, she was inclined to agree.

Reid lathered her hair with shampoo from the hotel bottle. Sometimes the length, halfway down her back, made it difficult to manage, but it framed her face perfectly, making her feel as if she were the younger woman almost every man perceived her to be. After all, when it came to men, she who mastered perception mastered the game. As much as possible she intended to control who perceived what. And when. And how. After the fiasco in El Paso, with her losing her job, and tonight, with those three idiots trying to rape her, she intended to master the game every chance she got.

Next, a coarse towel for her back, rubbing the tiny scars she preferred to ignore, and on to her long legs. The rough towel likely did a great job of exfoliating them, but they could use a razor soon.

Reid wrapped her hair in a second towel and brushed her teeth, fell into bed and started to reach for her latest paperback. Instead, she turned off the lamp and closed her eyes.

What might a new day bring? Certainly nothing to do with the police concerning those men. At the least, maybe the morning would bring a decent cup of coffee.

3

Sunlight attempted to stream through the faded hotel curtains and across Reid's face, warming her sunburned cheeks. She fingered hair from her eyes, checked the time, and rolled back over to stare at the yellowed ceiling.

She had seen a fair amount of Texas in the last few days, stopping along the border with Mexico to check various historical sites along her meandering journey. If her plans held true, North Carolina should welcome her in about two weeks. She studied the yellow highlighter mark she had made on the map from the nightstand. It traced a circuitous route through Virginia, along whatever stretches of the Blue Ridge Parkway appealed to her, and headed toward Highway 158 East.

She would work again but no time soon. Would it be law enforcement? Maybe, maybe not. Her recent experience, after doing what she had thought to be a fine job, had all but destroyed her faith in the system. Whatever. Maybe she would stay at the coast for a while, her planned-for destination in North Carolina. Become a waitress or something. Lie on the beach until the weather forced her inside.

Reid stretched. No time for a run. She could use an hour or two, since the miles on the Honda did nothing for her exercise routine. Her upper body could use gym time also. A pair of resistance bands might come in handy. Probably would fit in one of the Honda's compartments.

She slid a hand along the sheets. Dry as desert sand, which meant no nightmares. Sometimes she remembered, sometimes not, but the scars on her back and the sweaty sheets always reminded her, exactly like after her thirteenth birthday, when her mother used to remind her to keep a pad in her backpack for when her period might start. What a nightmare. As far as the other nightmare, the shrink had said they might lessen with time. They had, to an extent.

Her last clean jeans went over her last clean panties, so she would add a visit to a laundry mat to her to-do list, whenever she made a to-do list. The hotel coffee maker looked usable, but she decided against it. She had seen a diner specializing in breakfast about a mile back, so she would stop there for a quick bite. Later, since she had enjoyed her multiple pool games so much, she might try a few more. The police should have the trash in the alley taken to the morgue by now. Still, she better wait until early afternoon to make sure.

The Honda started with a turn of the key, and she allowed the engine to warm, enjoying the moment before strapping on her helmet. Even this dingy parking lot couldn't take the freshness out of the late morning air. Maybe her next overnight stop, she would pitch her small tent and camp. Sitting beneath the stars by a fire would be a great way to get ready for a good night's sleep, after a ribeye steak cooked over open coals and a beer.

* * *

Breakfast had been so-so, the coffee fine. What was it about those small diners located on the outskirts of larger towns? They almost always had great coffee.

The laundry mat was nearly empty, just a couple of moms with small kids running around, stopping occasionally to ask their moms endless questions about endless subjects. One of the moms took a book from her purse and read to her little girl. Good job, Mom, keep up the good work.

An hour later, Reid opened the dryer door. Hot air and floral dryer sheet smell hit her in the face. She piled the clothes on a sagging plastic table, started folding but stopped. A police car rolled by, slowing as the officer eyed the Honda. The car stopped and he faced the center console, probably running her plate on his PC. He pulled away a few minutes later, eyeing the laundromat. Good deal. Nothing to see. Just keep going. Don't ruin a former ICE officer's escape from Texas.

Reid finished the clothes, packed them into one of the Honda's many on-board compartments, and headed to the bar to finish her pool practice. The cops had to be done by now. Done searching the alley for clues. Done asking anyone if they had seen or heard anything. Reliable witnesses, as far as she was concerned, were a thing of the past. She had fired three times. Any supposed witness would say from one to thirty. If anyone had heard, that is. It had happened around 12:30 in the morning, and the police would be told anything from twelve until four. Again, if anyone had heard.

Reid cruised by. Not a police car in site. Except for the darkened L, the POOL sign blinked red again. Not so funny after almost being raped and having to shoot three jerks.

She parked across the street from the bar and removed the hot leather jacket. Sweat ran down the back of her neck. She fished a tie from a pocket, tied her hair in a ponytail, and crossed the street.

The place was deserted. Great, no one to ruin her day. She ordered a draft. The bartender placed the beer on the counter, along with a napkin, and considered her with curious but dull eyes. "Had some excitement last night."

Reid waited for the aggravating habit some people had of making a person ask them to continue. She waited no more. "And?"

"Had a good old-fashioned massacre in the alley down the street."

"Anyone I know?"

"If you knew the names of those three guys you pissed off, you did."

"They never properly introduced themselves. Far as I'm concerned, they were Larry, Curly, and Moe." Reid sipped beer. "Far as I'm concerned, they got what they deserved. None of them were ideal candidates for the Boy Scouts anyway."

The bartender grinned, revealing a missing tooth. "That's pretty good. Any of the Stooges ever Boy Scouts?"

"What do the cops say about this 'massacre' of yours?"

"It won't none of my doin'."

"Ever hear of something called a figure of speech?"

His expression went blank. "What's that got to do with anything?"

"Don't worry, figures of speech are harmless. You were about to tell me what the cops said?"

"Those guys had long rap sheets. Hell, they spent more time fightin' 'mongst themselves than they did gettin' along. Seen it myself plenty. They was all found dead by the guys runnin' the mornin' trash truck. One had a knife, the other two had guns. All I know." A faraway stare appeared in the bartender's eyes. "That ain't right. The cops said they found a bullet that went through one of the guys. Said they would check it out."

Reid sipped beer when she would rather curse a blue streak. How had the cops found the bullet when she had looked all over for it? Good thing she had left the Glock in hotel room. If the cops showed up and found it on her, she would be hard pressed to not allow them to take it in for ballistics testing. She had done nothing wrong in defending herself from rape, but leaving the scene of a self-defense shooting was wrong enough to ruin her plans for getting the hell out of Texas as fast as possible. Maybe the bullet was too beat up to test, and that would be the end of that.

"Any idea what kind of shape the bullet was in?"

"Damn if I know, lady. What am I, information?" He paused. "You left before they did, didn't you? See anything?"

So, this guy wasn't even sure whether she had left before the men or not. That meant the only thing linking her to the men, other than the bullet, was their interaction at the pool table.

"Nope, didn't see a thing."

The bartender eyed her. "I was wonderin'…"

"Yeah?"

"What did you tell them that made them let you be?"

"I told the tall one how my last boyfriend had to pee sitting down when I got through with him."

"Meaning?"

"You married?"

"I got an old lady. What about it?"

Reid slid the napkin from under her beer and over to him. "Can I get your address?"

"For what? And you never said why you asked if I was married. And you never said what happened to your last boyfriend, what made him need to pee sittin' down."

She drummed her fingertips on the counter. She was talking to a regular Einstein. "As far as being married, I wanted to know who I might send it to. Since you, as you say, 'have an old lady,' I want to make sure she gets it."

"Gets what?"

"The same thing I took from that last boyfriend of mine." Reid made a slicing gesture, one hand against the other. "Cut it clean off. Tends to happen to people, especially men, who ask me too many damn questions."

He took a step back. "You mean his…?"

"Anything else you need to know?" She slid the napkin closer. "I'm going to need that address if you do." The man wiped his mouth with the back of his hand and moved down the counter, where he grabbed a glass, wiped it with a grungy towel, and placed the glass under the bar. He grabbed another glass and started the sequence all over again.

Reid sipped beer. Einstein had finally figured it out. As far as the bullet, what could the cops learn from it? Regardless, if it had ricocheted, maybe hitting the street or the curb, it was possible they couldn't learn anything. Still, it could be evidence—useless evidence without her Glock. The pool table sat unused. No, the best thing she could do was get the hell out of town. She turned to leave.

Son of a—

A man, about six-two or three, entered. Dark hair, dark eyes, striped tie, pressed suit pants. Not the kind of man she expected in here. None of that caught her eye at first. The first thing was the badge attached to his belt. The next was the service weapon beside it. The last was the realization that he was a detective.

She eased back onto the bar stool and picked up the mug. Maybe he just wanted a damn beer. Wrong. Not while wearing the badge and gun he didn't.

The tap of his dress shoes on the hardwood floor came closer. He sat two stools to her left. "I understand you like pool?"

Reid kept her attention on the beer. "I think you understand wrong."

"There were a couple of people in here last night who'd have a problem with that statement."

"They were mistaken."

"They said you were pretty good."

"How would they know?"

"I guess they watched—and heard—the balls bank off the bumpers and fall into the holes. Why do you say you don't like pool?"

"I like geometry."

"Meaning?"

"Pool is geometry. Angles. Line of sight." She faced him. "I find that intriguing, more so than pool."

He placed his shoe on the rest beneath the stool between them. "One more thing I'd like to clear up." He waited for her to ask.

Damn if she would play his childish game, same as Einstein had tried. She placed her boot on the same rest opposite his shoe. "Spit it out. Since this fine establishment doesn't allow kids, act like an adult and be done with it."

"ID."

She took her wallet from her back pocket, removed her driver's license, tossed it on the counter. "See how easy being an adult is?"

He took the license. "Pamela R. Stone. The R is for …?"

"Reid. I prefer it to Pamela."

"Okay, Reid, what happened here last night?"

"I prefer Reid for people I allow to call me Reid. You aren't one of those people."

He returned the license. "About last—

"I was practicing geometry and three guys hassled me. The bartender told me they were found down the street in an alley. I guess that's why you want to know."

"Why were they hassling you? Do guys hassle you a lot?"

Reid untied the ponytail. Her hair flowed around her shoulders. His eyes opened wide. She slipped the tie in her pocket. "Some do, some don't. Wouldn't you?"

His mouth opened and closed. Thick auburn hair halfway down her back usually had that effect on men.

"I'm not into hassling anyone," he said. "I'm just trying to do my job."

"And I'm trying to finish my beer and leave town. Since you're determined to make that difficult, you might as well tell me your name."

"Detective Pete Anderson. Pete is fine for whoever. I'm pretty easygoing, unlike some people."

She stood. "So am I, as long as people—including detectives—don't ask me unsubstantiated questions. Let's hope I won't be seeing you anytime soon." She strode to the door. Being a man, no doubt he was checking her out. Too bad. Time to hit the road and watch Texas fade in the Honda's rear-view mirror.

"We found a bullet this morning, Reid. If you have a nine-millimeter pistol laying around somewhere, our ballistics guy would like to take a look at it."

4

Reid left the door, took a seat at table by the window, and kicked out the chair across from her. "Might as well sit. The quicker you finish, the quicker I can leave."

Anderson scraped the chair closer to the table and sat. "You have an interesting walk. Reminds me of the straight-up way a law enforcement officer walks."

A LEO her ass, he had checked her out while she was walking to the door like she had thought. "My walk has nothing to do with anything we're discussing." She nodded toward the bartender. "He says one of those guys carried a knife and the other two carried guns. How do you know they didn't kill each other? He also says they were known to be less than cordial concerning their interpersonal relationships. If that's the case, there's no more questions and I can leave, unless you know more than you're telling me."

"That's an interesting way to put it. 'Less than cordial concerning their interpersonal relationships.'"

"I like interesting."

Anderson placed his elbows on the table and rubbed his hands together. Good hands, clean nails, recently trimmed. She liked good hands.

He faced the window. "That your bike across the street?"

"Is it illegally parked?"

"I'd like to run your driver's license and registration. If I find nothing outstanding, you're free to ride away. Regardless, I need you to stay in town for the time being. I'd like to know where you're staying too."

Great. She hadn't found a decent place for breakfast either. Reid took her license and registration from her wallet and tossed them on the table. "I'll stay if I have to. Not forever, we clear on that?"

He left and started across the street, stopped for a passing car. His ass was okay. Maybe she should mention it and see how he liked knowing she had checked him out. No, it would probably puff up his ego even more. She took a breath. No, he didn't seem the type, so that might be an unfair assessment.

Behind the Honda, he took a small pad from his back pocket and scribbled. In his car, just like the cop at the laundromat, his hand hovered over the PC. After a bit of typing, he glanced her way. Probably found her service record, something she didn't care to discuss. There'd be no getting out of it, not without steering the conversation elsewhere.

Einstein the bartender was still wiping glasses. She raised a finger. "If you have a glass clean by now, can I get another beer?"

He dropped the towel on the counter and brought over a filled mug. "Three bucks."

She gave him a five from her wallet. "Keep the change. I ragged you pretty bad earlier."

"'Preciate it." He started to turn but stopped. "I was wonderin' 'bout your boyfriend. Did you really …?"

"I shouldn't tell you. That would spoil the intrigue."

His forehead wrinkled. "'In' what?"

"Intrigue is like a mystery. It's much more interesting to never know. Now you'll always wonder about me."

A slow smile spread across the bartender's face. "Don't take this wrong."

"I'm sure I won't."

"You'd be hard to forget anyway."

Reid raised the beer mug and returned the smile. "Thanks."

The door opened. Anderson returned to his seat, dragging warm air with him. "A clean but interesting record. One I have some questions about."

She set the mug on the table. "Have a beer."

"On duty." He offered the license and registration. "About what I found, what's this about—"

"Come on, Detective, lighten up." She returned the paperwork to her wallet. "At least have something to knock the dust of this county off your tongue. What town are we near anyway? Oh, yeah, we're on the northern outskirts of Laredo, right? While you decide what you want to drink, tell me where I can get a really good breakfast. Since you're making me stick around, I might as well make the best of it."

"You're about five miles north of Laredo. You know how it starts building up on the outskirts of bigger cities. I don't live too far from here myself. As far as breakfast, anything in particular?"

"Eggs all the ways they're good, which is any way. I'm partial to omelets—make a killer one myself. Potatoes, meaning hash browns. Shredded is okay but I prefer small squares browned in a cast iron skillet."

"Doesn't sound like you need a restaurant, sounds like you need to cook all that yourself." He licked his lips. "I haven't had a breakfast like that in a while. My wife used to—"

Reid finally had him talking about something else, so why had he stopped? "Is she a touchy subject? I still see the indentation on your finger where you wore a wedding band. I'd say it's been there quite a while."

"You're into detail, aren't you?" Anderson covered his left hand. "What happened in here last night? Before you answer, yes, she's a touchy subject. An off-limits subject."

Reid took another swallow of beer. "Didn't Einstein tell you what went down?"

"Who's Einstein?"

"The guy wiping the beer mugs and shot glasses. Must be the cleanest assortment in town."

Anderson glanced at Einstein. "I'd rather hear it from you."

"I already talked to him. His story will be my story. Word-for-word."

"You admit it?"

"I *admit* nothing, except to being intelligent enough to corroborate what he's already told you. He might tell you a bit more now, like what I told those guys that made them leave me alone."

"Why can't you tell me?"

"It won't be as amusing." She leaned the chair back on two legs and raised her hands over her head to stretch and yawn. "Go ahead. I've got all day now, dammit."

At the bar, Detective Anderson talked to Einstein in low tones, and Einstein laughed. When Anderson returned, the slightest of smiles played at the corners of his mouth. "He said you taught him a new word—intrigue—which means a mystery. I think you have a fan."

"I can live with that."

Anderson slid closer to the table. "Did you do it?"

"Cut my boyfriend's ...?"

"Yeah, Einstein—I mean the bartender—thinks you did. That there's no mystery about it."

Reid cut her eyes toward the bartender. He gave her a smile, so she returned it. "Good for him." She faced Anderson. "You?"

"From what I've learned about you in the short while I've known you, I think it's damn well possible."

She smiled again, even bigger. "That's how I like it, Detective."

"Like what?"

"Keeping men thinking I'm capable of almost anything. They're a lot less likely to take advantage of me. Or try to. About that breakfast …"

"How about dinner? Red meat, preferably rare. The horns knocked off and the moo barely silenced."

"That's a fine guess. Steak it is. Medium-rare, which is minus the 'moo.' Good salad bar, potato bar, ice-cold draft."

He gave her the same slight smile, this time with the added benefit of a faint crinkling of his dark eyes. "I think I've found my soulmate."

"Don't go there, Detective, not even as a joke."

"Because?"

"How long did you date your wife before you made that 'soulmate' comment?"

Anderson's dark eyes lost their crinkle. "I see what you mean." He glanced at his watch. "You have a phone number?"

She pursed her lips. "Want me to put some lipstick on and write my number on a napkin and kiss it for you? That's how it's normally done."

He took the pad from his back pocket and a pen from his shirt pocket. "Not necessary."

While Reid gave him her cell number, she considered his penmanship, much smoother and more elegant than the average guy. His wife probably didn't think so. Since he was a cop, a cop who had a bad history with women, well, with his wife—ex-wife maybe—why had she been flirting with him? That didn't make sense, not after she had given him such a hard time when he first came in. Who knew, but it might be a good idea to keep a potential enemy close.

"Any reason you can't put my number on your phone, or are you afraid a girlfriend might see it?"

"Not a problem." He wrote another note and gave it to her. "I hate restaurants. Do you mind dinner at my place?"

Reid checked his address. "I'm not dumb enough to turn down free food." She folded the note for her pocket. The tactic of getting Anderson's mind off of those three jerks she had left in the alley had worked perfectly. Use that angle until he either cleared her or she had to leave in the middle of the night. Then again, since he had invited her to his place, maybe all he was interested in was a replacement for his wife.

She stood. "I prefer a rib-eye. Plenty of marbling. If you overcook it, you're deader than the cow it came from."

"I'll run by the store after work. Come any time after six. That's when I'll light the grill."

Reid left the bar. At the Honda, she slipped the jacket on, making sure to tuck her hair in. Helmet on, she glanced at the bar. Anderson remained at the table, looking her way. Had him wrapped around her little finger already. Had even managed to leave without telling him where she was staying, unless he had completely forgotten about it. Figuring out which tonight, as well as what was going on between him and his wife, might be an interesting endeavor.

5

As Reid neared the hotel, she glanced at the clock on the Honda's dash. Since she had time, why not visit the mall advertised on a billboard she had passed on the way here? One of the department stores might have something special to go with her green eyes and auburn hair. Something that might interest her as well as Detective Anderson.

At the mall, she parked, locked her jacket and helmet in one of the Honda's compartments—if she kept traveling around the country, she would have to consider a trailer—and strode to the double glass doors.

Conditioned air hit her in the face, chilling damp areas on her body where the jacket had made her perspire. One of those mesh-vented jackets would come in handy for summer riding. She stopped and glanced around. Perfume and cosmetics straight ahead, as evidenced by the scents. Men's wear to the left, lady's wear to the right.

Women of all ages and sizes were sliding hangers from side to side with a clatter. She did the same at the first rack of summer dresses that caught her eye. Yellows, blues, pinks, prints, colors she had never seen—polka dots? Yuck. What color would go well with her auburn hair? She slid the next rack aside, and a green dress, almost a mini, appeared. The tag read teal. Lucky her, in her size also. She plucked the hanger and searched for a dressing room. The dress fit perfectly, accentuating her modest-sized breasts, narrow waist, slender hips, and complimenting her dark-red hair like nothing she had ever worn. Her bare feet stood out, stark white, and her toenails needed attention. Pedicure? Nope. She would pick up a clipper and polish, maybe a color similar to the dress, and shoes also.

In street clothes again, she visited the shoe section, where nothing caught her eye. When a clerk asked if she needed help, she told her she was just browsing. The woman looked her up and down and hurried away, high heels striking an aggravated tune on the white linoleum. Why were some women so damned judgmental, based on clothing or appearance or a combination of the two?

Rejecting the selections on display, Reid started opening boxes. At the third from the top, she stopped. A pair of gold high-heels with thin straps lay within the white folds of crinkly, tissue-thin paper. The label said they were a half-size small, but they didn't pinch or bind. She slipped her scuffed, black western boots back on, tucked the box under her arm, and strolled the store, picking out the rest of the items on her mental list.

A cashier on the other side of the perfume department stood at the ready. Reid headed that way, pausing to spritz a few samples of the slightly sweet but alcoholic scents on her wrists. She sniffed a variety, and nothing appealed to her. At the last counter, she tried a brand advertised for teens. The scent, like something she might have worn twenty-five years ago, when she experienced her first kiss at a friend's neighborhood dance, reminded her of yellow roses. The boy, whose name was Jeff or James—something with a J—had been so nervous, he had kissed her on the cheek. She told him to be still, because that wasn't how a first kiss was supposed to be. She didn't tell him she had read that in one of her teenage romance magazines. The kiss hadn't lasted long, and Jeff or James or whoever he was had taken off to a group of boys, apparently to tell them he had scored. Where had the time—

"Ma'am, can I help you?"

A young girl, likely not much older than Reid in her daydream, smiled, perfectly plucked eyebrows rising. Reid didn't see a new bottle of the perfume on the counter, so she pointed at the sample. "Do you have this, but new?"

The girl took a new bottle from beneath the counter. "Getting something for your daughter?"

"Pardon?"

"You're about thirty, thirty-five, right? You have a daughter, maybe around ten. Lots of younger girls like this scent."

Reid blinked her eyes once, narrowed them, and leaned across the counter. "Let's just say I'm young at heart."

The intimidating stare worked perfectly. The girl took a step back. "I didn't mean— Well, I hope I look as nice as you do when I'm your age."

"Let's hope you look as nice as I do when you're forty, young lady. Proud of every year."

"Wow, I would have never guessed you're—"

"I'm sure." Reid took the perfume and spun away. Yes, just where *had* the time gone?

In the sweltering Texas sun again—too damn hot, even in September—she loaded the bags on the Wing, the name that Honda Gold Wing enthusiasts called their oversized toys. She considered the jacket, but that would be like wrapping herself in an electric blanket. It wasn't far to the hotel, so she left it packed away. Helmet on, face shield raised to catch any available breeze, she left the parking lot. The Honda growled contentedly as she ran through the gears.

She hadn't seen much of the city—she hadn't even realized she was near Laredo when she had checked into the hotel—so she drove along the outskirts, sometimes entering an inviting side street.

On one such lane, kids played in a yard. On another, people led their dogs along shaded sidewalks. On yet another, someone's mom must be cooling some kind of fruit pie—apple, maybe peach—on a window sill. Did people still do that?

Further down the street, a mower revved, its engine popping, and she ran through an invisible wall of cut-grass aroma. It was like stepping back in time to her childhood, to when she and Mom baked cookies and when Dad made time after dinner to play catch. She loved those memories because they were all she had left of her parents. All that mattered. The house was still hers, and she had a decent income from her inheritance and her dad's life insurance. That and the money she had saved from her job would easily get her by until she needed—or wanted—to work again.

Reid checked the digital clock on the Gold Wing's dash and drove in the general direction of the motel. After a few twists and turns, she ended up behind a car that had to be a near antique. Not only was it old, dust covered its drab green surface. She wouldn't have been able to tell the color if it hadn't been daytime. Dust even covered the license plate, the letters a reddish-brown blur. Maybe this guy had taken a wrong turn too. He must live outside of town for the car to be so filthy.

The neighborhood grew rundown. Broken windows of abandoned houses stared accusingly. Grass tall as hayfields. One white frame structure partially caved in. At the next corner stood two women, both dressed in short skirts and high heels, a man beside them. As the filthy car moved closer, the women strutted back and forth while swinging their hips. The guy, likely their pimp, pointed at the old car, and the women wiggled into the street.

The car slowed to a stop. Through the dingy back glass, Reid tried making out the head of the man inside. Gray hair? Probably bought the car new and wore it out like he was worn out. No way he would pick up one of the prostitutes. Maybe he wanted to ask directions so he could find his way back to wherever he lived.

The two girls said something through the open window, and the man leaned out. Yes, old, both hair and beard steel gray. He waved the pimp over, who eased toward the car. The old man jabbed his hand out the window with something black in it. Three quick pops followed. The girls screamed and took off, high heels flying in the air. The pimp fell in a heap beside the sidewalk, hands scraping at the asphalt while his feet scrabbled for a foot hold on the reality of having a bullet—or bullets— piercing his body.

The filthy car accelerated. A cloud of choking blue exhaust trailed it down the street and around a corner. Reid pulled the clutch lever. Go after the old guy or not? Not. She hadn't ridden the huge Honda long enough to commit to a high-speed chase through narrow streets. Besides, the idea of one less guy who made a living off of human trafficking appealed to her.

The pimp lay still. She dropped the kickstand and checked him. Two holes in the chest, blood pooling beneath him, eyes open and glassy. If he were alive, he wouldn't last for an ambulance. Had the girls called one? That was probably the last thing on their minds. Reid climbed back onto the Honda. No need to stick around and see if they had.

She made her way through the streets until she found the main drag where the hotel was located. Ten minutes later, when she unlocked the door, the alarm clock's red numbers changed to 5:00. According to the address Anderson had given her, and the GPS on the Honda, it would take thirty minutes to get to his place. He probably wouldn't mind if she showered and changed there. She bagged her purchases and bathroom items, stowed them on the Honda, and climbed aboard.

On the way, she recalled the shooting. Why would an old man shoot a pimp? It looked like an execution. Maybe he had a daughter who worked for the guy, and he wanted her out of that lifestyle. She could see that. She would've done the same thing.

It had been one of the strangest things she had ever seen, and she had seen—and been a party to—a lot of strange things— things Anderson would likely bring up tonight since he had run a background check on her. She would deal with it. She had nothing to hide and not a damn thing to be ashamed of.

Anderson's neighborhood consisted of a row of unoriginal houses on both sides of a narrow, shaded lane. Mowed lawns, shrubbery, and family sedans parked in short driveways lined each side of the road. Up ahead on the right, a mailbox with Anderson's address—black numbers on a white surface that could use another coat of paint—extended from an overgrown bush of some kind. She parked beside a full-sized four-door pickup in front of a closed garage. Huh, she had him pegged for a sedan. Something reasonable. Something safe. The front door opened. Anderson, in shorts and a T shirt, a towel around his neck, walked out.

"This is a first. Anytime I've ever asked a woman to be somewhere at a certain time, she was at least thirty minutes late, not early."

Reid removed the helmet. "Complaining or complimenting?"

"Complimenting. Come on in. I took a run and need to clean up."

She took two bags from the bike. "If you've got a guest room and a shower, I'd like to do the same. I didn't want to ride over in anything decent."

He opened the door. "Hot water might be a problem. You know, since we'll be showering at the same time. You won't shoot me if you run out, will you?"

She considered the obvious comeback: if they showered in the same bathroom at the same time, they would have plenty of hot water, but she decided against it. "I haven't shot anyone lately. Might need to. It's been a while since I got my violent tendencies out of my system." She followed him down a hall.

He stopped at a bathroom. "This is it." He tapped a closed door opposite the bathroom. "Guest room's here." He pointed down the hall. "Towels and washcloths in the closet if you need any more. Anything else?"

She looked in one bag and frowned. "I forgot my razor. Mind if I use one of yours for my legs?"

"You're kidding. That would mean we were engaged, or at least sleeping together."

She entered the bathroom. "I wanted to see if I could get a rise out of you." His mouth opened but he didn't say anything. She smiled and locked the door behind her. The sound of his footsteps faded down the hall.

Would he lock his bathroom door? Probably. After all, he had questioned her about killing those three guys. Since that was the case, why invite her to dinner? Then too, why hadn't she asked herself those questions earlier today? She shrugged and looked in the mirror.

Her hair lay flat and limp from the helmet. She sometimes braided it but not now. Her skin looked great, just a few freckles that had appeared since she had started traveling on the Honda, despite sunscreen. Might have to step up the SPF rating, especially for her nose. Eyebrows could use a light plucking, but she hadn't brought tweezers. She would do it soon. No one she knew, including herself, cared for the uni-brow look.

In the shower, the water sprayed ice cold, raising goosebumps and forcing her to step from the stream until it warmed.

Anderson.

Had he taken her comments as overly flirtatious? As much as she enjoyed sex, she was extremely choosy about it. Careful too. As far as safety, safe sex hovered at the top on her list of priorities, zooming to number one when necessary. A guy had to be intelligent and decent looking too. Being well-read was a plus.

The water streamed over her with delicious warmth. Shampoo twice. Conditioner, just a touch. Her hair tended toward oily, and too much conditioner made it worse. She lathered a washcloth and scrubbed herself from head to toe, shaved her legs and rinsed. Good thing, because the water had turned cold like earlier. Men liked to complain about women using all the hot water. Yeah, right.

She climbed out, wrapped a towel around her hair, and glared at the fogged mirror. She had forgotten to turn the exhaust fan on, and it was too late now. It was damned difficult to get completely dry in a bathroom when it steamed like a sauna.

She wrapped a towel around herself, intending to make a dash across the hall to the guest room, and peeked out the door. The sound of a shower came from the room down the hall. Uh-huh, using every last warm drop. Good, that would allow her to slip across. In the hall, the wood floor chilled by the AC cooled her feet. She turned the doorknob; the door wouldn't budge. She bumped it with her hip and it moved. She bumped it again and her towel fell off.

Anderson opened the door at the end of the hall, wearing a robe. "Problems?"

Reid turned sideways and crossed her arms over her breasts. "So much for you being a gentleman, gawking at me."

"Took my contacts out. All I see is a flesh-colored blur, honest. Why didn't you grab a towel?"

"I was wrapped in one until it fell off while I was trying to get this stuck door open." She stepped backward, dragged the towel with her foot into the bathroom, and shut the door. Contacts her ass. "Just open the door."

He thumped the door open. "Yep, it sticks on occasion."

"Why this occasion?"

"Lucky I guess. Be back in a few."

She peeked again and slipped across the hall, shoved the door closed and locked it. He could open it again if it stuck.

With her body dry, she used the towel on her head to squeeze the leftover moisture from her hair. The air conditioning must be going full blast. She shivered as goose bumps rose on her skin worse than in the shower. Too bad she didn't have a blow dryer. She could use it on her arms and legs before her hair.

She slipped on panties clean from the laundromat. The new dress. Shoes. Checked herself in the mirror on back of the door. Not bad, even with damp hair. She unlocked the door and shoved it open. In the bathroom, she found a hair dryer under the sink. "Thanks, Mrs. Anderson, wherever you are."

The steam had cleared. She plugged the dryer in and finished her hair. Much better. Full, soft, and entirely too sexy. She eyed her reflection. Nothing would happen tonight. Not a thing. Get to know him. See why he asked her over. Take it from there.

Tomorrow night, however, or maybe the next.

She ran a brush through her hair once more, holding the ends to get every inch, and looked in the mirror again.

She had almost forgotten about the old man shooting the pimp and would have to ask Anderson about it. That kind of thing intrigued her.

6

While Reid put the hairdryer away, Anderson stopped at the door. "I see you're making yourself at home."

"I see you found your glasses. Good thing."

"Why's that?"

She followed him down the hall. "It might mean you were telling the truth. Who knows, you might even turn out to be a gentleman. Still, it's too soon to be absolutely sure."

They entered a kitchen, where he opened a refrigerator. "Ready for a beer?"

She twisted the cap off the offered bottle, dropped it into a trash bin by the end of a counter, and took a long swallow of the cold, deliciously-bitter liquid. "This was next on my agenda, after the hair dryer. Would your wife mind me using it?"

"I'd prefer we leave my wife out of the conversation." He opened his own bottle with a quick, savage twist.

She held out her hand for the cap. "Sorry. I usually think before I speak. At least when I'm working up an especially cutting sarcastic remark."

He dropped the cap into her palm. "Seems like you haven't had to think up any of those remarks since you got here."

"I do my best work under stress." She leaned against the counter and crossed her ankles.

"You were stressed at the bar but not in the hall?" he asked. "Getting caught nude by a stranger, I'd think, would be something to stress over. I noticed all your smart commentary fell in the floor with your towel."

"Very observant. I still haven't decided if you were lying about seeing me."

"Flesh colored blur."

"Detective, don't you think it's time to light that grill I see in the back yard through the window over the sink?"

He offered his hand. "My friends call me Pete."

"I guess Reid will do." She took his hand and let go. "Until you start asking about those three guys. Then it'll be Ms. Stone."

He took a pack of steaks from the refrigerator and placed it on the counter. "Open these and put them on a couple of paper towels, okay? Plates are in the cabinet behind you." He aimed a thumb to his right. "Paper towels over there." At the door he faced her. "I'll get the grill going."

"How about a knife to cut this plastic? I assume I can help myself to another beer."

"In the drawer by the sink. You know where the beer is." He closed the door and left her alone in a stranger's house. Were they strangers now? Didn't seem likely, not after the hallway incident.

Strangers or not, she intended to get answers to more than a few questions this evening, like why Pete had invited her and why she had accepted so easily. Unless it really was because she wanted to "keep the enemy close," as she had told herself at the bar.

She tended to the steaks, swallowed the last of the beer, and opened another.

What if Pete's glasses were for reading only? If they were, that meant his far vision was fine, that he didn't wear contacts, and that he had seen her as naked as the day she had been born. Not that she needed the compliment, but he hadn't mentioned how she looked. In her estimation she looked great, especially with the new dress and shoes. Maybe he wore contacts and needed new ones, or maybe whatever was going on with his wife, a huge question mark, still affected him.

She stepped to the window. He knelt in the shade of a tree, fiddling with something beneath the grill.

A wooden deck. Fair sized backyard. No swings usually meant no kids. No toys either. Yard had been mowed recently. The lot was small, so he had likely used a push mower.

On the other side of the kitchen, she entered a doorway leading to a living room or den. A recliner and a flat screen. Maybe a fifty inch. Book shelves built into the walls, something she had always wanted for her own home, when or wherever that might be. Lots of paperbacks, mostly crime thrillers and a few about the Vietnam War. Further along, an entire section of World War II non-fiction hardcovers filled a space. Anderson must be fascinated with the stuff, or had a relative who served.

On one shelf near the middle, about head high, a portrait took center space. Likely his parents, the man resembled Anderson—Pete she should say—with grayer hair. The woman's hair was still dark. Skin too. Hispanic descent from Mexico like so many people around here? Pete's dark hair might be a clue, as well as his complexion. He looked as if he had spent a lot of time in the sun, so it may be inherited and not a tan.

After looking the shelves over, she glanced around the room. No wife pictures? No hopes of getting back together? Maybe their conversation would progress to the point of him sharing that knowledge. It didn't seem likely, unless a few more beers loosened him up.

On the far wall, next to the doorway to the kitchen, a certificate of some kind hung there. Outstanding Service for Our Community.

Reid raised an eyebrow. Service for what exactly?

Shoes thudded on the deck. She hurried to the kitchen, and Pete closed the door behind him. "Grill's lit." He knelt by a cabinet and took out two potatoes. "Ever do these in the microwave?" She said no. He washed and dried the potatoes and rubbed them with olive oil. "I'll take care of them when I bring the steaks in. Doesn't take long."

"Anything I can do?"

"In the bottom of the fridge there's stuff for a salad. Onions too, if you like them. I do, not too many."

She rinsed the knife she had used to open the steak package and dried it with a paper towel. "Going to make me cry already?"

"I don't have to eat onions."

"Thanks."

While he sprinkled some kind of spice on the steaks, she opened the refrigerator. "There's mushrooms too," he said. "Broccoli, carrots, whatever you want, grab. As far as dressing, I like a little olive oil and red wine vinegar. You?"

She placed everything on the counter. "Sounds good to me. Kiss."

He jerked his head up. "Say again?"

"K-I-S-S. Keep it simple stupid. Never heard of that?"

"Not from a gorgeous redhead standing in my kitchen making a salad." He snapped the cap closed on the spice container. "Nice dress." He glanced at her feet. "Shoes too, much better than boots."

"Took you long enough to notice."

He grinned, ever so slightly. "I may wear contacts but I'm not blind. The green toenail polish is wild. Glow in the dark?"

"Teal, matches the dress. No glow that I know of."

He took the steaks to the door. "Medium rare, right? That's what you said at the bar."

"Anything in the neighborhood."

He closed the door behind him. She went to the window over the sink. Smoke rose as he placed the steaks on the grill, and her mouth watered. She could almost hear the sizzle of the meat on the hot grates.

At the counter, Reid opened the bag of pre-cut greens for the salads. She enjoyed being around a man who liked to cook almost as much as one who noticed her appearance, even if it had taken as long as it did. She didn't consider herself vain, but to have her efforts appreciated meant something.

He was a bit hard to figure out. Somewhat quiet. Somewhat serious. Especially about his work. She had witnessed that by his questioning of her at the bar.

The certificate on the wall was another piece of the evidentiary puzzle. Community service was a fine thing, and plenty of communities, towns, and cities near the border possessed their fair share of opportunities.

Had the old man who shot the pimp performed a community service by removing him from the criminal food chain? She would have to ask Pete about that later. It wasn't a priority at the moment while eating was.

Reid filled the bowls with the greens and other ingredients and took them to the refrigerator. Potatoes in the microwave? She could've done that if he had told her what to do.

She started toward the door to ask him but stopped. A laptop sat on a far counter. The internet: a search-savvy woman's best friend.

She raised the screen. A desktop picture of a woman appeared. Dark hair and eyes. Laughing eyes. A huge, bright smile. Pete's wife? She was stunning, obviously happy. Better times, no doubt. What broke her and Pete up, law enforcement stresses? That was the norm in that line of work, and Reid had seen her share. Sad faces of men she had served with. A woman in uniform standing at her locker while looking at pictures taped inside the door, tears running down her face. Another crying in a bathroom stall. Once, while standing out under the stars about half-mile from the border, her partner had punched the side of their Jeep after confiding about his own breakup. What a screwed-up job. One she had loved. One Pete had probably found while performing the background check on her. Pamela R. Stone. Fifteen-year veteran of ICE, otherwise known as U.S. Immigration and Customs Enforcement.

The door opened, and she whirled around. "Damn, Pete, you sure know how to sneak up on a girl."

He eyed her as she closed the laptop. "Something I can help you with?"

"Didn't want to bother you. I was going to do a search on how to microwave potatoes. Now that you're here …"

He took a roll of foil out of a drawer and a plate from the cabinet. "Stick them with a fork, I forgot while ago. Set the timer for five-minutes, turn them and go five more minutes. Go ahead, steaks should be ready when they are." He returned to the grill.

She followed his instructions and went to window over the sink.

What would she and Detective Anderson discuss this evening? The possibility for topics was almost endless.

7

The microwave dinged. Reid turned the sizzling and steaming potatoes and reset the timer. Pete opened the door and placed a foil-wrapped plate on the counter. "Good timing. I can use that last five-minutes to let me know when to take the foil off."

She closed the microwave door. "Salads in the fridge. I don't know where you keep the olive oil and vinegar."

Pete got those items from a cabinet and placed them on the counter, gathered butter, the salads, and two more beers from the fridge. "Did you want another beer?"

More alcohol or not? Probably not. She would rather be in control for the rest of the evening. "Ice water. Lemon if you have it."

"The stuff they put in a plastic lemon okay?"

"I'm not hard to get along with."

He smiled, just a hint, and the microwave dinged again. "If you'll handle that, I'll cut the steaks."

She opened the microwave door; a cloud of steam caressed her face. "How do you know I wouldn't rather cut my own meat?"

He looked up from the plate. "I like it thin. If you'd rather ..."

She smiled. "Just yanking your chain."

He finished the steaks. She cut and buttered the potatoes. Her mouth watered like when he had placed the meat on the grill's hot grates. She slid the plates over. He placed juicy slices of meat beside each potato. "If you take the salads to the table, I'll bring the plates and come back for our drinks."

She did so and sat. The chair's wooden seat chilled her thighs. Maybe the dress *was* a bit too short. He followed with the plates, left, and returned with his bottle, her glass filled with ice and water, and the yellow plastic lemon. "Didn't want to assume anything about that."

She squirted the liquid into her glass. "Good practice to keep, especially with women."

He drizzled olive oil on his salad. "Wish I had learned that a while back." He handed her the bottle, and Reid took it.

Was he referencing his wife? Sounded like it. Better let him bring that subject up on his own. "It takes us a while to learn our lessons," she said. "Some longer than others."

"Sorry about snapping at you earlier, when you mentioned my wife."

"I'm sure relationships with law enforcement personnel aren't the easiest to maintain."

He chewed and swallowed. "How about we avoid any controversial topics while we eat? We eat and talk after, when proper attention can be paid to the conversation."

"I can do that." Reid raised her glass and tipped it toward him. "The meal's great, here's to your prowess with a grill. I appreciate the invite too." He smiled as he had earlier, that same slight grin that seemed afraid to grow into a full-blown expression.

She took another juicy bite. Pete sure knew how to handle a steak. She swallowed. The evening should be interesting, but even though he knew how to handle a grill, she doubted he had learned how to handle her.

***

Pete rinsed dishes while Reid loaded them into the dishwasher. He offered another beer and she declined, choosing more water and fake lemon. Sipping from the glass, she strolled toward the room with the bookshelves and stopped at the entrance.

"I looked around in here earlier. Hope you don't mind."

Pete took another beer from the fridge. "Anything interesting?"

She entered the room. He followed as she headed toward the picture. "Your parents?"

"That's them, Mr. and Mrs. Anderson."

"Is your mom of Spanish descent? I noticed her dark hair, yours too."

"She is."

"Do you speak any?"

"Spanish? Enough to get by. Comes in handy with the work. People tend to trust you when you've made an attempt—weak as mine might be—to learn their language. Mom wanted to learn English well enough to speak as a native, and she did. Maybe that's why I learned."

"Podríamos así obtenemos las preguntas que tienes para mí fuera del camino."

"I think you said you have some questions for me."

"Since you gave me the opening, I was wondering about the paperbacks. Most are based on wars." She pointed. "A lot of those are about Vietnam."

"Dad served. He never talked about it and I wanted to read up on it. It was a hell of a war. I guess that's why he kept it to himself."

"You keep using past tense words. Is he dead?"

"Five years ago. Heart attack."

"Your mom?"

"Early onset Alzheimer's. She's in an assisted living facility."

"Nearby? You get to see her often?"

"San Antonio. I drive up once a month."

"That's got to be tough."

"For her, not so bad. She's pretty sharp yet. When she forgets, she forgets. I was afraid she might wonder away from home and get lost. She likes the place. Says she's on vacation. Whatever eases her mind, you know?"

"Yours too."

"As far as my translation of your Spanish a minute ago, you said I was 'close.' In what way was I off?"

She sat on the couch. "Basically, I said we might as well get the questions you have about me out of the way. Questions about what you found when you ran your background check on me."

"I'm not sure where to start." He sat at the other end of the couch. "That was an interesting background check."

She crossed her legs; the dress slid up her thighs. Definitely too short. She hadn't thought about that when she tried it on. She tugged it down, trying to be nonchalant. Had his eyes followed her hands? "Start with what makes you the most curious, Detective. Do that and everything else is pie."

Pete stood and shook his beer bottle. "Getting another and making a side trip to the bathroom. Need anything?"

"You're getting up when you're about to ask me your most burning questions about who I am?"

"I don't want to get up in the middle of the story."

"I'm good."

As he left, Reid tugged the dress down again. She didn't mind looking good but not X-rated. Still, he had seen her in the hall nude. No, he claimed to have seen a flesh-colored blur.

Regardless, she didn't care to sit within arm's length of him with half her bottom hanging out. Besides, he was wearing his glasses.

A couple of minutes later, Pete rattled bottles in the kitchen. Must be putting more beer in the fridge. Drinking problem because of the situation with his wife?

He walked in, beer in hand. "Sure I can't get you anything? Popcorn for the upcoming theatre?"

"I guess you're intimating to our upcoming conversation. No, but ..."

"Yes?"

"Could I get something to cover up with? I'm a bit chilly." His eyes. Was he looking at her legs?

"I can turn the AC up."

"You'll be too warm."

He was probably already hot if he was checking out her legs. Was she imagining it, or was she *hoping* he was checking out her legs?

He shifted his weight from foot to foot. "Dealing with the grill made me sweaty. I'd just as soon stay cool, be right back."

He returned to hand her a lightweight quilt. She unfolded it while he sat. Needlepoint patterns covered its surface—flowers, hummingbirds, butterflies, dragonflies—all in their corresponding thread colors. "I've never seen one like this, not even in a store."

"You won't either. Mom did all that."

"She's quite the artist. Does she still sew?"

"On her good days she'll do handkerchiefs and doilies, stuff like that."

"It's good to have hobbies."

"Do you have any, other than riding your motorcycle?"

"I read."

"That's where you got it."

"Got what?"

"Your vocabulary. I don't remember the last time I heard anyone use the word 'intimating.'"

"Reading definitely helps." She sipped water and placed the glass on a coaster on the coffee table in front of the sofa. "Time for your questions."

His beer joined her water. "The one I'd really like to know is why you aren't with ICE anymore."

"No surprises there. I was with ICE from 2001 to 2016. Started when I turned twenty-five, right after five years of college and a year of training."

"Impressive, what happened?"

"Which is the all-consuming question of choice, right?"

Pete picked up the beer, tipped it back, and placed it on the coaster again. "I'm waiting."

She did the same with her water.

"Wait a minute," Pete said. "Those dates would make you … with legs like those you're forty? What the hell did you look like when you were twenty?"

"Good genes I guess. I run too, when I can."

"You're doing a great job. I'm thirty-seven and look five years older. Hair's thinning, all of the above that comes with more years. I need to step it up."

"The stress of being in law enforcement doesn't help."

"Didn't hurt you any. That reminds me, you haven't answered my question about why you're no longer an ICE agent."

She paused. How would he take it? There was only one way to find out.

"Murder."

8

Pete tilted his head to one side. "Exactly what do you mean by 'murder,' like in killing someone for no reason?"

"You think I'd do that?"

"I don't think—or know—anything. At least not until you tell me what happened."

"What do you want to know, every little detail?"

"I'm the detective—you talk, I'll listen. I'll ask when I have a question."

Reid held the quilt over her legs while turning sideways on the sofa to face him. She hated reliving that night. It had led to her feeling betrayed by a system she had trusted completely, but not anymore. Too many people in government ignored inconvenient facts about immigration—like its toll in human trafficking—and for nothing but power and greed and votes.

"Try to be open minded. If you start spouting all kinds of crap about why I shouldn't have done what I did, you might get your ass kicked in your own home."

"Never happen, Reid."

"Shut up and listen."

"Go ahead."

"My partner and I were stationed about a quarter mile inside the border, him in his Jeep and me in mine about 100 yards apart. We would sit facing known trails with the headlights off, using high-tech listening equipment. When border crossers got close, we turned the headlights on. You never knew who you might see. There were a lot of drug smugglers. If their packs were too big to run with, they would drop them and take off. We were good with that, more drugs off the streets. What we wanted to catch were human traffickers. The average American gets to sleep in their bed, go to work, come home, eat dinner, help their kids with homework, and start all over again—all without knowing that women are kidnapped and brought across the border for sale as prostitutes. You live in southern Texas. When's the last time you saw that kind of story in the news, local or national?"

"I get your point. We have our share of Hispanic prostitutes. Many are brought here that way. For the most part, the ones arrested come here illegally, trying to make ends meet and send money back home."

"Human trafficking—making a profit off of people like they were a commodity of some kind—is something I have no tolerance for."

"Did the event you're telling me about happen because of your 'no tolerance' policy?"

"I'll tell you the rest and let you decide."

Pete placed an elbow on the back of the sofa and rested his head in his hand. "I have an idea how it went, and how your job ended too."

Reid shifted on the sofa and pulled the quilt around with her. "We'll see."

"That night it was dark—I mean absolutely pitch black—no moon, overcast, no stars, nothing. We liked it like that, no reflections off the vehicles. You hear lots of things, especially when there's no wind like it was that night. Animals scurrying through the underbrush. Armadillos, deer, you never knew that to expect. Then you'd hear coyotes yip-howling. I never got tired of hearing that."

Pete reached for his beer. "When I was younger, I'd drive to the outskirts of town—far enough to lose the traffic noise and get away from the lights—and listen to them. Haven't done that in a long time."

She sipped water. "Not trying to distract you with the animals, so I'll get to it. People walking through brush make a different sound. Their pants legs rasp against branches. Nylon jackets sometimes. When they get closer, their shoes pound the trail. They might talk, they might not. This night they weren't making a sound. By the sound of those feet hitting the trail, I could tell it was more than one. As soon as I knew they were in front of me—we always parked on an exposed area so we could catch them in the open—I hit the lights. It was a man wearing a backpack with three women behind him. The first thing that struck me was they didn't run. In fact, they came closer. I got out, thinking they wanted to be taken in to the nearest sorting station. They do that a lot of times. I couldn't have been more wrong. I told them to stop. That's when I saw the rope tied to the women's wrists. The man had the end tied around his waist."

Pete took his hand from under his head and sat up straight. "The guy was trafficking women for prostitution?"

"No doubt."

"And you did what?"

"Nothing. Until he grinned and said, "Será la cantidad habitual ser suficiente?" I took a step closer and shot him dead center in the forehead. He wore a knife on his belt. I wore gloves, so no fingerprints. I cut my arm with his knife and dropped it beside him."

"He offered you money, the usual amount, 'suficiente.' He had probably been paying another agent to look the other way. It would've been impossible to find out who."

"Right. His grin would have disappeared at the first question."

"The women?"

"They thanked me. Profusely. Said he had been doing it two years or more. Said other women from their town were gone because of him. They promised not to say anything about the knife. My partner heard the shot and drove over and called it in. My lead agent investigated and decided it was a good shoot. Everyone headed in for the night. The women were turned over for processing, and I thought that was that."

"But ..."

"One of the women thought she could cut a deal to stay in the good old US of A, I'm assuming."

"At least you didn't get prosecuted."

"They didn't care to do that to a fifteen-year veteran. Make the agency look bad. Get more questions asked. Get the media involved. You know how it is."

"When did all this happen?"

"Two months ago. I said the hell with it and bought the Honda the next day. After I got somewhat used to riding that monster, I bought a map and a GPS and hit the road a week ago. Been riding and checking out some of our great state's historical sites. I intended to stop for a while on the Outer Banks of North Carolina in another month."

"And I'm keeping you from getting on your bike and heading east."

"That you are."

"You realize, with everything you just told me, I can see you killing those three guys I questioned you about."

"What's keeping you from it?"

"Lack of evidence, because the bullet was badly damaged."

"You didn't mention that about the bullet back at the bar."

Pete shrugged. "You know we hold information until we can use it. Besides, the casings we found had their fingerprints on them."

Reid was tempted to ask about the lack of gunshot residue on Runt and Beady Eyes' hands. Hell, maybe they'd been target shooting out in the desert before they came to the bar, which meant she was totally in the clear. Still, the detective could've pressed harder, like getting a search warrant for her hotel room. Since he hadn't, time to tease him with a question. "Are you clearing me for any other reasons, like from their records and what Einstein told you?"

Pete chuckled silently, the rise and fall of his shoulders giving it away. "Since I'm clearing you, what're my chances of getting you to stay a while?"

"Ulterior motive, Detective?"

"Best dinner in town."

"How's breakfast?"

He paused to run the tip of his finger across his lips. "We'll see."

"Sorry I have to mention it, but does it have something to do with your wife?"

"You could say that."

"Don't tell me you want me on standby in case you two don't get back together?"

"Can you trust me and stay a while? I'm sure the hotel's expensive."

"Stay *here* you mean?"

"The guest room's yours, no expectations. I'd enjoy your company."

I'll have to sleep on it." Reid waggled a finger at him. "In my hotel room." She picked up the TV remote. Finding the shooting she had witnessed on the evening news would make bringing the subject up a lot simpler. "Care if we catch the news? I want to check the weather. I might head out of Texas instead of taking you up on your offer."

"Go ahead."

Disappointment in his eyes?

Reid turned on the TV and changed channels, until she found a newscast. A young woman, in a dress similar to hers but not as skimpy, held a pointer while telling the weather.

Reid swallowed. Had she missed the major news?

After the five-day forecast, a man and a woman appeared behind a desk in a studio. The woman picked up a piece of paper. "We have breaking news. A man was shot this afternoon—apparently while walking on the south side block of Rosemont Street. Two rounds struck him in the chest and one missed, hitting the abandoned house behind him. The man was known for having ties to prostitution. There were no witnesses. If you have any information, please call ..."

Reid punched the remote, ending the news. Had the street been Rosemont? Didn't matter, the description fit perfectly.

Pete took a long pull from the bottle and returned it to the table, empty.

"That's interesting," Reid said. "I don't know how I could have forgotten about it."

Pete jerked his head her way. "What do you mean?"

"I saw it."

He sat up straight. "How?"

"I went to the mall this afternoon. That's where I bought my dress and shoes. On the way back to the hotel, I took a ride around a neighborhood or two and turned down that street—Rosemont. I got behind an old dust covered car. Couldn't even read the tags or see through the back window. The car stopped near a couple of prostitutes and their pimp. The guy in the car stuck his head out the window and waved the pimp over. Then he stuck a gun out the window and fired three shots. The girls took off screaming. I guess they didn't call it in, since there were no witnesses. Probably glad their boss was no longer their boss."

"You saw the shooter?"

"Not until he stuck his head out the window. I guess he couldn't see me behind him for all the dust on his back glass." Reid expected Pete to ask for a description. When he didn't, she went ahead. "It was kind of strange. He was some old guy. Gray hair. Beard. I thought maybe he had a daughter who was into prostitution and he was killing her pimp to get her out of it. It looked exactly like what I think it is, a premeditated execution."

"You didn't follow the car? What about calling 911 for the guy that was shot?"

"I haven't been riding that heavy Gold Wing long enough to chase a car through unfamiliar backstreets. Besides, I really didn't give a damn about one less pimp in the world to ruin women's lives. I checked him, he wasn't going to make it. You know my record with ICE. Then I had the displeasure of you questioning me about those shootings near the bar. I didn't care to get involved and got the hell out of there."

"I guess the shooter will get away with it."

"Maybe his daughter—if that's who he was doing it for—will go home." Reid paused. "Nobody told you?"

"Sheriff gave me a call. I asked him to give it to another detective."

"Because of what you're going through with your wife ..."

"He knows about it. Knows I'm somewhat distracted."

"He sent you to the bar."

"Our other detectives were tied up. Just lucky I met you, I guess."

Reid glanced at her watch. "Time to go." Pete stood and so did she. "Thanks for dinner. "If I decide to stay, I expect a better dinner the next night." She got her bags from the guest room. As she started toward the door, her cell phone rang.

"Expecting a call?" Pete said.

Reid checked the screen. "Damn."

"Something important?"

"Someone broke into my parents' house. I live there now. Have one of those alarm systems that texts me if someone is breaking in. The police will check it out, but I need to get back."

"How far is it? That's right, saw it on your license. You live in El Paso."

"On the outskirts. It'll take over ten hours straight through. I'll go in the morning."

"After a good night's sleep, right? I'd offer to drive, but ..." She started for the door, and Pete said, "Don't you think you better change?"

Reid stopped. "Very observant of you, Detective. Wouldn't want a bug up my dress."

She changed but paused before returning to the living room. Why hadn't Pete asked her to give a description of the man who'd shot the pimp? Drumming her fingers on the dresser, Reid eyed herself in the mirror and shrugged. She wasn't about to ask why, not if it might cause further complications with law enforcement.

9

After a quick breakfast at the same diner she had visited the day before, Reid set off toward Highway 35 north, where she would connect with the same series of roads she had recently traveled, which would eventually get her to I-10. She didn't care for the interstate, its long-haul trucks, its numerous cars with drivers weaving back and forth while on cell phones despite laws against it, but it was the fastest way back home. At least she would only have to travel it less than half her drive.

Two hours into the trip, Reid sat up straight to stretch her stiff back.

What was up with Pete's offer to let her stay in his guest room, apparently for as long she wanted to stay? "No expectations. Sure Mr. Detective, whatever you say."

His comment about her legs, including his eyes following her hands when she pulled her dress down, were obvious hints as to what was on his mind. The proposal had its attractions, Pete being one of them. He hadn't offered any criticism after she had told him about being fired from ICE, so that meant he understood what she did and why. That comforted her. Few men understood her, even a small part of her, and that unexpected surprise tempted her to stay and see how their relationship might progress.

Did she want it to progress? If she were honest with herself, the answer would be a resounding no. Still, at forty-years of experience—she hated calling it age—there were times when she considered the positives of a steady relationship, even marriage. She had worked with women who described their marriages as "found their soulmate" or "married their best friend," and their descriptions were similar to the too-short evening she had spent with Pete, even with the less-than-ideal subjects they had discussed.

Three hours into the drive, black clouds gathered in the west, low on the horizon and thickening. She could stop for the rain suit, but even with the Honda's tall windshield, treated to repel water, she would rather not ride through a storm. Del Rio was about twenty-minutes away. Breakfast had become an afterthought while hunger gnawed at her stomach. Maybe a hamburger place. Order one all-the-way with a pile of hot fries. Run an extra mile or too when time permitted.

Ten miles later, as lightning flashed in the distance and a smattering of huge raindrops splattered on the windshield, the first signs for Del Rio loomed ahead. A billboard advertised a number of restaurants that included one called Harry's Burgers. Had to be something better than the fast-food chains. She flipped the signal and slowed for the turn.

The gravel lot held few cars, a motorcycle or two, and a pickup. Reid kicked the Wing's stand down and checked her watch. Early lunch crowd. She had left at seven and made decent time, arriving at ten-thirty. If the storm passed quickly, she could be on the road in thirty minutes. If she included another stop or three to stretch the miles from her back and shoulders, she should be home by six.

She removed her jacket and patted her right side under her shirt. The Glock's familiar form met her hand. She locked the helmet, covered the Honda, and entered Harry's.

Standard burger joint. Aroma of hot oil in the air. A long bar with a few people sitting on red stools that would spin. A kid with a mop of brown hair was doing that down near the end, his untouched plate on the counter. Reid took a seat in one of the red booths lining the windows, down from two bulky men with tattoos sitting at the bar up from the kid. Her stomach growled. Kid better watch out before she stole a french fry.

The typical waitress—young, harassed, hair in a ponytail—asked if Reid wanted water. Along with that, she ordered the House Special, consisting of a double burger with all the trimmings. She almost didn't add the fries, since she wasn't getting much exercise from all her riding lately, but she did anyway. The waitress left and hung the ticket on a rotating wheel at an opening to what must be the kitchen. "Order up, Harry!"

The cook's name was really Harry? What were the odds? Might the burger and fries be as genuine as the joint's name? A sizzling sound came through the opening, followed by the wet crash of fries dropping into hot oil. It didn't get more genuine than that.

Reid raised the ice water, the glass cold from the ice and wet from water condensing on the sides. While she sipped, one of the men gave her a glance, winked, and mumbled something to the man beside him. She raised her shirt, revealing the Glock, and waited. The men laughed. The other man turned, did a double-take, and elbowed his pal, who turned, smiled, and also did a double-take. Without another glance, both paid their bills and left.

Reid sipped water through a smile. Glock should hire her for an advertisement. She could see it now, on one of the billboards she had passed during the drive. Her in her riding outfit, consisting of a black leather jacket, faded jeans, scuffed and worn black leather western boots, and the jacket opened to show the Glock. Underneath the caption: Glock—A Girl's Best Friend.

The waitress arrived with her food, open-faced burger sizzling, fries steaming. Reid thanked her, salt and peppered the fries, and dove in.

A couple of minutes later, the waitress returned, lips tight, nostrils flaring. "I'm going to have to ask you to leave."

Reid chewed and swallowed, sipped water and eyed the woman. "Might I enquire as to why?"

"Someone complained about you having that gun. I don't care for it myself either, all their good for is killing."

Reid picked up a fry, took a bite, chewed, and swallowed. There were things she didn't care for either, like people who were afraid of an object for no other reason than "just because."

"I'm not paying for a partially eaten meal." She pushed the plate away. "However, since you could use some much-needed perspective, I'd like to explain something about a gun before I go."

The waitress glared but said nothing. Reid went ahead.

"You've heard it before, I'm sure, and scoffed at it. This gun" —she patted the Glock— "is nothing more than a defensive tool. In the right hands, a gun can fire a bullet and hit a target at a thousand yards. With a gun, a hunter can take a wild turkey for Thanksgiving dinner. My dad did that when I was a little girl. Best turkey I ever ate too. A gun can allow a woman to defend herself from a possible rapist—or *rapists*—without relying on someone else to do it for her. Do you give one fancy damn about any of that?"

"You just need to leave. The customers—"

"I'm a customer—a customer who was thinking of giving you a better than average tip. Help put some groceries on the table. Put some gas in your car. *Was,* that is. As far as customers, remember those two guys sitting at the bar? One winked at me and said something to his buddy. You like it when guys treat you like that? I don't. Any idea what made them stop hassling me and run like their asses were on fire? Me raising my shirt so they could see I don't put up with children, regardless of age.

Reid slid from the booth. As she passed the cash register, the door by the order window swung open, revealing a man wearing a stained white apron and a hair net over his bald head. He held his hands up as if to stop her. "Ma'am, I just caught the tail end of that conversation and I'm sorry. I didn't know those guys were bothering you. As far as Katrina here, I've tried to make her understand the same thing you said about guns. You know how some folks just don't get the practical side of that subject. She told me someone complained." He faced Katrina. "You want to tell me the truth about it, or do you want me to write your last paycheck for lying?"

Katrina placed her hands on her hips. "I didn't lie, Harry, I just—"

"She didn't lie." The women sitting by the seat-spinning boy faced Reid. "I complained. Maybe I shouldn't have said anything, now that I know what happened. I heard that man say something—something I won't repeat. I didn't know he was saying it about you. I must not have seen him looking at you."

"See, Harry, I didn't—"

"Hush, Katrina, we'll talk about it later." Harry faced Reid. "Ma'am, please finish your lunch. A slice of pie on the house, if you'd like."

"Thanks, it'd be a waste to throw that fine meal in the trash." Reid returned to her seat, slid the plate close, and took a bite of the still-warm burger.

"Are you a cowgirl?" The seat-spinner boy eyed her. She couldn't help but grin at how his eyes squinted at the seriousness of his question.

"Might be. Why?"

"You gots boots like mine, 'cept yours are black and mine are brown. You gots a gun too. I bet it shoots real bullets."

"I bet yours shoots caps."

"My dad says when I get old enough, he'll get me a BB gun. He said I gots to be safe when I shoot it at stuff."

"Your dad's a smart man."

"I think so. He—"

"Jeremy." The mother spun his seat toward the bar. "Let the lady eat in peace."

"I was just—"

"You were just hushing up is what you're doing. Eat so we can get back on the road." The woman sighed and faced Reid. "I'm sorry, ma'am. I'm sorry about the other too."

"I realize guns can make people nervous. I wouldn't have shown mine if it hadn't been necessary."

"I'll let you finish your lunch." The woman turned around.

Reid dipped fries in ketchup. Seemed she had made some friends, or at least influenced a person or two. Not Katrina though. Plate emptied, she left the money on the table, tipping the tight-lipped waitress anyway.

Outside, while grinning a snaggletoothed grin, the boy waved as his mother backed out of a parking place. Reid waved back.

The storm had passed to the south, thunder still booming in the distance, but the smell of rain hung in the air. She worked herself into the rain suit, turned the key on the Honda, and set off on the next leg of her grueling drive.

Back on the highway, she glanced at the time on the dash. Might make it home by six, but it'd be close. Best step it up a tad. No need to be on the road after dark, when deer started moving around.

The sky ahead was clearing, vibrant blue, with wisps of white clouds and airliner contrails painting the horizon. A pickup roared by, passing her before she could get up to speed. Long blonde hair filled the back glass at the driver's seat, and Reid barely had time to read the personalized tags before the woman swerved around the eighteen-wheeler ahead of her. MA'AM'S? That woman couldn't be old enough to be called "ma'am."

Regardless of all the "ma'am-ing" Reid had received in Harry's, neither was she.

10

Nine hours later, after five stops that included a thirty-minute wait under an overpass while a storm rumbled directly overhead, Reid pulled into the outskirts of El Paso. Tired couldn't describe the ache in her arms and lower back. The Honda rode as smooth as any vehicle she had ever driven, but the hours, as well as the pounding the sections of I-10 under construction had given her, had worn her out, including making her bottom feel like it had been jackhammered. Once she secured the house, she would fall into bed right away.

As she drove through the first residential streets, North Franklin Peak, the highest mountain in the Franklin Range, rose beyond the city. A few more turns later, she made a right onto the familiar narrow lane. In the driveway of the third house from the corner, the first thing that caught her eye was a large piece of plywood over the porch window. Her dad's best friend of thirty years, Bob Brindley, had likely taken care of that. She parked and stretched, trying to ease the stiffness in her neck and shoulders, and opened the door of the fence that separated the houses. Her dad had told her how fences could make good neighbors, but after he had known Bob three months, both had agreed how adding a door would also make them great friends.

Bob stepped out onto his porch. "Thought you'd be getting here soon, Pammy. Maybe in a day or so, but not now. Had that Wing in the wind, didn't you?"

Reid smiled at the pet name her dad had given her. After her parent's deaths, Bob had adopted that as well as her, not legally, but in every way that mattered. "Let's just say I outran all the tumbleweeds, Bob. How've you been?"

"Fine as dust. You see your lawn and mine? Desert's about taken over. I cut what I could, but I should give you your money back."

Reid hugged the man who was so much like her father—tall and wiry and stubble-chinned with gray whiskers—who also had her father's bad habits of trying to grow a garden and flowers in spite of the lack of rain, beers on the porch after dinner, and, of course, sharing the occasional bottle of Jack Daniels. They usually did so at dusk, in the form of a few shots while the sun set in a cloudless sky behind the mountains. On Saturdays, they sometimes stayed up long after the stars had winked into view, talking and laughing about anything from the latest sit-com, to corny jokes about how they lived in a virtual desert.

"Keep that money, Bob. Cutting my weeds gets you some exercise."

Bob laughed. "There you go, making me chuckle when serious things are afoot. I guess you saw what I did with your window."

"Dad would be pleased."

Bob slid his hand around her waist and led her to his porch. "We might as well sit while I tell you about it."

They walked along the flat stepping stones that Bob and her dad had set into the thin soil, who knew how many years ago, and took seats in two wicker chairs on his porch.

"I never heard such a ruckus," Bob said. "Glass breaking, April barking up a storm. I didn't know what to think. Then your alarm went off and I knew what to think. I made sure the Remington had a full mag of buckshot and turned on the porch lights."

Reid wanted to laugh at her imagined scene of Bob getting ready to do battle, his poodle, April, barking in the background, but she didn't. "Did they stay, or just …?"

"About the time I got the front door open, the car took off down the road. Police showed up thirty minutes later. Good thing you had that alarm. Gonna get one myself. I'd hate to have to splatter someone's guts all over my new carpet."

Reid laughed. "Bob, you are too much. Thanks for watching out for me."

"Glad to do it. Told your dad I would in the hospital."

"He told me." She patted his knee. "You know, before he died."

"I sure miss him and your mom. April's decent company but she's not folks."

"You should get out and meet a nice widow at the grocery, or at church."

Bob chuckled. "Okay, Miss Matchmaker. Let's see what those hoodlums did."

Reid inspected Bob's handiwork in covering the window and unlocked the door.

"Good thing you left me that key," Bob said. "It's not too much of a mess inside. Guess they didn't have time to do much damage."

She opened the door, and Bob followed her in. "I didn't clean up in case you want to claim it on your homeowner's insurance."

A few framed pictures lay on the floor, along with shards of glass and several books that had been raked off the shelves her dad had made. Maybe they thought something was hidden behind the books.

She picked up one of the pictures. Her mom and dad. Thirtieth anniversary. Good thing she hadn't been here. There'd be lots of blood mixed in with the glass, and it wouldn't have been hers either. Bastards. Her life had been shattered in more ways than most and now this. Did fate waltz around, picking and choosing who it ruined, or—

"You okay, Pammy? Want me to get a broom and sweep this mess up?"

She patted Bob's shoulder. "I'll call the insurance company first and see how they want me to handle it."

"Hungry? Got leftover pizza in my fridge."

"I'll scrounge something up before I go to bed."

"Give me a call if you need help cleaning up after talking to those hoodlums."

"You mean the insurance people, not the guys that broke in, right?"

"No pulling the sagebrush over your eyes, is there? I hope they don't come back" —Bob winked— "for their sakes." He stepped to the door. "Sleep tight."

As he closed the door behind him, Reid stepped to one of the windows without a piece of plywood over it. The Honda's yellow reflectors glittered until Bob turned his porch light off. She needed to get the Wing in the garage. After getting her here safe and sound, it deserved to spend the night indoors.

With the Honda secured, she locked up. In the kitchen, she searched the cabinets and found a few cans of tuna barely in date, crackers a month out of date, and what she really looked forward to: one of three ice-cold beers left in the fridge.

She ate and then walked the house, turning off lights, checking windows, checking doors, took a quick shower, brushed her teeth, and climbed in bed, this time reading a paperback. Before long her eyelids closed. She tried again, until the book touched her nose. The red letters on the clock on the nightstand changed. Five after nine. She turned the lamp off, turned it back on, and went to the den, where her dad's gun safe sat bolted to the floor and the wall. The Remington twelve-gauge, a twin to Bob's, from when he and her dad used to quail hunt in the fall, sat cased in the corner. She found buckshot in the back. They used to hunt dear as well as turkeys, but if any would-be thieves showed up tonight, she would hunt human game. She loaded the chamber and filled the magazine, locked the vault and returned to her room, where she leaned the shotgun against the wall beside the bed. The Glock already sat on the nightstand. She slipped under the cool sheets. Good thing she had lowered the temperature on the thermostat an hour ago. All the activity had left her wide awake, so she read again, until her eyelids grew heavy.

A second after she clicked the lamp off, faint light flashed in the window of the darkened room. Lightning? A car? More seconds passed. Thunder boomed in the distance. She closed her eyes. Unlike being on the highway while driving the Honda, a coming storm would be welcome while snug in bed. Listening to the muffled patter of rain on the roof would be a great way to fall asleep.

Light flashed in the window again, bright enough to penetrate thin curtains and closed eyelids. She waited for thunder. Instead, the faint rumble of a car engine came from the driveway.

Reid climbed out of bed. The car door slammed. She pulled the curtains back. A car sat in the driveway, blue and unfamiliar. She slipped on her robe, a pair of tennis shoes, and grabbed the shotgun. As she eased down the stairs, adrenaline hit her blood stream, and her heart pounded faster and faster. She swallowed, willing herself to be calm.

The doorbell rang. Either the person was a polite thief or they were making sure no one was at home. Another knock followed, soft and then harder. She crept to the door and unlocked the deadbolt, careful to keep it from clicking. The person knocked again. Persistent, weren't they? So was she. She raised the shotgun, slowly turned the doorknob, and jerked the door open.

A woman stood at the door, eyes widening at the fact that a shotgun was aimed at her chest. "Pamela, it's me, Carletta!"

Reid lowered the shotgun, hands shaking, heart almost beating out of her chest. She had come within a hair of shooting the woman who had kept her when she was a child.

"I'm sorry, Carletta. I thought whoever broke in had come back." Reid flipped the lights, and Carletta entered.

"Bob called and said you were home. I should have phoned."

"It's not your fault but I wish you had. When I think of what might have happened ..."

"It didn't, thank God. Just in case, my Amara, I will call next time."

Carletta held out her arms. Reid hugged the short, dark-haired woman, pressing her face against the wrinkled cheek. How long had it been since she had heard the Spanish nickname Carletta had lovingly bestowed upon her? Names always intrigued her, and she had come home and asked her mother what Amara meant. "Imperishable," her mother had said, and Reid had asked what that meant. "Never-ending, sweetheart," she had said. Reid had grinned and ran to her room.

A few years after that, there had been times when she wished she could have ran from the world.

She ended the hug. "As good as it is to see you, I wish it was without plywood covering the window."

"Bob did an excellent job."

"Want something to drink?" Carletta answered that she did and followed Reid to the kitchen, where Reid took the next to last beer from the refrigerator. She would need more before going back. Going back to where? Had she decided to take Pete up on his offer without knowing it? "What can I get—"

"If you don't mind"—Carletta took the other beer—"I will have your last beer."

"You know I'd never mind."

"I'm teasing, Amara. Let us go back in the living room so I can rest my bones."

Carletta sat on the couch, Reid at the other end. "Are you still keeping children? If so, I imagine your bones—and the rest of you—need a break."

Carletta sipped beer. "Ah, *deliciosa*. If my Armando knew I was drinking, he wouldn't allow me back in the house." She clinked the bottle to Reid's. "Until time for breakfast, that is. Yes, I still tend the little ones. They are like little seeds I love watching grow."

"How's my other papa doing? Is his belly as round as ever?"

"The doctors are making him lose weight. They tell him no more beer and all the foods he loves. I'm sure you know what kind of mood that puts him in, especially when I place a salad on the table in front of him."

"I think I remember you giving us kids carrot and celery sticks one time. He said that was food for goats."

Carletta smiled, even white teeth shining in the lamp light. "And now he is the goat, eh, Amara?"

Reid fell back on the sofa and laughed. It came from down deep, pure and simple, until her sides ached. Carletta laughed with her, and when they stopped, she patted Reid's knee. "It is good to see you laugh like that. How long has it been?"

What a question, one Reid didn't know the answer to. Before being fired? Before her parents died in the car crash? Before …? "I'm not sure."

"Things have been difficult, have they not? No person should have to bear so much. I wish your parents were here to help you with your troubles. They would tell ICE what a good person they have fired."

"I wish they were here too. That night was one of the worst of my life."

Carletta placed her hand on Reid's. "For mine too. Why do young men do such things, driving and drinking? My brother's youngest ran a couple off the road last month. At least they weren't hurt badly. He's in jail, waiting to be deported."

"I'm sorry to hear that."

Carletta stood. "No need, Amara, it will be as God wills." She breathed a deep sigh. "I must get home to Armando, or should I call him by his proper name, cabra vieja?"

Reid smiled and shook her head. "Not to his face. He might not like being called 'old goat.'"

"Do not worry, this old woman has not lost all her sense." Carletta went to the door. "You're continuing with your journey?"

"It's something I need to do." Reid hugged Carletta again. "Te amo. Buenas noches."

Carletta pulled her down by her shoulders and kissed her cheek. "I love you too, Amara. Dulces sueños."

Carletta drove away. Standing on the porch, Reid wrapped her arms around herself. "Sweet dreams?" She had to get back to sleep first. Then she would see what her dreams brought her.

She would rather they leave her alone.

Reid locked the door and returned to her room to sit on the side of the bed. Her reflection in the dresser mirror stared back, but it faded, changing into an image of her when she was a few months older than fifteen. Shorter hair, brighter red, more freckles across her nose, she held the back of her shirt up while her mom sat beside her, cleaning dozens of small cuts with a warm wash cloth, following up with alcohol on a cotton swab. Reid winced with each touch, tears running from her eyes in a continuous stream. When her mom finished, she mentioned how Reid might have tiny scars on her back, like lines on a crossword puzzle. Mom had been content to believe the story she had told her, that she had slid on loose rock and lost control of her bike while riding home from soccer practice.

If only that had been the truth.

Her present-day reflection appeared, with tears from the past slipping down her cheeks. She shoved them aside with the palms of her hands, pressing hard enough to feel the sharpness of her cheekbones. How long would the memory haunt her? How long before that nightmare jarred her awake to find the sheets damp with sweat and her throat raw from screaming?

She would stay here long enough to get the window repaired, clean up the house, work around the yard, and then make the drive to check up on Pete. Maybe the nightmare wouldn't follow her. It hadn't in the last five years, but her fifteen-year-old self hadn't appeared in the mirror in the last five years either.

11

The next morning, after Reid showered, she asked Bob for his opinion on someone to replace the window. He recommended someone who did such work on the side for close friends, who she could count on for it to be done well, and who could start within the week. When she asked if the person could start sooner, Bob hurried to his garage and returned with his tool box, a cap on his head, a huge smile on his face, and a tail-wagging April at his side. A hug and a cash payment of his estimate sealed the deal.

Two days later, after completing work around the house that included changing the oil in the Honda—Pete would find that interesting—and washing it as well as all the clothes she had taken on the trip, Reid turned the Wing's key and headed east.

The uneventful return trip to Pete's consisted of another, more welcome stop at Harry's. This time it included a slice of peach pie with vanilla ice cream. A clear blue sky without a hint of a storm accompanied her for the duration, and she even managed to avoid the eighteen-wheelers that had harassed her the first time around. Still, when she reached the exit that took her off the interstate, the relief at not being forced to inhale exhaust fumes calmed her, allowing the tension in her arms to ease for the remainder of the trip.

On her last stop to fuel the Honda, she left Pete a message at his home number, saying she would stop by in an hour if the invitation still stood, then set off on the last leg of her journey to the outskirts of Laredo.

At Pete's, his truck sat to one side of his driveway. She parked beside it and rang the doorbell. A minute later, Pete opened the door. "Got your message." He moved aside. "Hope the robbery wasn't too bad."

"I rung the bell to make sure you weren't in the shower or something before I got my stuff." Reid returned to the Honda. He followed.

"Does this mean you're taking me up on my offer?"

"If it still stands." She started taking bags out of the Honda's compartments. He placed his hand on hers, stopping her.

"Like I said, no expectations." He offered his hand. "Deal?"

She took his hand, slightly damp from some activity, and shook it. "Why's your hand wet?"

"Sweat from cooking." He wiped his hands on his jeans. "Thought you'd like barbecued chicken on the grill."

She gave him two bags, took two for herself and a small backpack, and closed the compartments. "Cold beer too, I hope, preferably on ice."

In the kitchen, Pete pointed at the refrigerator. "Got a few beers in the freezer. When I got home and heard your message, I thought you'd appreciate it." He followed her to the guestroom, where Reid dropped her bags on the bed.

"You realize I could get used to this, Detective. Trying to spoil me?"

He smiled the same half-grin he had smiled the last time she had been here. "I doubt that's possible. I need to check the grill. If you need to unpack or clean up, you know where everything is." She followed when he left the room.

"I'll shower later. Maybe that beer will wash the taste of diesel fumes from my mouth."

Pete gave her a beer from the freezer. "Is it that bad? I'd think the wind—at what, seventy-miles-an-hour—would take care of that."

She twisted the top off the icy bottle. "You think I go that slow? I hang with the big boys on the interstate. Even pass them when I can."

At the door, he gave her that same half-smile. "Like I'd think otherwise."

When he raised the grill lid, smoke billowed. Reid could almost taste the chicken, especially if he did as good a job with that as he did the steaks. She walked across the shaded deck and through the sparse grass that could use water.

"You asked about the robbery. I lost a window and nothing else, far as I can tell. They made a mess in the living room before the alarm gave them a hint that they needed to leave or get caught."

He nodded, his attention on turning the chicken. "Glad to hear it. Glad you made it back safe too. That's a long ride, regardless of what you're driving."

She sat in a nearby chair, crossed her legs, and swallowed beer. "You've never ridden a motorcycle? It didn't sound like it when you asked about the fumes."

"I rode dirt bikes when I was younger." He closed the grill lid and sat in the chair beside her. "Too bad you don't have another helmet. You could take me for a ride on the open road and let me taste those diesel fumes."

"Don't you have one of your old helmets from your dirt bike days? If you do, you're not driving."

Pete ran a fingertip across his lower lip. "Wouldn't dream of it. Otherwise, I wouldn't have the chance to wrap my arms around a gorgeous redhead."

Reid said nothing. Was he flirting or not? Hard to tell, but the thought of them speeding down the interstate at eighty, wind whipping around them, his body pressed against hers while his arms held her tight, caused a twinge deep within her that she hadn't experienced in too long a time.

"You'll have to stop by the nearest cycle shop and pick up a helmet. Unless …"

"Unless I can't handle it, right? You never know, I just might do that after work tomorrow."

She rubbed her nose, trying to hide a grin, and turned her head left to right, as if studying a fly on his head. "Better get a large size for that big head of yours, maybe even an extra-large. Do they make a size larger?"

He nudged her foot with his, smiling that damned half-smile. What the hell kept him from letting go and simply enjoying himself, his wife?

He stood and raised the grill lid. "Mind getting me a plate? I already have two salads in the fridge." While Reid walked to the back door, he added, "I think the chicken might be a bit longer. How about grabbing me a beer?"

She continued toward the door. So much for him spoiling her.

* * *

During dinner they discussed her trip, her stop at Harry's, the work she had done at the house, and how she had such a great neighbor in Bob. She mentioned Carletta and her story about Armando's new nickname, cabra vieja, and Pete chuckled. Still, he never really let go, never really showed her what was inside. The thing with his wife must be more serious than Reid had thought. If that was so, and it hurt him to that extent, why had he invited her over?

Afterward, she rinsed while he loaded the dishwasher. This was the last thing she thought she would be doing on this trip. The simplicity of their working together eased her mind away from things she would rather not dwell upon, like the vision in her mirror at home. Their continued talk of her trip made her feel … what? Almost at home? Dangerous thoughts, ones she shouldn't be having about a man who doesn't know if his marriage is over or not.

Pete closed the dishwasher door and opened the refrigerator. "Think I'll have another beer, you?"

Reid shrugged her shoulders. "Why not? After the last few days, I deserve it." They twisted off the bottle caps and threw them in the trash. In the living room, they sat on the sofa as they had before. Reid reached for the remote. "Any more news about that shooting I saw?"

"Not that one."

She whirled toward him. "He did it again?"

"When the police asked around the neighborhood this time, someone claimed they saw the car leaving. Same description you gave, including the old guy driving."

"What's the investigation turned up so far?"

"Seems like we've got some kind of vigilante killing going on, but with the damnedest cowboy I ever heard of."

"That's it?"

"The car doesn't stick out unless you're looking for it. It's like any other vehicle driven on the dirt roads around here."

"Your Chief hasn't started checking farms for anyone who might drive a car that fits the description?"

"Needle in a haystack, Reid. With no probable cause, it'll never happen."

She swallowed the last of the beer and stood." Time for that shower. Coming?"

"No expectations, remember?"

"Just kidding, remember?"

In the kitchen, she dropped the bottle in the trash, then retrieved her bathroom items from the guestroom. In the bathroom, she made sure to turn the exhaust fan on. The blades whirred overhead while she undressed. The slight updraft caressed her skin, still damp from perspiring on the long ride back.

Reid filled the tub this time, wanting to soak the aches from her muscles. Pete had the AC pumping, so the water steamed as she slipped in, luxuriating in the slow immersion of hot water. She soaked until the water cooled, reliving the days before meeting Pete, the days when she had returned home, and now, while she sat naked in his bathtub, experiencing the same twinge as she had when he had mentioned having his arms around her.

She drained the tub and washed her hair, shaved her legs beneath the shower and donned the robe brought from home before crossing the hall to the guest room.

The cloth bags only took a minute to unpack, mostly jeans and sweatshirts to keep warm when she rode north and east. She hadn't tried the electrically heated coverall that connected to the Honda yet.

How about a robe instead of dressing? Would Pete be able to handle knowing she wore nothing but panties while sitting within reaching distance? Not an easy question to answer but one interesting to explore.

After blow-drying her hair and brushing it, she found Pete dozing on the sofa. She sat. Blinking like an owl, he gave her the quilt she had covered up with when she had been wearing the skimpy teal dress. "I left this out in case you were chilly. You're liable to freeze this time."

She spread the quilt over her legs. "I'm still warm from the shower." He glanced at her again but quickly faced the TV he had turned on.

In spite of what she had said about being warm, the conditioned air had chilled her, so he must've noticed she wore no bra. She extended one long leg out from under the quilt and stretched. "Over twenty-hours of riding the last few days has made me wonder what it would be like to have a massage from a genuine masseuse. You ever have one?"

He kept his eyes on the TV, but his head had turned slightly when she stretched her leg out.

"Not a genuine one." He faced her. "How tall are you? Those long legs must come in handy while straddling your bike."

"True." She stretched her other leg out from under the quilt. "My last physical I measured five-ten, barefooted."

"Must be hard finding a dancing partner. Can't imagine what you'd look like in four-inch heels."

"Haven't danced in ages. My dad used to try and teach me. Got any music, we could give it a shot?"

Pete's throat muscles worked with a hard swallow. "Look, I'm glad you're here—more than glad. If things were different between me and my wife, you'd about have your way with me. As it stands, I'd rather not be tempted."

She pulled her legs back under the quilt. "I was wondering if you found me attractive. I'd hate to think I'm losing it."

"No worries there. As far as my wife, what's going on between us is personal. Can we not discuss it?"

"If there's anything I respect it's privacy, as well as honesty. Since you're being honest, I won't pry."

"Thanks." He faced the TV again but turned her way after a few seconds. "You mentioned your dad earlier. Since you're forty, your parents are still alive, right?"

Reid, not ready to talk about the subject so soon after doing so with Carletta, limited as the conversation had been, took a deep breath to ready herself to tell the entire story. He had told her about his parents, so he deserved to hear about her own.

"It's a fairly common story. The variations are anyway. Two guys enter the country illegally and buy an old beater used car. They stick a cooler full of beer in the back seat and get blind drunk. Pretty soon, someone dies. In this case it was my parents. They were run off the road. Mom died right away from head trauma. Dad lingered in the hospital a couple of days from internal injuries. We spoke before … well, before he passed."

"Damn sorry to hear that, Reid. We get those around here too. Not often, but often enough. When did it happen?"

"Right before my graduation I didn't attend. I knew I'd be crying the entire time."

"They say it gets easier as time passes. I still have dreams about my dad."

"It's the same with my parents. I've had a good support group. I told you about Bob—he's like a second dad. The woman who used to keep me when I was a kid is great too. Carletta's from Mexico. Her and her husband, Armando, immigrated. He started his own business after working in construction."

"I'm glad they were there for you."

"I'm not quite sure what I would have done without them." Reid paused. What would he think about it? Didn't matter. She believed in honesty, and that's what she would give him.

"I saw a counselor for about a year after. Even though I had Carletta and Bob, sometimes a professional can make you see things about yourself you may not realize."

"Help's help, no matter where it comes from. You had the intelligence to recognize that. Do you ever wonder about ...? No, I don't think you'd be that way."

Reid frowned. "You're going to have to expound on that if you expect me to answer whatever question is on your mind."

Pete sat up a little straighter on the sofa and ran his fingers through his dark hair. "Since Hispanics had something to do with two extremely traumatic times in your life—your parent's deaths and you losing your job with ICE—do you have any particular animosity toward them?"

"That's an honest question that deserves an honest answer—no."

"Because?"

"Because I've asked myself that and so has the counselor. It's been a while since I've seen her. Remember Carletta and Armando? During summer, when school was out, I lived in their home ten hours a day. I know the difference between good people and bad. Background or ethnicity has nothing to do with either."

"That's as good an explanation as I could have gotten. One that more would do well to follow."

Reid stood, making sure to keep the robe snug around her. No need in tempting Pete. "I think I'm ready for bed. You going now or ...?"

"I'll catch the news and have another beer. I'm back to the grind in the morning."

Reid took a step and stopped. "How about a key? Unless you plan to keep me locked up in your castle tower like Rapunzel."

Pete stood, took a ring of keys from his pocket, and removed one. "Rapunzel was blonde, not a stunning redhead." He tossed her the key. "Goodnight."

12

Reid woke and sat on the side of the bed. She ran her hand across the sheets. No sweat. No nightmares. Maybe the streak would continue. After having that surreal vision in her bedroom mirror back home, she didn't know.

She stood, stretched, and glanced at the clock on the nightstand. Ten hours? When was the last time she had slept ten hours? She gave up trying to recall and slipped her robe on.

In the kitchen, she found a note from Pete, telling her to make herself at home, to have coffee, eggs, whatever, and that he would be home around five. After locating coffee and filters in a cabinet, she started a pot. Minutes later, two pans were heating on a stovetop. Two eggs over easy, bacon, toast, and coffee would start the day perfectly. She also found french vanilla creamer in the fridge. Pete's? Not likely. Maybe his wife's.

Reid went to a large dining room window overlooking the backyard. Typical September Texas morning, in the mid-nineties by noon. How hot would it be in the Blue Ridge mountains, cruising down its famous Blue Ridge Parkway, or wearing a string bikini while standing knee deep in the surf on one of North Carolina's famous Outer Banks' beaches? She had read how October was one of the best months for surf fishing there, and imagining herself doing that tempted her to leave.

Just slightly.

With breakfast ready, she filled her plate, poured coffee, and placed everything on the coffee table in the living room. She found the news on TV and took a bite of egg. The weather forecasted the same sultry day. Possible storms. The headlines included a follow up on the two shootings. "The investigation will continue." As far as she was concerned, more pimps needed to be taken off the streets. Hell, maybe the old man was a damned hero. Might have gotten a fair number of young women out from under the control of two pimps.

She glanced at the picture of Pete's parents and then the framed document that mentioned his "service." What might that "service" be? Crunching bacon, she studied the other side of the room. Beige curtains hung over a window facing the street, a table underneath, maybe mahogany, maybe—

On the table sat Pete's laptop.

Reid scratched an unfelt itch on her cheek. Should she? Since he had left it out, it was possible he didn't mind her using it. When she had told him about researching how to cook potatoes in the microwave, he hadn't said anything about *not* using it.

Laptop on the coffee table, she opened it, and the picture of the same dark-haired beauty appeared. Silky jet-black hair surrounded the dark complexion. Dimples from a stunning smile. Intelligent eyes, not quite as deep brown as Carletta's. It was easy to see why Pete wanted his wife back. If her intelligence matched her looks, Reid understood completely.

No.

She didn't.

Whatever the problem, why not talk it out instead of having another woman in the house? Maybe Pete didn't see the truth of the situation. If he and his wife weren't on speaking terms, it might be time to move on. Better to—

Do what, see what he had right under his own roof? Reid shook her head. Crazy thinking. She wasn't ready to settle down any more than he was ready to give up on his marriage.

Then why stay? Could her imagined vision of him behind her on the Honda, his arms around her, body tight to hers, be keeping her here? Maybe, maybe not. Could it also be that she had stayed in a home other than her own without a single nightmare? That had its attractions. Though she had only spent one night here, that one night's sleep had been the best she had had in years. None of those answers satisfied her, so she shrugged the whole question away to finish breakfast.

While Reid finished the meal, she considered Pete's wife staring back at her from the laptop, its sign-in block ready for a password. No wonder Pete had left it, since she couldn't access it. His wife's name? What the hell. She typed "Maria." Password Incorrect. "Casandra." Password Incorrect. Reid ran a fingertip back and forth across her lower lip while the beautiful woman's eyes bored into hers. When she had opened the laptop the other day, one of the first descriptions that had come to mind had been "laughing eyes." She typed and the desktop opened. Reid laced her fingers together and leaned back against the sofa. She shouldn't be doing this. If the roles were reversed, she wouldn't expect an invited guest to invade her privacy.

Privacy be damned.

She slid a fingertip across the touchpad to move the pointer toward the file marked "photo album" and tapped the pad.

More pictures. Pete and his wife getting married. Friends. Her parents, possibly. Pete and her standing on a beach, maybe their honeymoon.

She moved the pointer toward another album, raised her fingertip—

The phone rang.

She hurried to the kitchen and waited for message to end and the person to speak.

"Reid, if you're around—"

She raised the handset. "I'm finishing breakfast and running water into the sink. It's just a few dishes, no need for the dishwasher." She stretched the cord and turned the water on. "Something up?"

"Wondering how you were doing. Finding everything okay? Coffee? Anything else you might want but couldn't find?"

"I used some of your french vanilla creamer. Hope that was okay."

"Might want to check the date. Don't want you throwing up all night and keeping me awake."

"Keeping *you* awake? You mean you'd get up and hold my hair for me?"

"You'd have to be pretty sick for me to do that."

"When I get sick, I get sick. Sounds like I'm coughing up a lung."

"I'll bring home a new bottle. Can't have you disturbing the neighbors."

"I had no idea you were so thoughtful."

"With neighbors I am. Been out yet?"

"Might take a ride later."

"See you around five."

Reid hung up. Water splattered over the edge of the sink. She shut off the faucet and drained the water, wiped up the mess in the floor and retrieved her dishes from the living room and started all over again, this time using hot water, dish soap, and keeping an eye on the water level. Might have to rethink this settling down thing. She pressed her palm to her forehead and closed her eyes. After doing dishes every day at home, what happened this time? Dumb question, Pete happened this time. She shook her head, placed her hands into the hot, sudsy water, and found a dish.

Yep, Pete happened this time. Why was that? Who the hell knew.

Reid finished the dishes, filled another mug with coffee, and returned to the living room, where the laptop was in sleep mode. She slid a fingertip across the pad again. The screen asked for the password again. Could she find something else that might lead to knowing more about Pete and his wife's separation? Not likely, probably more pictures and nothing else. Anything revealing might be in his email, but even if she could, she wasn't about to invade that far into Pete's privacy. She closed the laptop and returned it to the table beside the window.

Her morning bathroom routine took twenty-minutes. Dressing, which included attaching the inside-the-waist-band holster to the double-thick belt and slipping it within her jeans, adding a button-up shirt, boots, wallet, and her Glock, took five.

Reid started the Honda and allowed it to warm up. Heat waves rose from the roof of Pete's house while the attic fans whirred. She engaged the reverse, extremely handy on the big Gold Wing, and backed out of the driveway, keeping the bike balanced as she steered into the street. Her long legs *did* come in extremely handy. If Pete's wife didn't return anytime soon, he might discover exactly *how* handy.

She started down the quiet lane, stopped at the sign, turned left, and headed toward the main road, where her hotel was located. At the intersection, she took another left that led into Laredo. Might as well punch a few holes in paper at the gun range she had noted when planning her trip: Big Jake's Gun Range, if she remembered correctly. While she waited at a stoplight, she activated the GPS, entered the saved address, and twisted the throttle when the light changed. The Gold Wing smoothly accelerated across the intersection.

From what she had read about Laredo, the city's population neared 260,000. It bordered Mexico on the American side of the Rio Grande, opposite the Mexican city of Nuevo Laredo, with a population nearing 400,000. ICE maintained a large office and detention center here. Stop by to say hello? Not no, *hell* no.

Reid entered the city, evidenced by building traffic. Beeping horns, exhaust fumes, and frustrated glares from motorists caused her to pay more attention to her driving. A few high-rises dotted the near horizon. Laredo was a fair-sized city but not the metropolis some of America's larger cities were. Fine with her. She couldn't imagine cruising down a New York or Los Angeles city street on the Wing, but she wouldn't mind visiting Washington, D.C. to check out the museums, including the Smithsonian. She would have to add that stop to her itinerary, if she ever made an itinerary.

There was a certain attraction to being free as the wind, which was one of the reasons she had bought the Gold Wing.

The GPS announced the gun range location. She slowed and pulled into the lot to park between two pickups. With the helmet locked and the jacket stowed, she entered the building, where the cooler temperature enveloped her. She stopped at a counter to read a brochure. Five pistol ranges. One rifle range. Ammo. Decent prices. She could even try out a fully automatic .223 rifle. Been there, done that. She had even become proficient with a fifty-caliber Barrett sniper rifle to the point of rating marksman. If nothing else, ICE trained their people well. Unfortunately, for her self-defense instructor, he hadn't cared for working with her after she had scythed a hard elbow into the side of his padded helmet, knocking him completely unconscious. Lucky for him he was wearing the helmet. Lucky for her too. She might have killed him otherwise, and he didn't deserve it. Not that she knew of.

The man behind the counter cleared his throat. "Can I help you?"

"I'd like some range time. A twenty-five-round box of nine-millimeter target ammo too."

He raised a bushy eyebrow. "I could rent you a .380. Less recoil. Need some hearing protection."

Reid raised her shirt tail to show him the Glock. "Just the ammo and a pair of foam earplugs."

He placed the items on the counter and rang them up. She paid and took the receipt. "Happen to have a Barrett around here?"

"Fifty cal? What would you know about that?"

"How long's your rifle range?"

"Not long enough. You'd blow a hole as big as a bowling ball through the concrete backstop."

"Too bad. I bet I could still hit a standard human silhouette target at 800 yards."

The guy smiled. "You've got the look about you. Seeing as we're here on the border, would you be with ICE?"

"Not anymore. I stopped by because I like to stay sharp."

He slid the ammo her way and pointed. "Down the hall, first door to the left. Couple of guys in there now. Targets on a table by the door. You know the drill."

Down the hall, the random pops grew louder as she moved closer. Nines or forties by the varying sound, no cap gun .380's. Earplugs in, Reid entered the door, gathered five standard targets, and stopped at the first open stall. She attached one target to the clips and pressed a button. The target zipped away to the end of the range, about twenty feet away. She unloaded the hollow points from the Glock's magazine and ejected the one from the chamber, filled the magazine with the target rounds and racked the slide.

"Mind if I watch, little lady? Might learn a skill or two." The voice was similar to her dad's or Bob's, or one of her older instructors in Georgia. She raised the Glock to align the green tritium front sight with the red dot on the target and fired a series of three double-taps.

Pop-pop! Pop-pop! Pop-pop!

Six neat holes appeared, four around the red one-inch circle with two in the red. Gray smoke laced with the smell of burnt gunpowder drifted in the air. She fired again. More holes appeared, four in the red with two surrounding it.

"Great day in the mornin'," the man said. "Your name Annie by chance, as in Annie Oakley?"

Reid pushed the button; the target zipped back. "No, sir." She clipped another target to the holder, sent it downrange, raised the Glock, and fired the last four rounds in two double-tap groups. Four holes appeared in the red. "Practice makes perfect is all." She checked the open slide and released the magazine, placed it and the Glock on the carpeted platform in front of her. "How about you?" She turned around. "Do you practice much?"

What the? Gray hair, gray beard. He could be a double for the old guy who had shot the pimp. No. She hadn't gotten that good a look at him, just his profile. Maybe she was seeing things.

"You okay, little lady? Look like you seen a ghost?"

"Smoke's getting to me." Reid rubbed her nose. "They need to check the ventilation in here."

"Pretty rough when all the lanes are full. As far as me practicing, I come in once a week or so." He patted his right side, where it bulged from the shape of a pistol beneath his shirt. "Try to at least stay good enough to hit the paper." He nodded toward her target still hanging at the end of the lane.

"Not practically blast out the red like you just done." He started to the door and stopped. "Enjoyed your performance. Maybe you can give me a lesson next time." He left before Reid could answer.

The gray hair, the beard, both the same steel gray shade … couldn't be. She shook her head. Or could it? No, there'd been no dust-covered old car in the parking lot.

Reid brought the target back, clipped another, refilled the magazine, and repeated the firing sequence, this time with all the rounds in the red except two. Good enough. Experience told her should could do the same out to twenty-five yards, but the groups would open to about three inches. *More* than good enough.

She reloaded the magazine with the hollow points and fired another double-tap with the same results. It was always a good idea to check accuracy of carry ammo. She would replace the two spent rounds when she returned to her room at Pete's.

On the way back, Reid stopped at a grocery. Maybe she could return the favor of Pete cooking for her two nights. When they had met at the bar, she had mentioned her ability to make a "killer" omelet and hash browns. She had cooked the last of the eggs, so she picked up a carton, and since she was pretty sure she had seen more potatoes under the counter, the only other items she placed in her basket were spinach, tomatoes, extra-sharp cheese, and various spices to add to the omelet. No meat, Pete. How'd he like a meatless dinner? Men. At least he would have potatoes.

Outside the grocery, she laughed. She was just as bad.

She packed everything on the Honda and drove the final mile to Pete's, arriving at two-thirty. More than enough time to pick a book from Pete's shelves to read while taking a leisurely bath before starting dinner.

Back in Pete's kitchen, a red number one flashed on the answering machine. She played the message, similar to this morning's message. Mighty nice of Pete to keep a check on her. Now, if she could only get him to loosen up and forget his wife for a while. No, that wasn't fair; he obviously cared about his wife. Fine, but he better not sleepwalk. If she found him in her bed in the middle of the night, she would *not* be held responsible for what happened.

With the groceries stored, she chose a paperback about the Vietnam war, ran the tub half-full, stripped, pinned her hair up, and slipped into the hot water. As the warmth seeped into her muscles, all her thoughts of the last few days drifted away. After a few pages of the paperback, she dropped it to the floor and closed her eyes.

13

Reid awoke to cold water. In the open bathroom door, Pete was smiling bigger than how he usually smiled. "You looked so comfortable, I hated to wake you."

"You didn't drive home with your contacts out." She covered her breasts. "Enjoying the view?"

Pete opened his mouth but nothing came out. She threw a towel at him. "Close the damn door and bring me a beer and leave it in the hall. That's the least you can do for looking at me lying here naked for who knows how long."

Pete closed the door. A minute later he knocked. "Enjoy."

She retrieved the bottle, twisted the cap off, and drank. What a jackass.

Reid finished the bath, forgoing her hair. It'd be okay another day, and she wanted to start dinner. With the robe on, she examined her fingers. Prune hands, great. In the hall, she looked for Pete in the kitchen but didn't see him. "Don't start anything, dinner is planned."

He stuck his head around the corner. "Omelets? I see you bought eggs. Want me to cube the potatoes and get out my cast iron pan?"

"Quite the memory, Detective. Out in a minute."

Reid slipped on a pair of faded jeans and a men's button up white shirt—no bra since Pete already knew what they looked like. She brushed her hair out and padded barefoot into the kitchen. Pete waited at the counter, beer in hand. "All presentable I see."

"You *saw* plenty."

"I'd just gotten home. I hadn't been standing there more than five seconds."

"Five minutes is more like it."

"I couldn't have handled that long."

"Like I didn't know that already. If you're not going to cut the potatoes, go in the living room and watch TV. Anything. Do something. Read a book. I like to cook without being watched."

Pete tipped the bottle her way. "Yes, ma'am. Right away, ma'am."

She eyed him as the left the kitchen, then took the heavy cast iron pan he had left on the counter to the stove. Maybe this was why she had never found a husband. Even the decent guys could be a pain.

To her, omelets were an art form, the more colorful the better. The spinach, tomatoes, spices, and cheese sprinkled on top of the creamy egg resembled a fancy pizza, but much better nutritionally. She shrugged. Wouldn't offset the potatoes.

She plated the omelets and potatoes, left everything on the dining room table, and stuck her head in the living room. "Come and get it."

On the sofa, Pete turned around. "Smells great."

"I poured orange juice. Didn't think you'd want beer with eggs."

He followed her to the table and sat beside her. "I could make Bloody Marys."

"Shut up and drink your orange juice."

"Yes, Mom." Pete took a bite of the egg, a bite of the potatoes, and washed it down with juice. "You should open a place that serves nothing but this exact combo."

Reid sipped juice. "Not the kind of life I want." She raised a fork filled with egg, but it slipped off the fork. As she leaned over the plate so the egg wouldn't fall on her white shirt, Pete looked her way. Maybe he was a breast guy. He had already seen them so why keep looking? "Glad you like everything. Anything else catch your eye?" In the middle of a swallow of juice, Pete coughed. Reid smiled and took another bite of egg.

Pete cleared his throat, wiped his mouth with a napkin, and took another swallow without issue. "You're a distraction—a fine distraction. Maybe I shouldn't have asked you to stay."

"You mean that?"

"I like having you here. Still, you're attractive to *my* fault. You're intelligent too, and funny. I guess I don't act like it."

"I think I've seen you genuinely smile only once since I've been here. I don't think you've laughed at all, wife on your mind?"

"Constantly."

"That's saying a lot, especially since I can't distract you from thinking about her. Not that I'm trying."

"Didn't think you were. I imagine with Pamela Reid Stone, what you see is what you get."

She tapped her glass to his. "One of the best compliments I've had in a while."

He stood, empty dish and glass in hand. "I'll wash these. It's the least I can do since you cooked. Won't take a minute."

At the counter, Reid placed her plate and glass by his. "I saw the shooter's twin today."

He stopped rinsing dishes. "When you were out? I thought you might be, since you didn't pick up when I called. Where at?"

"I like to keep my shooting skills sharp. I drove into the city and stopped by a range I had noted when I planned my trip."

"Jake's? I've been there. How much does he charge to rent a pistol? I always carry my own."

"Is that his name? Big guy, bushy eyebrows? Why would you think I'd rent a gun?"

"I just assumed you would—"

"Right," Reid said, holding up her hand to silence Pete. "You would assume I'd shoot a popgun .380 like Jake did. No, I've got my own Glock 19 with me. Best friend I've ever had."

Pete held up his hands as if to surrender. "Okay, okay, I sometimes forget you're an ex-ICE agent with fifteen years of experience. How'd you do?"

"Be right back." Reid hurried out to the Honda for the target she had shot after warming up and returned. "You tell me."

He took the target and looked at her through the ragged hole in the middle. "Guess that answers my question." He put the target on the counter. "Singles, doubles? First target, last?"

"Second. Three double-taps, followed by three more, followed by two."

"We won't be having a gunfight anytime soon. How's your speed drawing?"

"Fast enough."

"Fast enough to have taken out those three guys in that alley? Two shots were close to their hearts. One was straight through the heart. They were practically dead on their feet."

"That case has been closed, remember?"

"Tell me about the guy you saw."

"It was only for a minute. He came up behind me while I was getting ready. He sounded old."

"You didn't see him?"

"I fired, he complimented, I turned, we said a few words, he left. He did remind me of the shooter. Same steel-gray hair and beard. I didn't see any dusty old car in the parking lot."

"He could have washed it."

"There were no old green cars. Did I tell you it was green?"

Pete faced the sink. "I better rinse these dishes and get them in the dishwasher." He glanced over his shoulder. "You might as well take it easy like I did while you were cooking."

She dropped the target in the trash. "I intend to do just that."

The hum of the dishwasher came from the kitchen. Pete joined her on the sofa while Reid flipped channels. Finding nothing interesting, she turned the TV off. "How's the investigation going with the shooter?"

"Same as the last time we talked about it."

"Maybe he got the ones he wanted and that was that."

"As much as I like seeing pimps taken off the street, I'm not crazy about seeing them leave in a body bags."

"Is prostitution that big a problem in Laredo?" Of course, Reid knew it was, like in every border city.

"It ebbs and flows," Pete said. "We think only a few main rings exist. Most of those are probably directed from bigger bosses in Mexico."

"Who traffic the girls in against their will."

"No doubt."

Reid pointed. "That document on the wall that mentions your service, what's that about?"

Pete glanced toward the wall and back. "I helped disrupt one of those rings."

"There had to be more to it than that."

"All I did was hand out cards from the women's shelter in Laredo. It wasn't that many, but the word spread. Before you know it, about fifty girls abandoned their pimps." He glanced toward the certificate. "The city made a big thing out of it. Got some press. I agree with you, the human trafficking thing is just— I can't imagine being kidnapped and taken away from your home and your country and being forced to sell yourself for money. Then the pimps only leave you with just enough cash to scrape by. Maybe I should take up where that guy left off."

Reid appreciated how he cared about the subject. "All of that makes up a large portion of why I shot the Coyote who had those three women tied to him, which got me fired for my troubles. That and knowing I wouldn't be able to track down the agent taking his money."

Pete shook his head. "It's a screwed-up world."

Reid didn't answer. She wanted to bring up his wife. Sitting there talking about things they had in common, enjoying meals together the last few days, even their bickering about dinner, had been enjoyable, welcome even. He was attracted to her and she was to him. If his wife wasn't coming back, not likely it seemed, what was keeping that attraction from continuing down its most natural path of progression?

His arm was stretched along the back of the sofa. She ran her fingertips along the top of his hand. He turned his hand over and she placed hers within it. His fingers closed, and he traced small circles on the back of her hand with his thumb. "I've really enjoyed the past few days."

"Sometimes it's hard to tell if you do or you don't. We get along great, except for snapping at each other like my parents did. Yours too, I'm sure." She took her hand from his and sat up. "I'm done acting like a coy school girl. I want to know where this might lead, don't you?"

Pete's shoulders bounced with one of his silent chuckles. Reid smacked his hand still on the sofa. "What the hell is so funny?"

"The idea of you being a 'coy school girl.' No way, no how, not in a million years. I mean, look at you. What's not to be attracted to? When I saw you in the tub …"

She patted his hand. "Go on, I'm not stopping you. Wait a minute, you hurt something when you closed the door, right?"

Pete glanced down at his crotch, closed his eyes, shook his head, and raised his eyes back to hers. "Damn near."

Reid laughed, as long and as hard and as lusty a laugh as she had enjoyed when Carletta had told her about calling Armando an "old goat." Catching her breath, she fingered her hair out of her eyes and faced Pete. "Wow, forget I said anything. That was better than any sex I ever had."

"Your experience must be limited."

"Regardless of how I come off, I'm not a floozy, *or* that 'coy school girl' I mentioned earlier."

"There's a word you don't hear often."

"Floozy?" She checked her watch. Nothing interesting would be happening on Pete's sofa tonight. "Floozy pops up in some of the things I read. Oh, I borrowed one of your books. If you mind, too bad." She stood and stretched, giving him a show of her five-ten frame in tight jeans. "I'm going to bed."

"Borrow all you want, goodnight."

Done in the bathroom, Reid padded down the hall and peeked in the living room. Pete sat on the sofa, the laptop in front of him on the coffee table. He tapped the keys a few times and then shut it, almost slamming the screen down.

Reid padded back to the guestroom. Email from the wife, Detective?

14

Reid undressed, slipped between the cool sheets, and took the paperback from the nightstand. Except for her dad and Bob, she had never known anyone who had been in the Vietnam War. They would sit out on the porch while she played in the yard, and she would hear some of their descriptions of the war. It wouldn't be long before she would either go back inside or run around to the back yard.

As she read, her eyes closed and the paperback fell to her chest. She left it on the stand and turned the light off, rolled over and snuggled the pillow.

* * *

Someone was screaming, loud and long. A lung-emptying shriek that lasted until the person gasped for air to scream all over again.

And again.

And again.

Reid jerked upright. Nightmare. Sheets wet. Just when she had thought—

"Reid!" Pete banged on the door. "You okay? Open the door!"

"I … I'm okay. Bad dream."

Pete stopped banging. "More like a nightmare. I never heard anyone scream like that. Your throat's got to be hurting."

She swallowed. Pete was right; her throat burned like the time she had strep throat as a kid.

She unlocked the door and returned to the bed, pulling the sheet up around her. "You can come in."

Pete entered. "I hope the neighbors didn't call 911. If I didn't know any better, I would've thought someone was raping you."

Reid blinked stinging tears from her eyes. Then they filled to overflowing, leaving wet trails down her cheeks.

Pete sat on the side of the bed and rubbed her back through the sheet. "I hope I didn't say something wrong."

Reid collapsed onto his chest. "Dammit, put your other arm around me." He did as she asked. Her shoulders shook as she cried like she hadn't since she was fifteen.

Pete continued to gently rub her back, cradling her head on his shoulder while her tears soaked his T shirt. He allowed her to finish without saying anything. When her sobs ended, she pulled away. "It's been a few years since I cried like that."

"You said something about seeing a counselor. Was it because of the nightmares?" He gave her a box of tissues from the dresser and sat again.

She ran her fingers through her hair and pulled the strands out of her eyes, tucked it behind her ears and wiped her eyes and face. "I started going because of the nightmares after my parents died, when I was eighteen. Took a while, but it helped. I went again, once a year or so through college. It was the strangest thing how they stopped altogether then. When I moved back home, I was afraid they would start back again, but they didn't. To say I was relieved was an understatement. I had an idea it might happen again when I went back to check on the robbery."

"How's that?"

"You'd look at me a lot stranger than you're looking at me now if I told you."

Pete pulled her close and kissed her forehead. "Sorry about that. It's just that I've never seen this side of you. Did something happen to make you have these nightmares, or did they just spring up out of nothing?"

She lay her head on his shoulder. "I *wish* it was nothing." She sat up to look him in the eye. "I've never told anyone this, not even my parents. I didn't tell the counselors what caused the nightmares, only how I was having them, so I'm not sure …"

"You're not sure about what?"

"I don't want you to think differently of me."

"Are you saying you *were* raped?"

She lay her head on his shoulder again. He wrapped his arms around her, rubbing her back like he had earlier.

Reid hesitated. Where to start?

"What I said about having an idea it would happen … it was a vision … a vision I've had before of me sitting on my bed with my mom while she was wiping my back with a warm washcloth. That vision, flashback, PTSD memory, whatever you call it, is exactly the same thing I saw in the mirror on my dresser when I was fifteen, when it really happened."

Pete stopped rubbing her back. "Is that what this is?" The sheet had fallen from her back. His fingertips touched her, gently rubbing the minute scars. "Feels like lots of tiny lines."

"Scars. They run a lot deeper than they look or feel. I haven't had the nightmare at home for a few years. Never when I was sleeping in another bed."

"Like when you didn't have them in college?"

"Maybe it was the stress of going home to a damn robbery and dealing with all that. If not, once I start on this trip, I might not ever stop."

Pete tightened his arms around her. "You don't have to tell me."

She smiled, surprising herself, and snuggled against him. "There you go, being Mr. Nearly-freaking-perfect again."

"Yeah, right. Want your robe? It's kind of strange sitting here holding you with nothing but a damp sheet around you."

"Pete?"

"Yeah?"

"Shut up. I'm tired and I'm going to lie down. You can hold me while I tell you what happened." She stretched out on her side, facing the other wall. He did the same beside her, his arm on top of the sheet over her waist. She took his hand and held it between her breasts. "I'll avoid details. Neither of us will care to hear them."

"Anything you say, Reid."

To calm her nerves, she swallowed. Regardless, tension crept into her jaw, arms, and shoulders at the thought of reliving that night again.

"I played soccer at a field a couple of miles from my house. There was a short section about half-way there with several rundown houses. Fences between them with paint peeling. A ragged box spring leaning against one fence. That box spring was there when I started riding my bicycle to practice and stayed there until the night I'm talking about. When I rode by on the way to the field, there would usually be four or five Hispanic boys sitting on the front porches. Teenagers of the families living there, I guess. They would wave, I would wave. Practice ran past dark this particular night. The coach let me use the phone in the fieldhouse to call my mom. I didn't know how late I would be. It was no big thing. I said I would be fine."

"It happened when you were coming home?" Pete asked. "At this place you're telling me about?"

"A couple of street lights were out. I was going slower because I had no light on my bike. The town was working on the road, and I didn't want to crash on the loose rocks. When I went by the section of fence with the box spring, a man jumped out and grabbed the handlebars. At that distance I could see his face. He was older than the boys I had seen. Before I could scream, someone else grabbed me from behind and covered my mouth and dragged me off the bike. I won't ever forget what the guy that stopped me said before ... well. *"Vamos, amigos, tiempo para ser un hombre.'"*

"'Come here, amigos, time to be a man,'" Pete said, his voice hard. "What a bastard, making young boys think raping a girl makes them a man."

"Everything was a blur of faces and pain. That's how I knew it was more than one. I don't know how many or how long. When they left, I could hear that same guy laughing."

"How do you know it was the same guy?"

"Before the rape started, he kicked the box spring down. That's where— Anyway, he held his hand over my mouth and laughed and blew smoke in my face. The tip of the cigarette turned bright red when he inhaled. I closed my eyes after that."

"Damn, Reid, no wonder you have nightmares. What did you do when they ... well ...?"

"Finished? All I could do was dress and go home."

"What did you tell your mom when she cleaned your back?"

"She kept asking me how I only got hurt there. I told her I wrecked my bike and flipped over the handlebars and landed in the rocks. The ends of the springs in that box spring must have been poking up and cutting me while they ..."

"What about ...?"

"My other injuries? I told her my period started when I left the soccer field and I didn't have anything with me." Reid turned over, her face inches away from Pete's, tears stinging her eyes again.

"I didn't want them to think their daughter was ruined. It sounds stupid, but you have to look at it from a fifteen-year-old girl's perspective. At least I didn't end up pregnant. No diseases, thank God. I guess it was those boy's—however many it was—first time. My dad might've have taken things into his own hands and ended up in jail if I told him. Doesn't that make sense?"

"It does. I'd probably kill every last one, but I'd start with that laughing son-of-a-bitch. As far as you being ruined, you're anything but."

The tension in Reid's jaw, shoulders, and arms released. "Do you know how good it makes me feel to hear you say that? To know you understand, to know you don't think I'm any less of a woman than before I told you? I was half-afraid you'd jump out of the bed."

"I'm sure it changed you. Emotionally not physically. I admire you for dealing with it as well as you have."

While Reid stared into Pete's dark eyes, she placed her hand on his cheek, inched closer, and kissed him lightly on his lips. He didn't move, didn't react, so she kissed him again. This time his lips moved beneath hers, just barely.

Until he rolled away and sat on the side of the bed. "I can't, Reid."

"You can't or you don't want to?"

"I want to ... but ..."

"Your wife?"

He nodded.

She rolled over, tears filling her eyes as she faced the wall. "I think I've done a damn good job of respecting your privacy." She swallowed. "But you've done a damn poor job of being honest with me about what's going on between you and your wife." She rolled over, facing his back. He sat with his elbows on his knees, hands clasped in front of him. "When you asked me to stay without expectations," she said, "it made no sense. No matter what a man might say, if he wanted his wife back, why would he do that? I stayed, thinking you were interested. Since I was wrong, I deserve to know why."

"I can't talk about it. You're going to have to trust me on that."

Reid glared at his back. "Trust you? I just trusted you enough to tell you about the worst night I ever experienced. Why you can't trust me enough to tell me why your wife isn't here?"

Pete stood. "That's all I can say."

Heat rose in Reid's cheeks. She had bared her soul to this man, and he had no better explanation than that? Keeping the damp sheet around her, she stood.

"I'm gone in the morning. I don't care if you've got to work or not, don't be here." She brushed by him and stood by the door. "Out. I'm putting as many miles as possible between you and me tomorrow as I can. I need my sleep."

"Reid, I—"

"Except for sitting down on that bed and telling me why your wife isn't here, there's not a damn thing you can say to make me change my mind."

"I can't do that."

"Fine. Maybe she's gone for good and you're in denial. In that case, the best way to get over her is to make love to me."

"I told you, I can't do that."

"Out."

She slammed the door behind him and locked it. She wouldn't have him now if he crawled into bed begging her. She would get up early, pack, and get the hell out of Texas and away from Pete Anderson as fast as the Gold Wing would carry her.

15

Reid tossed and turned all night, rolling over occasionally to stare at the clock on the nightstand. Around dawn, when Pete's truck rumbled to life, she rose, dressed, and packed her bags. When she stepped onto the porch, Pete, sitting in a chair, stood. "Morning."

She hurried by, bags in hand, and opened the Gold Wing's luggage compartments. He followed and stopped beside her. "We need to talk."

"I said all I needed to say last night." She stopped packing and spun to push him away. "You jerk. What did you do, drive around the block and come back?"

"You wouldn't have come out of your room otherwise. I need to talk to—"

"Get it over with, damn it, you're wasting my travel time."

"I need to drive you somewhere to show you something—something that has to do with my wife. Once I do, you'll understand what's going on and why I've been acting like I have."

"How far?"

"About ten miles."

"I'll follow and be on my way after."

"You'll get wrapped up in dust the last half-mile."

"Where's your sidearm?"

"Don't need it where we're going."

She lifted her shirttail to show him the Glock. "We go. You show me whatever. You bring me back. I leave. Got it?"

"If you want to leave. You might not after."

"Get your truck."

He jogged down the street, turned at the stop sign, and pulled into the driveway a minute later. She climbed in. He backed out, drove to the sign, and took a left.

Jaw clenching, knuckles white, he gripped the wheel with both hands. Whatever he was going to show her had set him on edge. Didn't matter. What could he possibly do or say that would make her change her mind?

"Don't you have to work?"

"Except for questioning you that day at the bar, which was a favor to my boss because our other detectives were busy, I haven't worked in three weeks."

"Pining for your wife?"

"Do you have to be so damned antagonistic?"

"When it's warranted."

He glanced at her. "It's not—not this time. Do me the favor of being quiet until we get there."

"Where's 'there?'"

He tightened his lips into a thin line and continued to drive. They pulled onto the road where the mall was located and headed away from Laredo. A few minutes later they passed the hotel where she had stayed. Her stomach growled.

"I could use something to eat."

"I'll make something when we get there."

"Fast food, not a full meal with you."

"Look, when I asked you to trust me last night—especially after you told me your story—I know it was hard to take. I'm asking you to trust me again. If you still want to leave when you know everything, I'll bring you back and you can be on your way."

Reid faced the passenger window. The last buildings she had driven by when she had arrived passed by. Soon they drove by small houses and scattered farms that gave way to occasional fences marking the borders of cattle ranches. Although trees and brush dotted the landscape, sand and desert extended to the horizon, creating the never-ending panorama of south Texas.

Maybe a mile later, Pete turned at a relic of a mailbox, red with rust and sitting askew its equally rusted post, and continued down the dirt path.

In the side mirror, dust billowed in the truck's wake. Pete had been right. No one would want to ride behind him in that.

As they drove over a rise, a house appeared, the heat making the vision undulate in the distance. Pete still gripped the steering wheel as if it were someone's throat, and veins bulged in his neck.

"Why's that house got you so upset?"

"It's my parents' house. I'm not upset, just tense. I never thought I'd be showing anyone this."

"Can I ask what 'this' is now, or …"

"I wouldn't tell you if you did. I have a good idea how you'll react, but I'm not sure."

He parked in a dirt yard. The simple white-painted wooden structure looked abandoned. Dust coated the windows while the dried remains of shrubbery wavered in the breeze like skeleton fingers tapping the glass to be let in. To the side sat two storage buildings, one with an attached shed covering a small, rust-coated tractor, one tire flat on its rim. Pete climbed out and Reid followed, toward the shed with the tractor.

"Was your dad a farmer?"

Pete stopped at the closed and padlocked double-doors. "He bought that old thing right before he died. Mom wanted a garden spot but he never got to use it. Mom never said anything else about it. I guess it was something she wanted them to do together. That wish died with him."

"I know how it feels to lose your parents. I'm sure that isn't why you brought me here."

Pete took a ring of keys from his pocket and unlocked the large padlock. He didn't open the door. "Look, when you see what's inside, a million assumptions will run through your mind. Don't speculate. I'll fill in the blanks."

"Is your wife's dead body in there? You'll never fill in *those* blanks."

"Didn't I just ask you to not speculate? I'll tell you the rest in a minute. You'll have plenty of questions to ask when I open these doors." Pete removed the lock, hooked it to the latch, and pulled the squeaking doors open.

At first Reid couldn't see anything because of the darkness. Pete went inside and flipped a light switch, illuminating a dust-covered car. She joined him and ran a fingertip across the surface. Green paint showed underneath. Her mouth fell open. She spun and stared. "Did you kill the guy and bury his body out here in the middle of nowhere?"

"Assumption one—wrong."

She eyed the car and then him again. "Did you—?"

He held up his hand. "No more questions. You'll have plenty in a minute."

He unlocked the driver's door with a key from the same ring, climbed inside and shut the door. Behind the car, she could see him doing something inside, but between the dust covering the back glass and the lack of light inside the car, it was hard to tell what he was doing. He opened the door a crack. "I'm rolling down the glass."

"Whatever."

Pete stuck his head out the window, or rather, the man who had shot the pimp, complete with the same steel-gray hair and beard, stuck his head out the window.

"You?" Reid retreated a step. "You're the shooter?"

Pete climbed out. "You okay, little lady? Look like you seen a ghost."

That voice—it was same as the old man at the gun range. Pete had changed his voice, adding a coarse, scratchy tone. Who was this guy? She had stayed in his house and had wanted to make love to him. Now she had to force herself to believe he was a murderer?

Pete took off the wig and the beard. Fake, like him. She snatched the Glock from the holster and centered the green tritium sight on his chest. "Who the hell *are* you?"

He held up his hands. "I'm me, Reid. I'm the same guy who held you while you cried. I'm the same guy you told your darkest secrets to. I'm *also* a guy who's desperate enough to do anything to save his wife."

"*Save?* You say *save* your wife? Save her from what?"

"Keep the gun on me if you want. I'm going inside to fix something to eat. Maybe while I'm cooking you'll remember who I am and put the gun away. If you can trust me one last time, I'll tell you everything, right from the beginning."

Something in his eyes, the same thing she had seen when he had said he understood about her not telling her parents about the rape. She returned the Glock to the holster. "It must be one hell of a story. Serious too."

He lowered his hands. "Life and death serious."

She followed him to the house and onto the creaking porch. A white rocking chair, its paint peeling, barely moved in the breeze. He unlocked the door and swung it open. "Come on in."

Floorboards sagged underfoot as she followed him down a hall leading to a kitchen, where a yellow dining room table with two matching chairs sat beside the far wall, beneath a window.

Pete dropped the keys on the table. "Have a seat." He took a carton of eggs from a scratched and dinged white refrigerator that had to be twenty years old and placed a pan on a stove. "Over-easy okay? I have bread for toast. No coffee, just milk."

"Whatever."

He placed a carton of milk and a container of margarine on the table, along with some kind of purple jelly inside a small Mason jar. "Grape. Mom made that. Good stuff."

"Are the vines out back?"

"Dad planted six but they never did much. Mom got those from the Farmer's Market in Laredo." He checked the eggs, flipped them, and dropped bread in a chrome plated toaster. A few seconds later, a wisp of smoke rose from the slots.

Reid pointed. "Is that normal?"

He glanced at the toaster. "No telling how many crumbs are in the bottom of that thing."

"You're supposed to clean them out."

The toast popped up. He dropped two more slices and plated the eggs, brought them over and took two dingy glasses from a cupboard, plus utensils, and returned with the last two pieces of toast. As he poured milk, she picked up her empty glass.

"You're supposed to clean these too, like every year or so. If not then, before you serve your guests." He rinsed her glass, fork, spoon, and sat back down.

"Mom was the last person to do any of that. I think I don't clean anything until I use it because I feel like I'm losing her."

Reid raised the fork. "Let's eat before you fill me in. I want to concentrate on every word."

While she ate, Reid ran the last few days through her mind, looking for hints as to what Pete might tell her. Nothing stood out, so she made a mental list of questions she wanted to ask, but in no particular order. Many of them would likely be answered as their conversation progressed, or she would have him fill in any blanks as he had suggested.

She swallowed the last bite of egg and emptied her glass. "Ready when you are."

He took their dishes to the sink. "Can't stay too long. I'm expecting something back home."

"Anything to do with your wife?"

Pete said nothing. Dishes washed, he placed the last one into a strainer. "Let's sit in the living room. These yellow chairs get hard quick."

Back down the hall and halfway to the right, they turned at a wooden archway and entered a room that held an ancient brown sofa and two of similarly upholstered chairs. Pete sank into one of the chairs. Reid took the other across from him. He leaned back and sighed. "Thanks for holstering your Glock. I can't imagine what was running through your mind." He sat up straight. "Remember that certificate on my wall?"

"The one you got for breaking up that prostitution ring?"

"That, apparently, was only the tip of the proverbial iceberg. It got the attention of the guy who runs most of them. Running them all is his goal."

"Are you saying he's having you kill the competitor's associates? Why not have one of his own guys do it?"

"I asked myself that same question. I think part of it is to get back at me for breaking up his ring. Temporarily anyway."

"No wonder it got his attention."

"That and he doesn't want to risk his guys getting caught. Having good people running things is a valuable commodity that's hard to replace."

"Where does your wife fit in? No, don't tell me—he had her kidnapped and he's threatening to kill her if you don't do as he says."

"Bingo, Reid. ICE lost a great asset when they let you go."

"Their loss, not mine. Any idea who this guy is and where he's holding her?"

"Enrique Martinez is his name. The bastard has the gall to sign his emails. He also says he has someone keeping tabs on whether or not I do what he says. He didn't mention that person's name."

"He probably knows you'd track him down and force an exchange."

"He's got his bases covered."

"Any idea where's he holding her?"

"Probably in Mexico with him. He lets her send handwritten notes so I'll know she's okay. They're short and simple. I'm sure he checks before he mails them."

"You're sure she wrote them?"

"Identifying handwriting isn't that hard, if you know what to look for. Using a magnifying glass—and the internet—I compared the notes to some letters she wrote me when we were dating. Almost every word matched perfectly."

"What about postmarks? That might give you a hint where she is."

"They have local U.S. postmarks. I think he sends them to the guy who's here. Then that guy puts them in new envelopes and sends them to me."

"Talk about covering bases. I'm sure you're relieved she's safe." Reid paused. But for how long? And would this Martinez let Pete's wife go after Pete finished his dirty work for him?

Pete's chest rose and fell with a huge breath. "Go ahead and say it, I've said the same thing. When—and how—will it end?"

"It won't, will it? As long as he's got you under his thumb, he'll utilize his asset for as long as he can. What about— Damn, Pete, I don't even know your wife's name."

"Concepcion. Her name is Concepcion."

"Pretty. It means 'conception.'"

Pete covered his face and lowered his head.

Reid couldn't imagine what he was going through, but— No, not that too? She left the chair to kneel in front of him. "Pete, is Concepcion pregnant?"

He raised his head. "Connie … I call her Connie." Tears ran down his cheeks. He wrapped his arms around Reid and cried. She held him, hoping he could get it out so they could concentrate on getting Connie back.

His shoulders eventually stopped shuddering. "He sat up and wiped his eyes and face. "I haven't cried like that since Dad died." He wiped his runny nose. "I call her Connie because Concepcion is a mouthful. She doesn't mind what I call her. Most of the time it's hon, honey, or sweetheart. I guess the bad guys studied our movements and waited for her when I was at work. That way they could catch her outside so they wouldn't have to break in. A shopping bag was on the kitchen table. Inside it was one of those self-pregnancy tests, so …"

"Did Martinez leave a note?"

"Probably his hired man did. I doubt Martinez leaves home to soil his hands with this type of thing. In the note he threatened Connie and told me not to involve the police. He also added that he would start sending emails with instructions after she told him my email address, which he assured me she would."

Reid returned to the chair. "Bastard."

"No doubt about it, along with a few more choice names I've called him. Have you figured out why I asked you over after I ran that background check on you?"

"Since I worked with ICE, you thought the insight might be useful."

"I said it already but it bears saying again—ICE lost a hell of an asset when they fired you. You're probably more intelligent than all of them put together."

"I'm intelligent enough to ask this—how long before you were going to ask me for help?"

"Until I was sure you'd help instead of turning me in to my own department."

"That should've been obvious after I told you how I got fired."

"Trying to be careful, Reid. I'm sure you realize this is nothing to play with."

"Don't worry, one way or another we'll get your wife back. As far as Enrique Martinez, if I have anything to do with it, and I do, that son-of-a-bitch won't live to see his next birthday."

16

Connie Anderson paced the floor of the small room where she had been held for three weeks. She expected Martinez to show up anytime, demanding she write another letter to Pete. The grizzled Mexican, who had to be near seventy, had assured her from the start that as long as she and Pete did what he said, she would be home within a month. Regardless, she didn't trust the man. He had an ominous laugh and would smile often, but she believed it was all show. Since he could have her kidnapped out of her own home in the middle of the day, he was likely to be capable of anything, including murder.

She dropped to the lumpy mattress. What were her options for escape? Dumb question. She hadn't thought about anything else since she had been taken. Could she have missed anything? It was possible, so she should consider it again.

She had no idea where she was. She and the two men had been on the road at least three hours in a van marked Mendoza's Home Improvements. The van stopped at her house when she arrived home from shopping, and the men met her at the porch, asking if she needed any work done. She said no, took her keys from her purse, and they left for the van. As soon as she unlocked the door, they forced her inside. After they gagged and handcuffed her, they forced her to the van. She spent at least an hour on the road in a hot, cramped box, beneath a false bottom in the van's rear. When they stopped and opened the top, light and cooler air washed over her, along with relief at being released from the coffin-like enclosure. The more she thought about being in the box, the more she believed they had hidden her in it while crossing the border into Mexico. When that thought had occurred, she had attempted to make a mental checklist of all the Mexican towns and cities within a three-hour drive of Laredo and had quickly given up.

Connie glanced around the room for maybe the hundredth time. A heavy wooden door. Plastered walls. A single air conditioning unit that ran constantly, complaining with a chattering, incessant whine whenever the compressor kicked in. Whoever installed the unit had somehow secured it so it wouldn't budge. There were no windows. At least it stayed cool enough to be somewhat comfortable. She had a bathroom, a lamp on a rickety excuse for a table by the bed, and a single chair at a table where she ate. She had considered taking a leg off the table and using it as a weapon. Even if she managed to escape, she had no idea where to go to for help, and she wouldn't make it home without it.

A key rattled in the lock. The door swung open, and a wrinkled, dark-skinned old woman entered. She carried a tray with a paper plate of food, a plastic fork, and plastic cup of water. Just outside the door stood Martinez and another man. Since Martinez never locked the door behind him, Connie assumed the second man accompanied him during his visits to wait outside. The woman placed the tray on the table, left, and Martinez closed the door behind him.

"Buenos días, Señora Anderson. Eat, eat, you must keep up your strength for your trip home. Your husband has performed admirably. I do not wish him to think I have mistreated you when you reunite."

She sat at the table and glanced at the food. Her stomach protested, but she picked up the fork. She didn't want to give away her pregnancy. That would give Martinez another hold on Pete.

Martinez clapped his hands, took a pack of cigarettes from his pocket, and laughed. "You are a very intelligent woman to listen. Your time here has passed quickly, sí?"

She glared at him, took a small bite of scrambled egg, and swallowed. She couldn't handle the corn tortilla. "Not quickly enough."

"Of that I have no doubt." He lit the cigarette and blew smoke into the ceiling. "Since you are enjoying your accommodations, you may be here a short while longer than I originally said."

She dropped the fork to the tray. "Why would I expect a man who kidnaps a woman and smuggles her into Mexico to keep his word?"

"Ah, you have made that conclusion, I applaud your intelligence." He placed the cigarette between his lips. *Clap. Clap. Clap.* "I hope your intelligence allows you to realize your safety rests on whether or not your husband does as I say."

Connie slapped the tray off the table. "Hijo de puta!"

Martinez removed the cigarette from his lips and flicked ashes in the floor. "Why insult my mother by calling her a female dog? Yes, I know that is a common curse you high and mighty Americanos toss about. Perhaps it is time you learned a lesson in manners, no?" He left. The key rattled in the lock.

Connie covered her eyes. Why had she done that? She knew better than to antagonize him.

A short while later, the key rattled again. Martinez pushed a young woman inside. She knelt to gather the tray and everything that had been on it and wiped the floor with a rag. When she stood with the tray and stepped toward the open door, Martinez closed it.

"Señora Anderson, this is my lovely Gabriella. A beautiful name for a beautiful young woman. I purchased her from her parents at fourteen years of age. She is now sixteen. Turn around and let this woman see you, Gabriella."

He circled the young woman, whose eyes darted back and forth between Connie and the door, then raised the simple white dress to expose her brown legs. "I hate to spoil such beauty. However, Señora Anderson, it seems you do not understand the importance of your husband's mission."

Martinez took a pair of pruning shears from his pocket. "My gardener keeps these sharpened so I can trim my roses. They are also my preferred way of teaching someone a lesson."

Connie swallowed. "Please, I … I won't do that again. You broke your word. Wouldn't you be angry if someone broke their word to you?"

Martinez's high-pitched laugh sent shivers up and down her spine. "I do not get angry," he said. "What I do is make people learn how they do not want to *make* me angry." He held up the shears and squeezed the handles twice, making a horrible *snick, snick,* sound. "I will give you the choice. Which part of my beautiful Gabriella will you sacrifice so you will learn to not make me angry?" He moved Gabriella's long, black hair aside. "An ear?" He squeezed the shear's handles. *Snick.* He held the shears by her face, and a tear ran down her cheek, leaving a wet trail shining in the lamp light. "Perhaps her lovely nose?" *Snick.* He raised her hand and placed the curved blades around the first joint of her little finger. "Or perhaps …?"

Connie could hardly breath. "Please, you don't … you don't have to. I won't do it again."

Martinez smiled.

Snick.

17

Reid stared out of the passenger window of Pete's truck. She better run the final pieces of the puzzle through her mind — pieces that Pete had supplied during the remainder of their conversation at his parents' house. She always did this whenever a particularly challenging problem affected her, and figuring out how to get Connie back was definitely a particularly challenging problem.

Pete had received the first email the day after Connie had been taken. In it, Martinez said more emails giving the exact instructions as to where the pimps could be found would arrive. He didn't care how Pete did the killing, as long as he did it within the stated timeline. So far that had been within a week of receiving the instructions. The one she had witnessed had been the first of a pair, given in the first email, the second being the one Pete had told her about. Last night, when she had seen him slam the laptop closed, he had been frustrated because Martinez had originally said there would only be two. Now he wanted more, with instructions to follow.

Reid expected as much. Once someone like Martinez gained control of a situation, they used it to their advantage. No doubt he considered himself untouchable in Mexico, especially since his threats against Connie kept Pete in line. In addition, since Martinez's man in Laredo reported Pete's activities, slipping inside the country to rescue Connie was impossible. Also, even if he could, his less-than-ideal Spanish would stick out like a cactus in the middle of a shopping mall. Success required command of the language, including insider information from people inside Mexico.

Working with ICE for so long, Reid possessed those things, but she needed to seek that insider information to discover where Martinez lived. She had no idea what to do afterward. With more knowledge concerning Martinez, a weakness in his armor might appear. A weakness she would exploit to the fullest.

As they passed the hotel where she had stayed, she faced Pete. Jaw set, hands white-knuckled on the steering wheel again, he glanced at her. "It's a hell of a mess. Any idea where to begin?"

"For me, yes, for you, no. I'm going home for my passport and tourist visa. From there I'm heading into Mexico to look up a couple of people who might have information on someone like Martinez."

"How do you know them?"

"From stopping them while they were crossing the border. They were brothers—Miguel and Juan Hernandez—small-time marijuana smugglers trying to make ends meet to feed their families."

"How do you know all that?"

"By talking *to* them, not *at* them. They weren't violent or arrogant, and they were unarmed. The last thing they wanted was to be in jail away from their families, so ..."

"You let them go?"

"I made sure they promised to stop trafficking drugs. I joked about coming to check up on them and they believed me. I guess it's not often they have a five-foot-ten-inch redhead— with her hand resting on a Glock at her side—towering over them while standing in the headlights of a Jeep. They even told me where they lived. Said I'd be welcome anytime."

"I'm not surprised. You *do* have that effect on people."

"I hope one of those guys can give me a lead on Martinez. Maybe they can help me get a gun too. I need a weapon when I go back for Connie. As you well know, smuggling one in is out of the question."

"You're not going to do it all in one trip?"

"Not going to rush it. I'll go in and find out everything I can. When I've done all the damage I can do, I'll come back to El Paso and we'll go from there."

Pete turned onto his street. "I wish I could help. If I don't show up when I get another kill order, Martinez's guy will report it to Martinez. Nothing about this is going to be easy."

"I'd take your help if I had a choice. I'll get by. Hell, if it were easy, anybody could do it."

"You're not anybody, that's for damn sure." He pulled into the driveway and parked beside the Honda.

Reid grabbed his arm before he could open the door. "I didn't see the old green car parked at the gun range. Why were you there in disguise anyway?"

"Practicing my makeup skills while I got in some range time. I'm rusty as hell. If any of my co-workers had recognized me, they would've asked why I couldn't work. One of the guys lives out beyond my parent's place. I didn't want to attract attention there either, so ..."

"You were wearing makeup?"

"Mostly to make wherever the beard didn't cover look old and dried out."

"When I showed up that first day—when you came out wearing shorts and saying you had been running—were you cleaning up after killing that first guy?"

"Trying to."

"Good thing you remembered to take off the beard and wig."

"No joke. I drove Connie's car to the gun range. I only took out the green car when I had to. Hers is in the garage."

"Are her parent's still living? What are you telling your friends and work?"

"The same thing I told you, we're separated. As far as work, she recently quit. She was considering school in the spring and getting a degree in counseling, since so many vets are coming back from the Middle East needing someone to talk to. Her parents live in Mexico. I told them she had gone to California to try a new job."

"Don't they speak on the phone?"

"I told them she would be too busy, that she would call as soon as she could."

"Pete, you are one devious detective."

"Because I'm forced to, Reid. You know that."

No problem, I get it." She opened the truck door. "I better hit the road. I've got a lot of miles to cover and a lot of thinking to do."

"You want a bite to eat, or something to drink before you go? I need to check my email in case Martinez sent something."

"I could use a sandwich and the ladies room."

After the bathroom, she joined him on the sofa, where he sat with the laptop open and a frown on his face. "Does your expression mean Martinez sent you a message?"

"He didn't. I don't know if that's good or bad."

"How often does he let her write?"

"Once a week. I usually get it on Friday, sometimes Saturday."

"We met this past Saturday. I went home Sunday and came back Wednesday. We had our falling out yesterday, Thursday. That means today's Friday. When's your mail due?"

Pete glanced at his watch. "Usually by now, I'll check the mailbox." A minute later he returned. "Nothing."

"Maybe tomorrow."

"Hope so. I count on those letters. Even though they're short, at least they let me know Connie's okay."

18

The familiar rattle of the key in the lock woke Connie Anderson. She turned on the lamp as Martinez entered, paper and pen in one hand, a small cardboard box in the other. She sat on the side of the bed. He closed the door and faced her.

"It is time for your weekly letter to your husband. I'm sending a package as well. Since you learned such a valuable lesson from our talk yesterday—and from Gabriella's contribution—I believe your husband may benefit from the same lesson." He placed the items on the table. "Write your letter and I will read it. If all is in order, you will place it in this box with his lesson."

Connie stood on weak legs and shuffled to the table. Morbid curiosity tempted her to look in the box. Instead, she picked up the pen, slid the paper in front of her, and wrote. Martinez expected a few sentences stating that she was well. When she placed the pen on the table, her hand trembled. "Is Gabriella alright?"

Martinez smiled his yellow-toothed smile. She wanted to shove the box down his throat.

"Because of your impudence," he said, "she is no longer perfect. Before you place the letter inside, write that what is in the box did not come from you. Include how it is a reminder to your husband of the seriousness of our understanding. He will receive it later than normal, which is just as well. Perhaps the mental strain will also cause him to strive to meet my goals."

After he read the letter, nodding with approval, she placed it inside the box that held a wad of bloody paper towels, which were likely wrapped around the tip of Gabriella's little finger.

Martinez took the pen and the box. "*Gracias, you* have been most kind. I am certain your husband will find this package, shall we say, enlightening?"

Connie kept her eyes on the table. Cackling laughter, he locked the door behind him. A silent rage overtook her until she trembled, followed by overwhelming nausea.

She ran to the bathroom and vomited.

19

After a quick sandwich and a few swallows of water to satisfy her stomach for the beginning leg of her ride, Reid set off toward home. She ran plan after plan through her mind the entire way, attempting to manage Connie's rescue. Mile after mile, nothing plausible revealed itself. By the time she reached the outskirts of El Paso, she had cursed under her breath at each stop sign or set of traffic lights.

At home, she pulled into the driveway and killed the engine. When she stepped through the fence door to tell Bob how much she appreciated his fine work on the window, he and April were already on the way over. Reid met them on the sidewalk in front of his porch. After a quick hug, she rubbed the poodle's curly head.

After again thanking Bob for looking out after her, she raised the garage door with the remote from one of the Honda's compartments and entered to take a look at her dad's pickup. It sat clean, filled with gas, and ready to go, exactly as if he were still alive. The truck cranked as soon as the starter whirred. Dad would be pleased.

Reid unlocked the front door and unloaded the Honda, backed the truck out of the garage and parked the tired Wing inside. She dropped to the sofa and called Pete, who answered on the third ring. "I take it the trip went well?"

"I plan to head out in the morning, after a good night's sleep. Got to have all my wits about me."

"Sounds like the smart thing to do."

"I try. Did you get any emails from Martinez or a letter from Connie?"

"Nothing. I still don't know how to feel about it."

"Martinez isn't going to hurt her. He knows the minute you stop getting her letters, you might head to Mexico and look him up, in spite of being watched."

"I wish I could figure out who Martinez's man is in Laredo."

Reid smacked herself on the forehead. "Do I feel stupid, that's a great idea. While I'm in Mexico, I'll not only enquire about Martinez, I'll check on his pal too. If anyone knows Martinez, they'll know his cohort. We might be able to use that information. In fact, that information might be more valuable than what I might learn about Martinez."

"How so?" Pete asked.

"Not now, my brain's worn out. I'll think more about it when I head south. By the time I get back, I hope we can use everything I learn to get a concrete plan together. In the meantime, let's hope you hear from Connie."

"I hope Martinez doesn't send me any more instructions. Even with the disguise and the car, I've been lucky."

"You were more than lucky and you know it. As much as you hate why you're doing it, the way you took out those pimps was ingenious."

Pete blew a soft breath into the phone. "I'm not proud of it."

"It's still the truth," Reid said. "Knowing that makes me believe we can pull this off."

"I'm glad you said that. I've been sitting around here feeling like hell. Look, I want to tell you how much I appreciate your help."

"Save it for when we get Connie back safe and sound. You can thank me by grilling another steak."

"I should let you get some downtime from that ride. Be safe."

Reid ended the call. Had she overdone the pep talk? She would start believing it herself as the pieces of useful information fell into place. First, that bite of something to eat, a shower, and sleep.

* * *

Reid slapped the buzzing alarm clock into submission. As the faint glow of sunlight lit the curtains, the familiar hiss of air brakes on the garbage truck came from the street. How many times had she lain here and heard that sound? She half expected her mom to yell to get ready for school and her dad to open the door and pull the covers off her, saying, "Rise and shine, Pammy, time to get up and face the world."

What would they think of the trouble she faced now? Didn't matter. She would make them proud whether they were here or not. As far as she was concerned, they were.

After a bowl of cereal and an apple, both borrowed from Bob, she told him she would be gone a while. He didn't ask questions. He trusted her as much as her dad had and knew she could more than handle herself.

She stored her Glock in her dad's safe in the den and took out her passport. The permit for driving the truck in Mexico stayed in the glove box.

On her laptop, she checked the State Department website for travel bulletins concerning possible violence to U.S. citizens in Mexico. Reid absorbed the possible dangers while reading the long list describing any number of precautions tourists should take depending on the area. Generally, Mexican citizens stood a better chance at being victims of these crimes, but foreigners could be targeted, specifically in casinos and resort areas. U.S. citizens, especially, were warned to not display expensive looking jewelry or cameras, and to maintain awareness of their surroundings at all times, avoiding situations that might separate them.

As far as the requirements for crossing the border into Mexico, four months remained on her passport and tourist visa, so everything should go smoothly. What was she thinking? Drivers were occasionally chosen for random searches, even when holding another document in her possession—a Dedicated Commuter Lane sticker attached to the truck's windshield, otherwise known as a DCL. This reduced the amount of time it took to cross the border. With this trip especially, it was an advantage, since she had no time to spare.

She packed light, including bathroom items and clothes for a couple of days, placed the overnight bag behind the seat of the truck, hopped in, and set out for the El Paso to Ciudad Juárez border crossing.

In the dedicated commuter lane, she stopped several times, waiting for traffic ahead and for the crossbars to raise and lower. The traffic moved but slowed again, this time for the red and green lights communicating to a driver whether or not to stop for a vehicle inspection. To her left, long lines of stationary vehicles not in the DCL waited to move ahead. The annual document was definitely worth the three-hundred-dollars. The regular lanes could take as much as two hours to get through. She slowed for the inspection lane, stopped, waited, and her light turned green. An involuntary sigh of relief escaped from her as she pressed the accelerator and headed toward the free bridge that DCL drivers used. Minutes later she entered the city of Ciudad Juárez, located in the Mexican state of Chihuahua.

During her years with ICE, Reid had visited Ciudad Juárez several times, mostly for the purpose of getting to know the people. The locals usually referred to it as simply Juárez. She also enjoyed visiting the city's rich historical sites. To her, one of the best ways to understand a nation's citizens was to understand their history. The first meeting between a U.S. and Mexican president took place here, the summit of William Howard Taft and Porfirio Diaz in 1909. Also, Taft was the first president to visit Mexico. Even then as now, border tensions created conflicts, and an assassin was captured within a few feet of the two presidents before he could harm anyone.

A trickle of sweat tickled Reid's neck. The truck's outside thermometer read ninety-five. She set the AC a notch lower, turned onto the north-south Mexico 45 Highway, and settled into the seat for the four hour-plus trip to Chihuahua City.

Rather uninspiring, the view consisted mostly of desert. Wisps of grass, tall and brown, waved on the side of the road as the lone long-haul truck ahead of her passed them. Never-ending scrub brush stretched to the horizon. Power lines paralleled the highway, shining in the sun as if they were spider webs wet with dew while hanging from her mom's flowers. An hour passed. She yawned and shook her head, ponytail swirling behind her, and drank from the insulated container she had filled with ice and water before leaving home. Forty-five minute later she stopped at Villa Ahumada for a soft drink, a bag of chips, and a restroom break. By the time she passed Medio Camino, mountains rose in the west. The next stop, if she made good time, was her destination of Chihuahua City, Mexico.

According to the laptop search she had made before leaving home, the city's population neared a million, the main attraction being industry. Maybe the Hernandez brothers held jobs in that growing sector, since they had promised to refrain from the marijuana trade. For their sakes, as well as their families, that was a positive. Drug trafficking attracted many, as well as killed many. Even though Chihuahua City thrived, those issues continued.

Reid turned onto Mexico 450 and followed the GPS prompts to the northern edge of the city. Five minutes later she arrived at the turn that would take her into the neighborhood where the brothers supposedly lived. She checked the time. Almost 11:30. Might as well stop for lunch, see what hotels were available, and wait until later in the day, when the brothers would return from whatever jobs they might have.

At the next light, she did a quick search on the GPS for restaurants, found one with "smokehouse" in its name, and programmed the GPS. On the way she licked her lips. The place likely served authentic Mexican ribs. If experience meant anything, they would be great.

After a few more lights, a few more turns, and one long wait at an intersection a block away from the restaurant, several law enforcement cars sped by, sirens screaming, lights flashing. She pulled into the parking lot, found a space, and left the cool of the air-conditioned truck to enter the midday heat.

Inside the colorful restaurant, with red tablecloths, white napkins, and waitresses in red dresses with low-cut white blouses hurrying about, a greeter seated her at a corner table. A moment later, when a young woman asked for her drink order, Reid pointed at the menu. "Cerveza. Cualquier tipo, siempre y cuando es de barril y la taza tiene hielo sobre ella.

The woman smiled. "Por supuesto. De inmediato, señorita." She hurried away, red dress swishing about her brown legs.

Reid liked the waitress's reply. "Of course. Immediately." And Señorita, not Señora, the term for married, usually older woman. This waitress had just earned a nice tip.

Minutes later, she returned with the mug of beer, or cerveza, as Reid had requested. She placed it on a coaster and took Reid's order of ribs, corn on the cob, and side salad. Reid raised the icy mug and glanced around the restaurant before drinking.

Several televisions hung from the ceiling, many showing sporting events, others tuned to unfamiliar shows. To her right, a female reporter told the day's events. The sound was down, but the closed-captioned words running across the bottom of the screen informed viewers about an ongoing gun battle between police and one of the drug cartels.

Damn shame that drugs controlled so many people, including those taking them. She had never tried anything resembling illegal drugs, not even marijuana, and rarely drank enough alcohol to feel its effects. Why muddle her brain? Life could muddle it plenty with all it threw at a person.

The waitress returned with a huge sizzling plate. Reid sliced off a sauced and slightly blackened rib from the full rack. TV could wait.

Halfway through the meal, the TV caught her attention again. Concerning the previously reported story, three cartel members had been killed, and one officer had been badly wounded.

The violence brought to mind Reid's reason for being here. Time to refer to her game plan.

First, she needed to know where Martinez lived. Second, she needed to get an idea of how big his place was and where Connie might be held. Unfortunately, that would have to be determined when she returned to carry out the rescue. Third, and possibly most important, she wanted to know where the man keeping tabs on Pete lived, likely somewhere near Laredo. He was probably in the country legally, under the guise of running a legitimate business, and kept a low profile while using other men to carry out Martinez's orders, such as kidnapping Connie. All three parts of the puzzle would be difficult to acquire. Still, men such as Martinez held known reputations, and men such as the Hernandez brothers, who had once been involved in crime, though not as serious as Martinez's crimes, might be able to supply her with that information.

The waitress returned. Reid asked for water. Thirty minutes later, she left a stack of rib bones, a corn cob void of corn, an empty salad bowl, and paid with a credit card, adding a twenty percent tip.

Outside, the sun sat lower in the sky, but it still took a moment for her sight to adjust from being inside the restaurant with its dim lighting.

Shading her eyes as she hurried to the truck, she took her keys from her pocket. As she opened the door, sirens wailed in the distance, sounding as if they were returning from their former destination. Then they faded, heading the other way.

She climbed into the truck and drove to a hotel she had passed while coming to the restaurant. On a TV in the lounge, the same reporter was giving the details of the shootout, so Reid stopped.

Pretty much the same: three dead cartel members, one wounded officer. Now the reporter was saying that the officer would likely not live. Reid scowled, turned, and almost ran into a young woman standing nearby.

Wearing black slacks and a white blouse with the hotel logo, the woman stopped. "Pardon me," she said, in accented English.

"That's all right." Reid nodded toward the TV. "Does that happen often around here?"

"Too often." The woman's dark eyes blinked. "I thought you might be an American, you're so tall. I suppose we Mexicans look like savages to your country's people."

"We have our share of drug problems too. Greed is greed, no matter where it exists."

The woman glanced at the front desk, where an older woman was eyeing her.

"Thank you for saying that," the young woman said. "Do you need a room?"

Reid appreciated her. Might as well calm down the desk clerk for her. "Can you help me check in? I don't speak Spanish very well. *Por favor?* Is that right?" She read the name on the woman's tag. "Margarita?"

"That's correct. I'll be happy to help if you tell me your name."

"Pamela." Reid followed Margarita to the desk, where she told the frowning woman in Spanish that they had a customer who was asking her for help with checking in, since she didn't know the language. Reid smiled and nodded. The desk clerk huffed, but with Margarita's help, they completed the transaction. It was all Reid could do to not laugh every time the clerk complained about *"estúpidos Americanos"* coming here without knowing how to speak proper Spanish.

Reid took the key and thanked Margarita, retrieved the overnight bag from the truck and hurried up the steps to the motel's second level.

The room faced the intense heat of the setting sun, like the one in Laredo. She didn't mind. A decent bed and a hot shower met her needs. What more could she expect? At least there was a breakfast area in the lounge. Considering the reason for the trip, what more could she ask for?

She unpacked the case and checked the time. Good thing hotel nightstand clocks were universal. 4:30, too early to visit the Hernandez brothers. She removed her boots and relaxed on the bed, enjoying the cool air blowing across her face from the air conditioning unit, with its steady, insistent hum. Around six would be better. They should be home by then, possibly having dinner.

Reid yawned. It had been a long day. With the added tension of being in a different country, not to mention the reason why, she could use a nap. She set the clock's alarm to 5:30, rolled over, and closed her eyes.

20

From the kitchen, Pete entered the living room, a bag with a fast-food burger and fries in one hand, a beer in the other. He sat and glared at his cell phone on the coffee table beside the laptop. All day he had alternated between checking for calls from Reid and checking for emails from Martinez. Neither made much sense, but it was hard to ignore the nagging thought that something was wrong. He still hadn't received a letter from Connie, which didn't help matters. He couldn't do anything about the letter or the email. Probably should call Reid if she didn't call soon.

He took a bite of the burger and opened the laptop. Connie's dark eyes met his. He swallowed, picked up a napkin, and wiped tears. What he wouldn't give to have her home.

He dipped the cold fries in ketchup, chewed, and forced the tasteless mass down with one long pull from the beer bottle.

What he wouldn't give to have his fingers wrapped around Martinez's throat.

He logged in and checked his email. Nothing, absolutely nothing. He closed his eyes, rubbed his forehead, and his cell phone rang.

Pete knocked it off the table and scrambled to his feet, grabbed the phone and checked the screen. "Reid, you there? You okay?"

"I was beat, so I took a short nap. Sorry about not calling. I will next—"

"Please do, dammit."

"Stressed out, Detective?"

"What the hell do you think? Have you talked to—"

"Don't you think I'd tell you if I had? I will soon. Did you get a letter from Connie or an email from Martinez?"

"Nothing. I still don't know what to think about it."

"Don't speculate, it'll stress you worse. I'll call as soon as I get back after talking to the brothers."

Pete ended the call and dropped to the sofa to stare at the burger and fries. He didn't want either, but he needed food.

He finished the meal, threw away the trash, and returned to the sofa with another beer. As he logged onto his email, his throat tightened. One new message from Martinez. Pete opened it, read, and stared at the screen. Martinez repeated his earlier message about having a few more "tasks" to perform, this time with not one, not two, but three competitors to kill. He included again how Connie could return home only when the tasks were completed.

Pete clenched his jaw. The bastard. How many more after that?

Martinez also added that a letter from Connie should arrive soon, this time in a small box. He added that the contents would make Pete understand the importance of doing exactly as Martinez requested.

Pete closed the laptop. He was tempted to sling it across the room. Instead, he downed the beer, leaned back on the sofa, and covered his eyes with his palm, still damp from the condensation on the bottle.

Even if Reid discovered Martinez's home, could she and Connie leave safely? What about Martinez? He couldn't be left alive to repeat his particular brand of madness. Pete had no problem with that, and Reid had made her opinion clear on the matter.

A dull ache pounded at the base of his skull. In the kitchen, he gulped four ibuprofen.

In the living room again, he started to drop to the sofa but went to the window instead. The postal carrier was pulling away from the mailbox. He ran outside and pulled the door open so hard it came loose from the hinge. Inside sat a brown cardboard box about six inches square.

He glanced around. Ever since Reid had mentioned getting information on the guy keeping track of him, including how that might be more critical than what she might learn about Martinez, he had been paranoid.

The street was quiet, not a single car, but down at the stop sign, a van marked Mendoza's Home Improvements rolled slowly by. Probably lost looking for the next customer. Pete clutched the box to his chest and hurried back inside. He would fix the damn hinge later.

In the kitchen, he took a knife from a drawer. Before opening the box, he checked the return address. It was the same as the letters, locally postmarked, no return address. The tape slit easily, too easily, and Pete cut his finger. He wrapped a paper towel around the cut, opened the box, and found a twin to his bloody paper towel. His chest tightened. He started to pull the paper towel out but stopped. Partially hidden, a folded note had worked its way to the side of the box. It was from Connie. He started to read, but as soon as he read that what was in the box wasn't hers, he sank to the floor. When his breathing slowed, he sat at the dining room table, box and letter in hand.

The letter mirrored Martinez's email, nothing more. Pete looked in the box, unsure as to whether or not he wanted to see the contents. He tentatively unfolded the paper towel to uncover a single, brown fingertip. By the size and skin texture, it belonged to a woman. No polish on the nail and no sign that there ever had been. Connie usually wore some type of enamel on hers, so the finger wasn't hers. Then again, her note said it didn't belong to her.

He shut the box.

Whatever Reid was doing, she needed to do it fast.

Damned fast.

***

Re-tying her ponytail, Reid studied her reflection in the dresser mirror. She was handling the strain alright, but it was definitely showing on Pete. No wonder. He had kept everything almost completely hidden the few days she had stayed with him. There had been subtle hints, like the slight grins that never broke into a full smile and the fact that he never laughed out loud. She doubted she could have done as well in his situation.

Outside the room door, the air was noticeably cooler, but the heat of the day still radiated up from the asphalt parking lot. The truck was no better, since she had forgotten to put the shade in the windshield. She set the AC on high, backed from the space, and took a left out of the parking lot.

During the route to the Hernandez brothers' address, a police car sat at every corner, parked at the curb. Apparently—no, not apparently—the gun battle earlier in the day set local law enforcement on edge.

She turned at the GPS prompt and slowed as she entered a quiet residential neighborhood. When the GPS announced the location within 100 feet, she slowed even more. Up ahead, near the location, two police cars were parked. She slowly rolled by. Four officers stood on the porch, talking with two women and one man. One of the women held a child of about two or three. The other woman cradled a baby with one arm while covering her mouth with her hand. Her shoulders shook as if she were crying.

Reid continued past and detoured back toward the hotel. She would try again tomorrow. Maybe the GPS was off by a house or two. Regardless, her inner ICE agent demanded she not stop and check.

Near the hotel, a fast-food sign advertising taco salads flashed red and green letters. She ordered one and a large beverage at the drive-through and returned to her hotel room.

The black cowboy boots dropped off with a nudge of her toes. She sat on the bed to call Pete. No need to keep him waiting. He answered on the first ring. "Go ahead."

"I need to wait until tomorrow. When I drove by the GPS location, four police officers were talking to a man and two women on the porch. Do I have to tell you why I couldn't stop?"

"Did you recognize the man as one of the brothers?"

"He was about the right height and build. It's not like I could stop and take pictures."

"Any idea why the police were there?"

Finally, something she could answer. "I didn't mention it earlier. While I was on the way to lunch, the police were in a gun battle with one of the cartels. Three bad guys died and one officer was wounded. He's not expected to make it, according to the TV reports. It's no secret why they're in an uproar around here."

"I hope one of your brothers wasn't involved. You said crime was off their agenda."

Reid shifted the phone to her other hand. "You assume I had that much control over them? What a hell of a thing to say. I'll let it pass, like when you whined about me not calling you when I got here. I *do* have a slight idea of what you're going through."

Pete exhaled into the phone for a count of three. "When you get back, you're welcome to kick my ass in my own house, like you said you could."

"What I might do is tell Connie how you stared at my naked self in your tub for who knows how long. She'll handle the ass-kicking then."

Pete sighed, followed by a chuckle. "I needed that. Okay, I know you can handle everything down there. I'll let you go and— Damn, I almost forgot. I got an email from Martinez and a package from Connie."

"A package instead of a letter?"

"The letter was in the package. She said what was in the package wasn't hers, and I needed to do as Martinez demanded. His email said he was going to have few more 'tasks,' as he called them, for me to do."

"We expected that." Reid paused. Ask or not? "Do you want to tell me what was in the package?"

"The tip of someone's finger," Pete said. "Female from the looks of it. Connie wears fingernail polish and the nail didn't."

"A sign of what he might do if you don't follow orders."

"Exactly."

"At least we know she's okay. We also know he plans to use you again. I'll continue with my plan to visit the brothers tomorrow. I'll call as soon as I know anything."

"I hope I'll be here and not off an another one of Martinez's so-called 'tasks.'"

"You and me both."

21

Reid rose early and grabbed a quick breakfast in the hotel lobby. The television mentioned nothing new about the cartel gun battle. Maybe things had calmed down, including in the neighborhood where the Hernandez brothers supposedly lived.

As she dumped her trash in a container, the young woman she had met yesterday, Margarita, entered the main doors. Head down, knotted tissue in one clenched hand, she shuffled closer. Red eyes too. Reid placed a hand on her arm to stop her. "Margarita, what's wrong?"

"I—" She glanced at the watching desk clerk. "I cannot talk right now. I need to start work." She hurried down the hall.

At the front desk, Reid faced the clerk. "Do you know why Margarita's upset? She seemed fine yesterday."

The woman sniffed. "No hablo inglés."

Reid placed her elbows on the counter. "Is that what you tell these young women to tell us estúpidos Americanos so you can avoid speaking to us? Reconsider your answer—I speak Spanish as well as you. If not, I'll tell your manager how uncooperative you are with his *paying* customers."

The woman nodded toward the hall. "The police shot her father yesterday. He was a very bad man. Cartel."

"You're making her work today?"

"She can attend the—how you say—memo, memori …?"

"Funeral, memorial service, servicio memorial. How damned civilized of you."

"No mis reglas." The clerk tapped the hotel insignia on her uniform. "Las reglas del hotel."

Smack! Reid lifted her stinging palm from the counter. What a joy it'd be to smack the smug expression off this woman's face instead of the counter. "'Not your rules? The hotel's rules?' Damn the hotel rules."

She strode down the hall and around a corner, to find Margarita pushing a cart loaded with sheets and cleaning supplies. Reid stopped in front of the cart. "I'm sorry about your father." Margarita glanced down the hall toward the front desk, and Reid lay her hand on the young woman's arm. "Yes, the clerk told me. Don't worry about her, I need to ask you something. What was your father's name?"

The young woman's eyes filled with tears. "His name was Miguel, Miguel Hernandez. I'm sure the clerk said he was a bad man. He was not. My mother, she has a new baby. We needed more money. Papa said he would only work with them until he could get another factory job that paid better wages."

"I'm sorry to hear that. Things got a little rowdy with the clerk. I'll make sure she understands it was because I was concerned about you."

Margarita nodded. "I need this job, now more than ever." She pushed the cart to a room and unlocked the door.

Back at the front desk, Reid apologized to the clerk for losing her temper. She hated to do it, but she would hate it more if Margarita lost her job because of her. The clerk smiled, probably enjoying an Americano begging her forgiveness, and said she understood.

Reid glanced at her watch while hurrying to the truck. She had wasted valuable time, but now she knew exactly where the Hernandez brothers—now the Hernandez brother—lived.

The neighborhood lacked police cars, but other cars lined the side of the road. She parked behind the last one, hurried along the street, and stopped in front of the house.

Men and women, boys and girls, stood on the porch. In the middle of them stood the man she had seen yesterday. This must be Juan Hernandez. He looked familiar, maybe a bit heaver. Would he remember her? It was likely since she had changed so little, and the experience of talking to her in the middle of the night had probably been one he would not soon forget.

Some of the people stared as she strode toward the house. Juan left the porch and met her halfway. "Why are you here, Señorita Reid? I have done as I promised." He glanced over his shoulder toward the porch. "I wish I could say the same for my brother."

"I'm sorry for your loss, Juan. I'm also sorry to intrude while you and your family are in mourning. Please forgive me."

"How did you know?"

"I met Miguel's daughter at the hotel where I'm staying. She told me."

Juan lowered his head. "I understand." He raised his eyes to hers. "Why are you here?"

"I need to ask about two men I'm having problems with. If you have time to talk, I need your help. It's important, Juan, *very* important."

"Let me speak to my wife first."

Reid waited by the cars while Juan spoke with one of the women who was one the porch yesterday. The woman looked her way, nodded, and Juan joined Reid. "Señorita Reid, I told my wife—her name is Rosa—about you when Miguel and I returned from the border after meeting you. She was very happy for me to stop working with the marijuana. She always said it would be the death of me. Who are these men troubling you?"

"Can we sit in my truck? I don't like standing out here in the open." Inside the truck, Reid cracked the window to allow a bit of the building heat to escape, then faced Juan. "I only know one man's name—he is Enrique Martinez. I think he lives somewhere around Nuevo Laredo. The other is—"

"No," Juan said, "he lives in Monterrey. The other man's name is Esteban Mendoza. They once lived here in Chihuahua. I see why you are, as you say, having problems with them. They are the worst of men, especially Martinez."

Reid held in a sigh of relief. "Do you know where Martinez lives in Monterrey?"

"I have a cousin who works at one of the country clubs. He tells me about Martinez and how he plays golf. He makes his fortune in bad ways."

"He runs a prostitution ring in America, yes?"

Juan shook his head. "Not *a* prostitution ring, many of them. My cousin said he overheard him talking about how he wanted to run them all, at least all those in Texas."

Reid glanced out the window. That explained it. What Martinez couldn't take, he would kill and take anyway. She and Pete had no idea how deep his reach was, or how deep he was trying to reach. She faced Juan, who sat with his hands together, staring at her.

"My cousin says Martinez lives on an estate south of town. He keeps an armed man with him."

"What's the name of this estate?"

"I do not know."

"Thank you, Juan, you've been a big help. Can you tell me anything about Esteban Mendoza?"

"He and Martinez are lifelong friends. They once were involved in drugs in El Paso, but one of the cartels forced them out."

"It seems I remember some rumors about that when I was about twenty."

"They gave up drugs for prostitution and moved away from the Cartel. You know how they can be."

"Anything else?"

"Since Martinez lives in Monterrey, it is likely that Mendoza lives in Texas and runs the operations. He was born there. Then he met Martinez and ..." Juan shook his head.

"You don't know exactly where Mendoza lives?" Reid asked. "I'm thinking he lives somewhere near Laredo."

"I do not know where he lives."

"What's the chance your cousin could find out?"

Juan shrugged. "I would not want him to endanger his life. Too many questions can do that around a man like Martinez."

Juan's wife appeared at the end of the sidewalk. He waved her to the truck. Juan and Reid climbed out. Rosa stopped beside Juan to offer her hand to Reid, who said, "Please forgive me for disturbing you, Señora."

"Do not apologize. My Juan may be dead also if not for you. It is unfortunate Miguel chose to ignore our warnings, as well as the warnings of his wife. Let us not speak ill of the dead. Has Juan been able to help you?"

"Very much so. Would you mind if I keep him from you a few moments longer?"

"I do not mind. Thank you for coming, though I wish it were not under such circumstances."

As Rosa reached the sidewalk, Reid faced Juan. "You have a fine wife."

"I do, Señorita Reid. Would you like to return to the truck?"

Reid glanced around. "I only have one more question. I know you said it might put your cousin at risk, but can you contact him and ask if he can find out more about where Esteban Mendoza lives? I can return later today or tomorrow, whichever is convenient for you and your family."

"I will call as soon as I go inside. Then I will call Margarita at the hotel and have her tell you when to return here. Will that be acceptable?"

"That will be fine, Juan. Thank you so much."

As Reid climbed into the truck, Juan yelled from a few cars away. "Señorita Reid!" He trotted toward her. "I remember something my cousin once said. He said Martinez was joking with some other men about his American business. He called it a 'home improvement' business. Perhaps Esteban is using that to hide what he is really doing."

"You may be right. I'll wait for Margarita to contact me."

Reid hopped into the truck. Finally, some useful information, especially about the "home improvement' business. She needed to ask Pete if he had seen any kind of work van around his neighborhood, but she had to ask in a way that wouldn't cause him to be overly curious. If he thought Esteban—or Esteban's men—were nearby, he might act before she returned. That could ruin everything, as well as get him killed and Connie made into another plaything for Martinez.

In the hotel lobby, she did a quick Yellow Page search on the computer, checking the names of plumbing contractors in Laredo. Satisfied that none matched the names she had in mind, she returned to her room. The clock on the nightstand showed she had been gone a little over an hour. She checked her phone. No messages, so Pete hadn't tried to call. She dialed and sat on the bed. Pete answered after a couple of rings.

"You're up early, I suppose so you could catch the brothers at home. What did you find out?"

"A few things I wasn't expecting. One is that one of brothers, Miguel, was killed in that shootout yesterday, and—"

"So he *had* gone bad? Dammit, Reid, I—"

"Pete, we've had this conversation before, give it a rest. I spoke to his daughter this morning. She works at the hotel where I'm staying. Miguel worked at a factory but was trying to earn extra money because he and his wife just had a baby. I didn't ask, but I will if you insist, what his exact duties were. I'm betting he was driving their car and got caught in the crossfire. Who knows, maybe he's the one who shot the cop. Then you can feel better about your damned attitude. Are you ready to shut up so I can tell you what I found out? I can always hang up and let you cool off."

Pete said nothing.

"You there, Detective?"

"I won't do that again. What did you find out?"

Reid told him everything except the name of the man in Laredo. She also left out the part about Martinez having Esteban run a home improvement business as a cover while operating his prostitution rings.

"So," Pete said, "Martinez is in Monterrey. That's a start. Now you have to wait for Juan to hear from his cousin."

"Juan's going to have Margarita let me know before I talk to him again. I'm going to grab a newspaper and a bite to eat. I'll let you know something as soon as I can. Before I go, I want to ask you about something Juan mentioned. He said Martinez might be running a cover business for the prostitution ring. That'd be a good way to launder the money. You see any—"

"Don't tell me—it's a home improvement business. I saw a van go by the end of the street when I went to the mailbox yesterday."

"Nope, not it. Juan specifically said it was a plumbing business. He didn't say anything about home improvement. I think he said the name on it was something like Zippy Plumbing, or maybe Snappy Plumbing."

"I haven't seen any plumbing contractors around. You had me fired up. If it had been the van I saw, I was about to go looking for it."

"You'd get arrested for assault."

"True. I'll let you go. Call when you hear something."

Reid slid the phone in her pocket. Another piece of the Martinez-Esteban puzzle had fallen into place. She wouldn't be surprised if Connie had been taken out of the country in the same van Pete had seen. Good thing Reid hadn't told him the truth. Now, if his desperation grew to more than he could handle, he would look for a plumbing van with some off-the-wall name she had made up. That way, he would stay out of trouble until she returned.

The night stand clock read 10:30. Too early for lunch. She wasn't hungry anyway. Breakfast in the hotel lounge had been surprisingly filling. She frowned in the mirror and shook her head. Sitting around waiting to hear from Juan through Margarita was a pain, so grabbing a cup of coffee would give her something to do. As her hand turned the knob, someone knocked.

"Pamela? It is Margarita." Reid opened the door. Margarita closed it behind her. "I saw your truck outside. My uncle said to let you know he spoke with his cousin in Monterrey. His cousin—his name is Martin—is afraid to ask anyone anything about the men you want to know about. He says it is too dangerous."

"The information I received from Juan will help. I need to speak with him again. Is he home now?"

"He is. He and Rosa are going with my mother for my father's body. We will have a wake this afternoon and tonight."

Reid didn't care to wait, but she didn't want to intrude on the family. "What time are they leaving? I need to go home soon."

"Sometime after noon. I am certain you will have time to see him if you leave now. The people who were there last night will not return until later."

Reid placed her hand on Margarita's shoulder. "I'm sorry for your loss. When I met your father about a year ago, I could tell how important his family was to him."

Margarita blinked; a tear ran down her cheek. She took a wadded tissue from a pocket and wiped her eyes. "He wanted great things for us. That is why I learned English. He wanted me to go school in America. He always said I would make a good nurse."

"I hope you can do as he wished." Reid followed Margarita to the door. "Thank you for letting me know what your uncle said. If I don't see you again, hasta la próxima."

Margarita gave her a weak smile. "I hope to see you next time also, Pamela. Adiós."

Reid packed her overnight bag. She could start back to Pete's immediately if Juan could help with getting a gun or two for her trip to Monterrey.

She started to the door and stopped. If Juan couldn't help her acquire a gun, she and Pete would need to figure out something else. She left the key on the dresser and hurried to her truck.

On the way to Juan's, she stopped by a florist and bought flowers, using her credit card again. In her rush to get to Chihuahua City, she had forgotten to get any U.S. dollars exchanged for Mexican pesos.

Five minutes later she pulled to a stop in front of Juan's home. This time, as Margarita had said, no cars lined the street. The slight tension that had been trailing across Reid's shoulders released. She hadn't realized it was there, but it was likely because her height and red hair made her all too obvious, and she had been afraid some of Juan's visitors might talk about her more than she would have liked.

She parked. Flowers in hand, her boot steps on the sidewalk echoed back and forth between the trees in the yard as she strode to the house. The empty porch looked out of place after yesterday. When she reached the steps, Juan and Rosa opened the door.

"Margarita just called, Señorita Reid. I wanted to wait for you."

Reid gave Rosa the flowers. "Please give these to— I'm sorry, I don't know Miguel's wife's name."

Rosa took the flowers and placed a hand over her heart. "We are sisters, twins. She is Rosa also. Our father said he gave us the same name, because to him, when we were born, we looked like two beautiful roses from the same bush. Mama said she was too tired to recall him telling the doctor what to put on the birth certificates. Later, she said she told him we couldn't be roses, because we would have thorns, like him."

"Your mama and papa remind me of two people I know in El Paso. The woman watched over me when I was a child. She is Carletta and her husband is Armando. These days she considers calling him old goat."

Rosa smiled and Juan chuckled. "See, Rosa, I told you that calling your father old goat would be acceptable."

Rosa poked Juan's arm. "You never did try, did you?"

"No, that would not have been wise." Juan faced Reid. "I am sorry for not asking you if I could be of more help. It feels good to laugh."

"I also have lost loved ones. Laughter can feel like it's healing the soul. One more question and I'll be on my way."

Juan opened the door. "Would you like to come inside?"

Reid hesitated. She didn't want to refuse Juan and Rosa's hospitality during their time of mourning, but she needed to get back to Pete. "I don't care to intrude at such a time. Miguel's Rosa will have more than enough visitors tonight."

Rosa sniffed the flowers. "You are right, Señorita Reid. Rosa said she will be glad when this is over. This is usually a time of family, but it can be overwhelming." She faced Juan. "I will take these inside while you finish your business."

Juan closed the door behind Rosa and motioned Reid to two wicker chairs. She settled into one, its worn seat crunching in protest. Juan sat, leaned forward, and rubbed his hands together. "I wish I could be of more help. I am sure Margarita told you about Martin and why he does not want to ask any questions about Enrique Martinez's man, Esteban Mendoza."

"The information you gave me about Martinez having a home improvement company will help." Reid noticed Juan's chest rising and falling with a sigh. He was probably glad she hadn't forced the issue. "However," she continued, "I need a handgun. Preferably two, along with ammunition."

Juan's eyes opened wide. "Whatever trouble you are having with those men, it sounds like you are planning on trouble yourself."

"Martinez kidnapped the wife of a friend of mine."

"I do not own a gun and neither did Miguel. The laws are strict. Mostly, it is only the cartels who have guns. Of course, they have them illegally."

Reid knew Mexico's gun laws well. A citizen had to acquire a permit at a military base and then travel to Mexico City, where the only gun store in Mexico was located. The average citizen didn't have a chance at defending themselves from cartel kidnappings and rapes.

"I'll manage." She stood and offered her hand. "If I ever return to Chihuahua City, I'd like to visit you and your family when you're not burdened with heartache. Perhaps I could take you all out for a fine dinner."

Juan took her hand. "Oh, no, Señorita Reid, if you return, that will mean you have been successful with the rescue of your friend's wife. That would require a feast at our home to celebrate."

"I understand traditional Mexican feasts are special. Goodbye, Juan. Please tell Margarita I'll be thinking of her."

Reid cranked the hot truck, hit the AC button, and buckled her seatbelt. A traditional dinner with Juan's family sounded like a great idea, but a gun or two would increase the odds of her living to do so.

22

Wanting to grab lunch before leaving town, Reid pulled into the parking lot at a burger place and also set the GPS for the return trip. She also wanted to call Pete. He answered after a couple of rings, and she told him there was nothing new to add, except she would be crossing the border at Ojinaga, the shortest route back. She ended the call. The quicker she returned to Texas, the quicker she and Pete could plan for her trip to Monterrey. Something nagged at her too. Maybe it was the feeling she had worn out her welcome in Chihuahua City, especially since she had no protection against any of the cartels except her brain, her hands, her elbows, and her feet, with her pointed-toe western boots. She grinned. Hell, who needed a gun? She frowned. Down here, she did.

With the burger, fries, and a large ice water tucked in the truck's console, she followed the GPS prompts to Mexico 16 Highway for the three-hour drive to Texas.

The lukewarm meal filled her stomach, nothing more, but the cold water refreshed her. Still, after less than an hour, when she turned right onto Mexico 80D, a dreary two-lane highway surrounded by the ever-present scrub brush and underwhelming mountain ranges in the distance, she yawned. It would be good to get back home and sleep in a familiar bed, even if that bed was in Pete's guest room.

Mile after mile she continued, rarely seeing another vehicle. When Mexico 80D became Chihuahua 67, she checked the GPS. The town of Potrero del Llano lay ahead. When the first buildings appeared, she kept a lookout for a restroom and a place where she could find another water. It wasn't much of a town, nothing more than several dilapidated buildings that included one white structure with three horses tied to a short bush of some kind. Although the red letters painted on the side of the white building advertised the availability of gasolina, no pumps were visible. The few trees lining the road and scattered between the buildings waved in the slight breeze like leafless skeletons, similar to those around Pete's parents' house.

She licked her lips, attempting to work up enough saliva to swallow, and pressed the accelerator. Time to get the hell out of here instead of driving though what could have been some artist's surreal rendition of a 1950's Mexican village, complete with vaqueros. No water or bathroom break here. She could wait for both.

At the last of the buildings, two heavyset men wearing western hats, boots, and jeans stood between two dusty pickups. Each also wore black leather vests, and each eyed her as she drove by. Reid checked the gas gauge. Good thing she had filled up before leaving Chihuahua City. She had no intention of learning any of the history of this so-called town, so she hit the accelerator.

Ten miles and ten minutes passed. She leaned back into the seat and focused on the road stretching out in front of her. According to the GPS, she should be in Texas in about thirty minutes, and the first thing she would do—

Beep! Beep-beep!

Reid jerked upright. A pickup truck filled the rearview mirror, right on her bumper. Another truck pulled out from behind that one and raced up beside her, slowing to match her speed. The driver, one of the two men she had seen while leaving Potrero del Llano, pointed toward the shoulder of the road.

A truck behind her, one beside her, two against one. She glanced to the right. About ten feet over, the shoulder of the road fell off into a deep ditch. Nowhere to go. She mashed the accelerator, shooting ahead of the truck beside her. It matched her speed as the truck behind closed in. This time the truck beside her pulled ahead and turned into her, forcing her off the road. A cloud of dust billowed from beneath both vehicles as she slowed. No need in wrecking Dad's truck, and she would have less of a chance at handling these two guys if she hurt herself.

She stopped. Both men climbed from their trucks. One strode to her door. She wasn't about to unlock it. The man who had forced her over pulled a crowbar from the rear of his truck, pointed at her window, and raised the crowbar, hesitating. She raised her hands and shook her head. He pointed at the door lock. They were fast—too fast. No time to even check for cell phone service.

Reid took a breath. Make a plan and fight—to the death if necessary. She unlocked the door and stepped out, leaving her right foot slightly behind her, thigh muscles tight, knee cocked and ready.

"Please, please—por favor— I have money, credit cards!" She took her wallet from her pocket and fumbled for her cash and credit cards, dropping everything to the ground at the feet of the man on the right. He squatted to his heels, put the crowbar down to go through the cash, and she drove her knee forward. His nose gave way with a sickening crunch of cartilage and bone. She immediately planted her right foot on the ground and twisted to the left, viciously slicing her right elbow into the side of the other man's head. He crumpled to the dirt beside his companion. Blood ran from his ear hanging on by a single shred of skin.

Shaking, Reid leaned against her truck to allow the intense adrenaline rush to leave her body. Her knee throbbed and so did her elbow, both preferable to anything these guys had in mind. She wiped sweat from her forehead, shaded her eyes, and looked up and down the desolate road. Nothing.

The man with the non-existent nose, just a bloody mess in the middle of his face with two holes where his nostrils should have been, moaned and tried to sit up. She planted her boot on his chest and pushed him back down. His vest fell open to reveal a black handgun in a shoulder holster. She removed the gun and racked the slide. Round in the chamber ready to go. Shredded Ear was still unconscious. She squatted and stuck the barrel into Bloody Nose's ear.

"Hola, amigo." She nodded toward the other guy. "What were you and your friend going to do with me after I stopped?"

The man blinked, swallowed, and opened his mouth to take a gurgling breath. "No hablo … no hablo inglés." He coughed and spat blood.

"Imagine that. I had the same problem with someone else recently. She wasn't very friendly either." Reid shoved the gun harder and asked him again, this time in Spanish.

The answer wasn't what she expected from a man in his situation. He bared his teeth, spat again, and in Spanish said, "American bitch, we were going to take all you had. Then we were going to rape you and leave you in the desert with a bullet in your head."

Boom!

The gun's blast reverberated through the silent desert. Reid stood and nudged Shredded Ear with the toe of her boot. He groaned and opened his eyes. She squatted beside him and took his gun as well. "Amigo, your friend told me your plans. Before I do to you what you were going to do to me, I want to thank you for the fine pistols."

Boom!

"Gracias."

It was a struggle, but Reid dragged the bodies off the side of the road and rolled them into the ditch. Then she eased the pickups to the ditch to keep any passersby from seeing them, along with rolling up the windows and locking the doors. With any luck, the men wouldn't be found until the vultures signaled their presence. From the look of the deserted road, the coyotes might dispose of the bones before a car showed up. Nature came in handy from time to time.

Reid kicked sand over the blood and brains staining the shoulder of the road. She gathered her cash and credit cards back into her wallet, climbed into her truck to place the guns on the seat beside her, and turned the key. Sweat ran down her neck as she pulled onto the road. She cranked the AC to high and aimed the vents until the icy air cooled her face.

With the problem of acquiring the guns conveniently solved, now she only had to— No, not solved at all. Smuggling the guns across the border wouldn't be worth the risk. She stopped, disassembled the pistols, and threw the parts out the window at half mile intervals. At least those two guns would never be used for crime again, including chasing down and raping any female travelers.

Thirty minutes later she drove into the city of Ojinaga, followed the GPS prompts to the border crossing that lead to Presidio, Texas, waited in line thirty minutes, and promptly received the red light to be searched on the U.S. side of the border. No matter the location, U.S. law enforcement just wouldn't let her be. Good thing she had disposed of the guns.

With the search done, she entered Presidio and stopped at a gas station to empty her aching bladder. A dirty toilet seat and a broken tampon dispenser never looked so good.

She filled the truck with gas, climbed back in, and checked the time. The trip had lasted three hours, including the few minutes it had taken to rid the world of two bits of human scum. That'd be the last time they tried to harm anyone again, even a man.

Still at the station, she called Pete to tell him she was in Texas, but she still had a long way to go. He hadn't received any more messages from Martinez, and she replied that she was glad to hear it. She also mentioned she was going to find a decent restaurant, where she could relax before starting back to his place.

A search on her phone for restaurants turned up only three, and none looked promising. The same search for the town of Shafter yielded similar results, but the town of Marfa, about an hour away, advertised a couple of interesting places where a person could sit down for a steak and a beer. Regardless, she needed to head north on Highway 67, the route toward Interstate 10 and Laredo.

The steak, juicy and tender, and the hot baked potato, with sour cream and butter, filled her empty stomach. Reid enjoyed one ice-cold draft at the beginning of the meal and another to wash down the last bite. At the truck, she loosened her belt a notch to reduce the pressure on her full stomach and climbed in.

An hour and a half later, after merging onto Interstate 10 and driving fifteen more minutes, she arrived at Fort Stockton. She fueled the truck, took another bathroom break, and headed south on US 83 toward Laredo.

Six hours later, with a few more stops to stretch her legs, one to call Pete, and one to pick up ibuprofen for her tender elbow and knee, Reid passed the hotel where she had spent her first night in Laredo. She checked the time. Almost nine-thirty. She yawned. Pete's shower and guest bed would be a welcome sight.

She parked at Pete's. He turned the porch light on and hurried to the truck. "Need a hand with your luggage? You've got to be exhausted."

She took the overnight bag from behind the seat, closed the truck door and locked it. "All I need is a good night's sleep."

He walked with her to the house. "I take it the trip back was uneventful."

Reid saw no need to tell Pete about the two men who had forced her off the road. "I'd like to get inside and sit on something other than a truck seat. I could use a cold beer too."

She left her overnight bag and boots in the guest room and sank into the sofa cushions, crossing her sock feet on the coffee table to wiggle her toes. Pete returned, handed her the beer, and sat. She drank the cold liquid that revived her somewhat. "Pete, I think I know how to get us into Mexico."

"I thought we agreed I needed the stay here in case Martinez gives me another order to take someone else out. He's already lined up the men, remember? If I'm not here to do that, and his guy tells Martinez, Connie will be in danger."

"That's figured into the plan." She took another swallow of beer. "We still have the problem of not having weapons. If everything works out, I'm hoping that problem will be solved. You have a couple of guns we can use, right?"

"Do I have to tell you what'll happen if we get caught taking them into Mexico?"

"We're going to take the guns from Martinez's man—and him—into Mexico."

Pete jerked upright. "How can we do that when we don't know how to find him?"

"Remember the Mendoza's Home Improvements van you saw?"

"Didn't you say it was a plumbing—? What a minute, you lied?"

"Remember what you said you would've done if you knew that was him?"

Pete leaned back on the sofa. "I get it." He rubbed his eyes. "What's your plan?"

"It hinges on Martinez's guy here. His name is Esteban Mendoza. Juan said they grew up together. Regardless of his loyalty, I think it might disappear like a tumbleweed in a windstorm if you shove the cold steel of a gun barrel into his temple." Reid swallowed the last of the beer while Pete rubbed his chin.

"I guess you want guns so we can find Esteban and have him take us to Connie. How does his loyalty come into play?"

Reid stood. "I just thought about something. If Esteban drove by that day, he may have come by while I was here and seen me or the Honda. I don't want to take a chance on him seeing me if he hasn't. I want it to be a surprise when we find him. I should head back to the hotel."

"We should be realistic and play this out like he's seen you." Pete touched his cheek. "Remember the makeup I used to disguise myself? I have an idea to help with that. You might as well stay."

Reid turned on the sofa to face him. "Okay, Detective, you tell me your idea and I'll tell you mine."

23

The next morning, after a quick breakfast, a trip to the nearest store, and almost two hours in the bathroom, Reid eyed her reflection in the mirror of Pete's guestroom. Pete stood behind her, nodding in approval. "Not bad. I've never cut or dyed hair."

Her hair was now shoulder length, dark as in almost black—with bangs. She stuck out her tongue. "I never liked bangs." She turned around. "Out. I've got to dress and you need to clean those two pistols."

"As you recall, I ignored that question while I was cutting your hair. They never get dirty because I clean them weekly. Satisfied?"

She glared at her reflection again. "With this, no, with the guns, yes." She shoved him out the door. "Scoot. Your days of seeing me naked are over." Pete closed the door.

Across the bed lay the teal dress. Aside from the dye, they had also purchased hair shears and a purse large enough to carry a gun. Even if Esteban had spotted her, he had never seen her in the dress or high heels. He hadn't seen her in red lipstick or sunglasses either, her other purchases. Dress and shoes on, she applied the lipstick and donned the sunglasses, completing the transformation. She hardly recognized herself in the mirror, especially with the bangs. Frowning, she shook her head and stuck out her tongue again, but from between red lips.

In the living room, where Pete waited on the sofa with the guns on the coffee table, he stood. "Wow, maybe I'm in the wrong business. Think I should open a salon?"

Reid picked up a pistol, racked the slide to verify a round in the chamber, and dropped it in her purse. "What you need to do is shut up and get your mind on our plan."

"I guess I'm nervous."

"You—make that we—have a lot to be nervous *about*. Since we don't know if Esteban drove by last night, we're taking enough of a chance on you driving my truck as it is."

"We both know I can't drive mine. He'll recognize it right away." Pete holstered the second gun and draped the tail of a floral print golf shirt over it.

Reid patted his cheek. "Look at you, the perfect husband indulging your wife's wishes for a kitchen remodel."

He pulled a matching golf cap on over his dark hair. "I don't give a damn what I look like as long as it fools Esteban. Let's go."

"Let's, darling. Don't forget your sunglasses."

Before they left the house, Reid took a long look out the window. The empty street stretched from one stop sign a half a block away to the other. They didn't need that van showing up now. "Ready when you are."

In less than a minute they were taking a right at the stop sign. Pete had already found the address to Mendoza's Home Improvements on his laptop. Reid entered it into the GPS while he drove. "He's on the other side of Laredo, next to the border. How damned convenient." She sat back in the seat. "Have you considered that van's alternate purpose?"

"Running women back and forth between Mexico and here? Maybe cash?"

"Pay attention, Detective. I said 'alternate purpose,' not main purpose."

He glanced at her. "You think that's how they got Connie into Mexico?"

"Would you be surprised? As you and I well know, smugglers use all kinds of modified vehicles to move things—and people—in and out of the country. I bet that van's got a false bottom in the back. I also bet that's where they hid Connie, at least until they got far enough into Mexico where they didn't have to worry about border security. Besides, what good would she have been to Martinez if she had died from heat stroke in the false bottom in the rear of a van?"

"Too bad we don't have a van like that. We could get our guns into Mexico."

"If all goes to plan, that'll work out too."

"I don't remember that part of the plan."

"If the van's got a false bottom, that's how we'll sneak the guns into Mexico. I thought you would've figured that out by now. Typical man, needing a woman to keep you in line. Did you bring Connie's passport? We need that when we bring her back."

"I put it in the glove box while you were getting dressed. See? I didn't need you to tell me that."

"Good to know. Shut up and pay attention to the road."

Thirty minutes later, when they drove by the address of Mendoza's Home Improvements, Pete pointed. "That's the van."

"Have you seen that pickup beside it on your street recently?"

"No. That means Esteban might not be alone."

"Do I have to tell you we only want Esteban?"

"Is that why you had me buy duct tape when I bought everything else?"

"You got it. Turn around at the end of the block." He did as she asked, and they pulled in beside the van. "Hang back behind me," Reid said. "I'm wearing a lot better disguise than you are, and—"

"They won't be looking at me, they'll be looking at your legs."

She looped the purse strap around her shoulder. "That's what I'm counting on."

The building resembled the standard small business: brick fronted, two large windows, sign overhead. For all Reid knew, Esteban actually worked a few jobs to keep up appearances. She pulled the glass door open, and Pete followed her in. An empty desk. Two empty chairs. Gone? It was too early for lunch. She faced Pete. "We might have to—"

The door swished open behind them, and a short, stocky man, dark hair slicked back, eyed them for a second. "Something I can help you with?"

Reid stepped around Pete. "Señor Mendoza? It's so nice to meet you, my name is Pamela Reid." She placed her hand on Pete's shoulder. "This is my husband, Bob. We'd like an estimate on a kitchen remodel. Do you think you could help us? Bob's all thumbs when it comes to working around the house. I'm sure you know what I mean."

The man glanced from her to Pete and back to her. His eyes roamed from her face down to her long legs and back up. "I'm Señor Mendoza. I'm not taking new jobs at the moment."

Reid frowned her most disappointed frown. "Oh my, what a shame. Perhaps some of your workers would like to help me? You know, a little weekend job? Are they around? I'd love to meet them."

"I only keep two men. They are busy enough."

"If I could just speak to them, por favor? Did I say that right? We just moved here and I'm trying to learn your beautiful language." She placed her hand on his arm. "I just love the way it rolls off the tongue. It sounds so sensual, don't you think?"

"I have always thought so." The tension that had been on Esteban's face since he had stepped in, in the form of slight creases in the corners of his eyes, eased. "I suppose I could do the work myself. You say a kitchen remodel?"

"Oh, how wonderful." Reid smiled her largest smile as she placed her hand on his arm again. "Could you start next week? Bob will be out of the way on a business trip. Of course, only if *you* can do the job." She licked her red lips. "Do you think you can do the job, Señor?"

"I am quite sure I can. Where—"

"Could your other men help too? If they aren't here, could you call them? I'm sure you do all your business on a cell phone. Many professionals handle their business that way."

"They are not here, they are quite busy." He took a slim smart phone from his pocket. "This is how I contact them."

He returned the phone to his pocket and Reid opened the purse. "I'll give you my card so you can call and set up a time to stop by."

She pulled out the pistol.

Esteban's jaw dropped. He took a single step backward, apparently forgetting Pete behind him. "What? What are you—?"

Pete grabbed Esteban's shirt collar and jammed the gun barrel into the back of his neck. Esteban winced, closed his mouth, and Pete lifted him onto his toes. "In case you haven't figured it out, I'm Pete Anderson, the guy whose wife you kidnapped. Pat him down, Reid."

She did so. "Nothing. Bet if we look around, we'll find a few guns." She nodded toward Esteban. "Or he can save us some time and tell us where they are."

Pete jerked Esteban's collar again, nearly lifting him off the floor. "Where?"

"When Martinez finds out what you are doing, your wife won't live long."

Pete spun him around and shoved him to the wall, placed the gun's barrel under his chin and forced his head upward. "It'll go a lot better if you cooperate, you bastard. Where?"

Esteban swallowed, throat muscles contracting. "Desk."

Reid opened three desk drawers and found a Glock 19. She found another one in the last drawer and held them up. "My favorites." She racked one slide and then the other. "Hollow points too." Guns in her purse, she kicked a chair over. "Sit him down for a quick chat."

Pete jerked Esteban from the wall to the chair. "Sit."

Esteban looked over his shoulder at Pete. "I told Martinez he should not have done this to you."

Reid perched the sunglasses on top of her head. "Too bad he didn't listen."

Esteban dropped to the chair. "What do you want?"

"Not now." Pete pressed the gun into Esteban's neck. "Call your men and tell them Martinez won't be giving you any more orders for me, not at least for another week. Tell them you're heading down to talk things over with him and for them to go on as usual. While you're at it, tell them to collect the money from the pimps instead of bringing it here, if that's how they do it."

"He will be sending instructions soon. You know what will happen to your wife if you don't follow them."

Reid drew the gun back, ready to knock some sense into Esteban, but didn't. She lowered the gun — to line the front site on the crease between his brown eyes. "Señor Mendoza, I'm tired of asking you to do as we say. I recently had the pleasure of blowing the brains of two of your countrymen across a deserted stretch of Mexican highway. Believe me, they deserved it." She raised her left hand and formed a thumbs-forward grip on the Glock. Had to be a hell of a thing, seeing that black hole in the end of the barrel staring at him. "Ready to make those calls?"

Esteban blinked. "I … I need my phone."

"Reid," Pete said, "what did you do in Mexico?"

"Not your concern." She gestured toward Esteban with the gun. "Make those calls on speaker. The barrel of Pete's gun will be in your ear. One wrong word …"

Esteban took the phone from his pocket and made the calls, swallowing and frowning every time Pete adjusted the angle of the gun barrel in his ear. He ended the calls. Reid held out her hand.

"Maybe you're not as dumb as you look." He gave her the phone. She gave it to Pete. "You've got room for this in your pocket, don't you? My purse is loaded." She adjusted the thin strap cutting into her shoulder. "Literally."

He took the phone. "Can't forget his passport."

"You heard him," Reid said to Esteban. "Where is it?"

"In the top drawer of the desk, in the back."

She pulled the drawer all the way out, found the passport, and opened it. "All in order. I think we— Wait a minute, are you married?"

"No."

Pete prodded Esteban in the back with the gun. "I'm not sure about that. Hold out your left hand."

Reid examined his ring finger. Tanned and no indentation. "Looks good to me. I was gonna make him call her to say he had to be out of town a few days. Okay, Pete, time to go. Esteban, you're driving your van and Pete will be right beside you. I don't have to tell you what will happen if you don't do as he says. We're going someplace where we don't have to worry about uninvited guests showing up. Then we're going to have a talk so you'll understand how you might come out of this thing in a lot better position than you are now, especially while working for Martinez. You might end up with more money than you're making now too. Get him up, Pete."

Pete grabbed Esteban's collar. "Up." Esteban stood. Pete shoved him toward the door.

Reid started to follow but stopped. "Turn him around." Pete did so, and she looked Esteban in the eye. "Where's your cash? I'm sure there's plenty around here."

Esteban's eyes twitched toward the desk. "I—it is at my house."

Reid walked around behind the desk. "Pete, remember telling me in the bar how I was 'into detail?' Our friend just took a quick glance at the desk. Any idea what that means?"

"A false bottom in a drawer?"

"That's one of those details I would've seen." She rolled the chair aside and pulled a square of carpet from under the desk. "Imagine that, a safe. So much for those people in Mexico who said I was estúpidos. Combination, Esteban."

Pete took a quick glance from Esteban to Reid. "Do we have time for this?"

"I've got something in mind for whatever money is in this safe. It'll only take a minute if our new partner shares the combination."

Esteban shook his head. Reid lowered the Glock's sites to his knee. "Do you have any idea how much it hurts to have your kneecap blown off?"

Esteban's brown complexion paled. "All right, all right, I will tell you." He gave Reid the numbers. She turned the dial. Seconds later she placed a cloth bank bag on the desk and counted thirteen thick bundles of hundred-dollar bills. She removed one and flipped through it. "Got ourselves quite a haul, Detective. If memory serves, there are one hundred bills in each of these thirteen bundles."

"130,000 dollars? Not bad. Can we leave now?"

Reid closed the safe, pulled the carpet in place, and returned the chair. "After Esteban gives me his keys. I'm going to lock up and flip that closed sign on the door."

As they forced Esteban into the van, Reid covered him through the open window while Pete climbed in the passenger seat. Pete stuck his gun in Esteban's side. "Do exactly as I say and you live. Maybe to have a better life than you have now. Understand?"

Esteban's eyes cut toward Pete. "You keep saying things like that. How I might have more money too. What are you talking about?"

"Not now." Reid dropped the pistol in the purse. "Pete, you two back out first and I'll follow." Pete nodded. Reid climbed into her truck. She shoved the bag of money under the seat.

During the drive, she checked the time. They had spent about twenty minutes at Esteban's. Not bad. Now the real test: convincing him to cooperate so Martinez would think things were going to plan while they traveled to Monterrey.

At Pete's, Esteban parked the van beside Pete's truck and Reid parked behind them. She took her pistol from her purse, climbed out with it hidden behind the money bag, and returned the purse to her shoulder, heavy from the weight of the two guns. She stopped by the driver's side window and Pete nodded. As Esteban climbed out, she showed him the gun. His jaw worked, and Reid said, "You've never been in a situation quite like this, have you? Yes, it can work out if you do as we say. Any choice other than that ends up with you dead." Pete rounded the front of the van and took Esteban by the arm. Reid followed them inside.

She took the money and her purse to the guestroom and returned to the living room, where Esteban sat on the sofa. "I'm going back to the truck, Pete. I'm not sure we can trust our guest quite yet. A few wraps of duct tape around his ankles and wrists will ease the situation, at least for us. Pete nodded. At the van, she glanced at the windshield. It would be great if— And there it was, a Dedicated Commuter Lane sticker matching the one on her truck. Made sense since Esteban probably spent time in both countries.

Duct tape in hand, she returned to the living room to give Pete the gray roll. She aimed her gun at Esteban while Pete applied several wraps of the thick, sticky tape to Esteban's wrists and ankles. When Pete finished, he stood. "Mouth?"

"He can't cross the border taped up." Reid glanced at her watch. "Where are our manners? Maybe he needs the bathroom or something to drink or eat before we make the drive to Monterrey. We can make better time if we do those things now."

Pete faced Esteban. "How about it? I'll even let you have a beer."

Esteban's eyes cut from Pete to Reid. "Why should I drink with you?"

"Fine," Reid said, "nothing for you. Pete, for the interest of speed, I'll make a few sandwiches and— You have bottled water, right? Thought I saw some in the fridge. How about a cooler?"

"Good idea, that'll keep us from stopping. There's a couple of smaller coolers under the sink. We can have one in each vehicle."

Reid started for the kitchen. Esteban cleared his throat and she stopped. He held his taped wrists up. "How do I use the bathroom like this?"

"Ask Pete. You're his problem, not mine."

She packed the coolers with water, sandwiches, and ice, and returned to the living room to face Pete. "Where's your gun cleaning kit? I want go over his two Glocks. I never trust my life to someone else's gun. I'm getting back into my traveling clothes too."

Pete pulled at his shirt tail. "Good idea. This thing is too damned conspicuous. My gun kit's in the garage on the shelf by the vice. Pliers too, if you need to pull a stubborn spring. No telling when he cleaned them last."

Fifteen minutes later, dressed in jeans, button up shirt, and boots, Reid returned to the living room and held up a small gun safe. "Saw this out there along with the key. I wrapped his guns and locked them up. We need to hide them in the back of the van, where they kept Connie."

Esteban's jaw dropped. "How do you know that?"

"Trade secret. If only you knew who I really was." She sat in a chair across from Esteban.

Pete aimed the Glock at Esteban's head. "Here's the deal—I want my wife back and Martinez dead. Simple, right?"

"What do you want from me?"

"That's simple too," Reid said. "We want you to stay in touch with Martinez. I'm sure you do that after he gives Pete orders to kill a rival pimp. Don't deny it, your kneecap's counting on you. Maybe both of them."

"Why should I do that for you? Then, when he" —he nodded toward Pete— "gets his wife back and kills Martinez, he'll kill me."

Reid gave him her most sincere smile. "C'mon on now, you've got us wrong. For helping us—for doing us such a great service—we'll not only allow you to live, we'll allow you to take over your boss's operation. All we ask is you never bother Pete and his wife again."

"Not a bad deal, is it?" Pete said. "You could even retire from your life of crime, which might allow you to live at a tropical resort somewhere."

Esteban licked his lips. "And if I don't help?"

"Easy choice," Reid said. "Need to think it over?" Esteban shook his head. She glanced at her watch. "This is how it's going to happen. You and Pete in the van, me behind in my truck. When we—"

"What happened to you and your 'details?'" Pete said. "I can't hold a gun on him while we cross the border."

"You're a LEO. Pepper spray will slow him down if he does something stupid."

"And have the border guards kill me in the process."

"At least he'll go with you." Reid faced Esteban. "Can we trust you to get us across the border? The DCL sticker on your van is one less complication, the other is you. We going to build a little trust here or not? Like we've been saying, you can come out of this with more money than you've ever dreamed of. I bet Martinez has safes filled with pesos."

"I have seen it with my own eyes. I have known him since I was a boy. With money he is very selfish. He does not treat his women well either."

"I've seen evidence of that myself," Pete said.

"How could you? You have never met him."

"You know he forces my wife to send me letters. I received one recently, in a small box. It included the tip of a woman's finger wrapped in a bloody paper towel. My wife said in the letter it wasn't hers, that it was a message from Martinez concerning the seriousness of my continued cooperation."

Esteban lowered his head. "He would only do that to Gabriella. She reminds me of my daughter, who died long ago." He raised his head. "Martinez has gone too far. I am not a good man, but he—he has the devil in him. Don't worry. I won't be, as you say, a 'complication.' Let us be on our way." He held out his hands. "I cannot drive with tape on my hands and ankles."

"Not so fast," Reid said. "We're supposed to believe you for no other reason than your feelings for this Gabriella?"

"I don't know what else I can say."

"She's got a point," Pete said. "You're asking a lot of us."

Esteban raised his taped wrists and rubbed his forehead. "I have been loyal to Enrique since he saved my life as a boy. I am not proud of turning against him. He made me do things— things I did not think it was proper to do then and things I know are not proper to do now. Kidnapping your wife was one of those things, Señor Anderson. A man should do his own work, not involve someone else, especially not his wife. I am an old man with many regrets. Esteban saved my life, but if I had not done many of those things to begin with, I would have never been at risk. I will help you get your wife back. I will return Gabriella to her parents, if that is what she wants. Maybe I can make up for some of the bad I have done. As far as Enrique, he can go to hell."

Pete eyed Reid. "Sounds believable to me."

"I guess so. Cut him loose and—"

"His phone is vibrating." Pete took the phone from his pocket and checked the screen. "It's Martinez. It's time we find out if we can trust our partner." Reid gave Pete her pocket knife. He cut the tape on Esteban's wrists and gave him the phone. "Before you answer, you should know my lady friend can speak Spanish. Put it on speaker."

Esteban did so. "Ola, Enrique, how are you?"

"I have sent our assassin another list of our competitor's men to handle. The same list should be in your email. Do you foresee any problems?"

"He was extremely competent with the first two. I'll check my email and call as soon as the first man is dead."

"He hasn't replied after an hour. I'll have you drive by his house if he does not answer soon. For his sake—as well as his wife's—he better reply soon. Adiós."

Esteban gave Pete the phone. "Where is your computer?"

"In the kitchen," Reid said. She returned and placed the laptop on the coffee table.

Pete sat, logged on, and slid the laptop in front of Esteban. "You first." He walked around the sofa behind Esteban, and Reid joined him. The message was what she expected, with the exception of this list being for three men instead of two. It included the streets where they frequented and the timeline for Pete to do the killing.

She pointed at the screen. "He expects you to kill the first man by tomorrow. Didn't he give you a week last time?"

"He did. If we can't get to Connie before then, Esteban can tell him I did the job on time." Pete returned to the sofa and checked his email—the same as Esteban's—and sent a short message acknowledging the receipt. "That's it."

He looked over his shoulder at Reid. "We need to get the hell out of here."

24

Reid backed out of the driveway and waited for Pete and Esteban to go ahead. She would follow, but she still punched the route to Monterrey into the GPS. Keeping up with their progress was a priority. The trip only took about three hours, but they still had the border crossing to deal with. The DCL stickers should help, but a driver never knew when they would get a red light to be searched or a green light that would allow them to continue. Odds were against red, but odds rarely worked, especially when a person hoped they would work in their favor.

About twenty minutes later, traffic slowed as they neared the border. Lines of vehicles formed to her left. She had been able to stay with Esteban's van so far, but when they entered the final section of road separating drivers from the CDL lane, an eighteen-wheeler swerved in front of her. The van disappeared, hidden by the bulk of the truck and its trailer.

Reid threw up her hands, re-gripped the wheel, and twisted the warm vinyl. Last thing she needed. Maybe they would both get a green light and she could catch up when they left border traffic.

The truck's brake lights glowed bright red. She slowed and passed the sign warning of the upcoming Search-No-Search area, with its traffic indicator as to whether a driver should pull over or not. As she passed the indicator, the light stayed green, so she wouldn't have to stop. She relaxed her grip on the steering wheel.

Ahead of her, the eighteen-wheeler accelerated, leaving a cloud of black diesel exhaust streaming overhead. She leaned left and right in an attempt to peer around its bulk and locate the van, chewing her lower lip the entire time. The huge trailer might as well be a moving brick wall made of shiny aluminum. She glanced in the rearview mirror and swore. Pulled over, Esteban's van had received a red light to be searched. It disappeared as she was forced to follow the DCL lane and the truck.

She must have missed seeing the van when she looked to the left. Her cell phone sat in the console. Calling Pete might make security nervous. Let them do their thing. She would pull over and wait somewhere.

A few minutes later, she turned in at a fast-food place, backed into a parking space by the road, and just as she killed the engine, sirens screamed in the distance. Seconds later, two Mexican patrol cars sped by, red and blue lights flashing while on their way to the border. Reid covered her eyes. The last thing they needed was for their guns to be found. Should she go back? Should she stay? Maybe she should—

Her cell phone vibrated. She grabbed it and checked the screen. "Pete! What the hell is going on back there?"

"Hold on, we're on the way. I figured you'd be worried. Didn't know if you saw us get pulled or not. I think a car behind us got busted for drugs. The officers brought the search dog out and it went nuts, barking and jumping on the passenger door. I could see it all in the door mirror while we pulled away."

She fell back against the seat. "You're on the way, right?"

"I just said that. Sorry about rattling you. You still on the road or—"

"I'm parked at a fast-food place about a mile from the border. Stay on the phone until I get behind you. I almost wet my jeans, and I *like* my jeans."

Pete gave a low chuckle. "Don't tell Connie. I'm kind of fond of them myself."

"I won't, as long as you feed me that steak dinner after all this over."

"We've got a way to go yet before— I see you. We'll pass after another block."

Reid waited. "You just passed. Be right behind you." She pulled out and accelerated. "I'm hanging up. Holler if you need anything. I'll do the same."

She ended the call. She may not have wet her jeans, but a bead of perspiration trickled down the back of her neck and stopped at her bra strap. Heat or nerves? She set the AC on high and focused on the rear of Esteban's van. If she had anything to do with it, and she did, it would stay in sight until she chose otherwise.

A few miles later, when they took the north-south exit to Mexico 85 Highway, the van leaned to one side as Esteban rounded the tight cloverleaf. Was he in a hurry to get them to Monterrey safe and sound, or would he turn on them as soon as possible? Reid was inclined to doubt his statement concerning his regrets. Could he really betray Martinez after being friends with him for most of their lives? What about the girl Gabriella? How could Martinez harm her so casually—if it had been her—by cutting off her fingertip? No doubt he was a greedy individual, but was he that deranged as well?

Given that, what about Esteban? Trusting him was difficult. She would only trust him to a point, and that point ended with their lives.

He had tried to keep the 130,000 dollars a secret. Certainly understandable. He, or rather Martinez, could do a lot with that money. She drummed her fingers on the steering wheel. So could she, a lot of good that is. That would have to wait. Also, Esteban hadn't really fought them, just mentioned what would happen to Pete's wife if Martinez discovered their plan. What had he said about Martinez taking Connie? That he told him he shouldn't?

Reid glanced in the mirror, and a single arched eyebrow rose. After adding all that up, even *she* had to arrive at a decent argument for trusting Esteban. That was the last thing she expected. Still, the argument was only decent, not foolproof. Not by any means.

The landscape, with scrub brush and sand to the horizon on each side of the road, similar to the desert during the trip to Chihuahua City, passed by.

A mile later, the van slowed to pull into a custom's checkpoint. She stopped behind them and took her passport and tourist visa from the glove box. When she had driven to Chihuahua City, this section of her trip had gone smoothly, a cursory glance at her papers and nothing more. It shouldn't be any different here.

Two Custom's Officers approached the van. Pete and Esteban handed their respective officers their passports. As the officer on Esteban's side raised his hand to wave them through, the other officer held up his hand.

Another trickle of sweat ran down Reid's back. At this rate she would be soaked by the time they arrived in Monterrey.

The officer waved for Pete to get out of the van. Reid clenched her teeth. If they ever *got* to Monterrey.

Pete opened the passport, pointed at it, and she opened her window.

"… but officer, my wife and I were in Mexico last—" The Officer pulled his sidearm. Pete froze and dropped the passport. Reid cursed under her breath. She hadn't checked with Pete to see if he had his tourist visa. That must be what—

Esteban climbed from the van, joined Pete, and the other officer pulled his gun.

"Por favor," Esteban said. "My friend was just telling me how he made sure to have his visa with him before we left. I believe he said it was in his passport. May I look?"

The officer who held Pete at gunpoint kicked the passport over to Esteban. He flipped the pages, frowned, and shook the passport upside down. A folded piece of paper fell out. He opened it. "Ah, we have found it." He gave it to the officer. "If you can, please lower your guns before my friend faints. As you can see, he's not very trim. I would need to help him back in the van."

The officer studied the passport, eyed Pete, rubbed his own stomach, and laughed.

Reid's shoulders relaxed. What about her? Not only would she pass out if this continued, she would threaten to wet her jeans again.

Pete and Esteban returned to the van and pulled onto the highway. Not wanting to seem in a hurry, Reid eased up to the checkpoint and gave the officers her papers. One took the visa, the other took the passport. After a quick glance at the visa, that officer handed it back, but the officer with her passport looked at her, eyed the passport, and motioned for her to get out of the truck.

She closed her eyes, opened them, and climbed out. What bullshit. The officer held up the passport, pointed at her photo, and pointed at her head. Not her head, her hair. He wanted to know why her hair was black instead of red.

Speak in Spanish or not? Play the innocent American woman or not? It had worked with the two men who had forced her off the road, so why not?

She ran her fingers through her hair. "My hair? I colored it. You know, from a bottle. Don't you like it?"

"Sí, sí, my wife also does that." The officer twirled his finger in a circle. Did he want her to turn around? She did. When her back faced them, he said, "Buen culo, eh, Antonio?"

As she completed the turn, the other officer frowned and shook his head. "Mmm, no. Demasiado flaco."

The officer returned her passport and nodded to his fellow officer, who also returned her visa. Then he added, "Volvamos al interior, donde hace frío," and they both shuffled toward the small, white building they had come from when she and the van had arrived, where an air conditioner hung out a side window, whining in protest.

Reid wiped sweat from her forehead, hurried to the truck, and pulled onto the highway, rear tires squawking slightly as she accelerated.

She glanced in the side mirror at the rapidly fading checkpoint. The officer who wanted her to turn around had said she had a "nice ass," while the other had said it was "too skinny." Neither cared for the heat any better than she did, since they agreed to return to the white building where "it was cool." Probably had a fridge with a few cervezas inside to enjoy while watching their favorite American TV shows.

A white dot about a mile ahead, the van's image shimmered in the heat waves rising from the road. She nudged the gas pedal and glanced in the rearview mirror at the customs check. On the return trip, maybe it would be manned with two officers who knew a nice "culo" when they saw one.

As the van's shimmering image cleared, she glanced at her cellphone. Pete likely had noticed her absence, so why hadn't he called? She checked the phone. No service. Of course no service. The land was as flat and barren with no cell towers like it had been when she had returned from Chihuahua City. At least the highway was four lanes, and at least the vegetation—the trees along the sides and the grass in the median—was a bit greener.

About an hour later, the cell buzzed in the truck's plastic console. She checked the screen. It was Pete. She answered before he could say anything. "Leave a girl to be harassed by those guys at the customs check, why don't you."

"Bet you didn't get a gun pulled on you."

"You stand corrected, Detective. Why do you think they might question my passport? Or should I say, my passport picture?"

"You have a few more wrinkles now than when it was taken?"

Reid glanced in the mirror. Hell no, not a wrinkle in sight. If she kept frowning like that, there would be. "Detective, you're treading on shifting Mexican sand. I'll give you a hint, it's your fault."

"My fault?" He paused, and Reid could almost see his forehead wrinkling, like when she had explained losing her job with ICE. "What's taking you so long?"

"I'm trying to think of an answer that won't get my butt kicked when we— Was it your new hair color?"

"Exactly. I had to play the dumb American woman. They even had me twirl around so they could check me out."

"I bet that impressed them."

"We won't talk about that. We're back on the road and that's all that matters. How's Esteban? I heard most of what he said at the customs check. Sounded calm as could be. Not like your whining about a previous trip you and Connie had taken."

"How do you know that wasn't an act?"

"By the way you turned into an ice statue when that officer drew his gun. Pee your pants?"

Pete growled. "Not a drop. As far as Esteban, yes, he helped me out. Otherwise, we're doing okay. We've had a sandwich and a bottle of water a piece."

"I'll do the same." She glanced at the GPS. "We've got about another hour and a half to go. We should plan on stopping somewhere to finalize our plans."

"I agree. We can't go in there blasting away. Someone might get hurt, and that someone might be Connie. Given it any thought?"

"Some. We all need to arrive in the van. We can't go driving my dad's truck in there, that's a given." She checked the time. "It's almost two thirty. Ask Esteban what kind of schedule Martinez keeps. If he knows, ask him what would be the best time to take him, or if there is one."

"I'll cover that with him before we stop. We'll have to after those sandwiches and water."

"Maybe Esteban knows a good place. Call when you want to stop. While you're talking things over with him, I'll try to come up with a concrete plan for getting in and out with a minimum of fuss and damage."

"Especially to Connie," Pete said, his voice sincere.

"You got it." Reid returned the phone to the console. Had she just said "a minimum of fuss and damage?"

That wasn't like her at all.

25

An hour later, Pete called again. Reid tapped the answer icon. "What have you got?"

"Esteban says there's a truck stop ahead with bathrooms and a fast-food place. He also says—and he's right—we shouldn't stop anywhere near Monterrey. Someone might recognize him."

Reid agreed with Esteban's idea. "Will my truck be safe there while we— Forget I said that. I don't plan on us being gone that long."

"What about your plan?"

"You won't like it. It involves— No, I'll wait until we stop. You'll want to have an empty bladder when I tell you."

"Tell me now, I can handle it."

"Like you did back at the customs check? I doubt Esteban would want to finish the drive with you smelling like urine."

Pete said nothing.

"Detective, you detecting anything?"

"I'm detecting your sarcasm."

"I usually get like this when my nerves act up. That's a sign I—and we—need to get serious. Like I said, I'll fill you in when we stop. I'll tell you now, most of it hinges on how much we can trust Esteban. I'd say he's done an admirable job so far. His speech back at your place, when he mentioned making up for his past, sounded as sincere as any I ever heard. You were there, what did you think?"

"I've thought about it off and on. It's not like we have a choice."

"That's for sure." A billboard advertising food and gasoline loomed ahead. "See that sign? Is that the place?"

"It is. See you in a minute."

The van pulled in and parked. Reid did the same. Had she returned the duct tape to the truck before leaving Pete's? They would need it if Pete and Esteban agreed to her plan. She found it under a jacket behind the seat and climbed out.

Pete waited beside the van. Lifting his hands over his head and shaking his legs, he twisted his neck as if trying to remove a cramp. "Long ride, huh?"

"I need a restroom before I pop."

"Me too. That water went right through."

Esteban joined them. "I stop here for that purpose on occasion. We should go in one at a time. We don't want people to think we're together."

"Good idea," Reid said. "I'll go first if no one objects."

"Go ahead," Pete said. "I can wait."

Done in the restroom, Reid returned. Esteban leaned against the van while Pete shifted from foot to foot, in obvious strain from needing to pee. "My goodness, Detective, you're a sight."

Pete started for the restaurant. Reid grabbed his arm. "Hold up a minute, I need to tell you something."

He turned around. "Damn, Reid, can't it wait?"

Reid faced Esteban. "You go ahead." After Esteban left, she faced the now squirming detective, trying not to grin. Her quirky sense of humor could rear its head at the worst times. "Remember what I said about you smelling like urine?"

"I remember you saying you'd wait to tell me what you had in mind until after I went to the bathroom."

"Changed my mind. Being married, you should know that's a woman's prerogative."

"Why can't I go?"

"I need you to hold it until we leave for Martinez's place. Then you can pee all you want."

Pete's mouth fell open. "What the hell are you talking about?"

"We're going to stage it like you found Esteban. I want it to look like he got the upper hand and decided to bring you here for a little personal attention from Martinez."

"Martinez won't believe that. He'll ask Esteban why he didn't call about capturing me."

"I don't care what Martinez believes. I'll have Esteban tell him he made the decision on his own because he didn't want to waste an effective killer. We'll see what he thinks. If he agrees, we'll decide the best time for going in."

"What else does your plan include? I doubt wetting my pants is all."

"Listen to you, doing your usual fine detective work."

Esteban walked toward them, hitching his pants. "We should get inside the van. I saw someone who knows me."

They all piled into the van—Esteban in the driver's seat, Reid and Pete in back in case the person came over. They waited and watched.

A few minutes passed. Esteban pointed. "That's him. He doesn't know I work for Martinez the way I do." He paused. "The way I *did*. He thinks I work on his house from time to time."

"When we were at your place," Pete said, "you acted as if you were going to do the work Reid lied about. You do that type of thing?"

"I only started working for Martinez about five years ago. We kept in touch over the years, but he knew I did not care to be involved in crime. However, when he insists, even friends listen. To answer your question, yes, I do the work. I enjoy making old things new again."

"Which is what you were doing until Martinez meddled in your life," Reid said. "I admire that."

"He'll meddle no more. Have you and the detective decided on a plan?"

"We need to get out one more time. I'll tell you while your friend finishes at the gas pumps."

While the man completed his fill up, Reid shared her plan with Esteban and Pete. Pete didn't care for his part, but he agreed to do whatever he could. Esteban also had his doubts, especially about Martinez questioning him for bringing Pete down here. He agreed how they had little choice, especially when Reid reinforced the fact that their options were quickly running out.

"Okay, Esteban," Reid said. "Now that we've figured this out, what's the best time to go through with it?"

Esteban didn't hesitate. "Enrique goes to bed around nine. We can get there before dark, possibly around eight. I need to see his reaction when I arrive. He will be angry that I did not contact him. When he is angry, he can be extremely unpredictable. Like with Gabriella, the bastard."

"You can have one of your guns. I didn't tell the detective here. Keep it tucked in the back of your pants with your shirt over it. If Martinez threatens you—I doubt he will—you know what to do. Just make sure his hired man isn't around. If it comes to that, you'll have to be ready to take him out too. I prefer to get in and get out with as little fuss as possible, so let's hope it doesn't come to that."

Pete eyed Esteban and then her. "If he's been lying …"

"Trust me, Pete. You've done it this far, don't stop now." Reid looked around the back of the van. "Any paper around here, Esteban? I need you to make a drawing of the layout of the buildings."

Esteban retrieved a pad and pencil from the glove box and sketched a road and several buildings. He touched the pencil to a large rectangle. "This is the main house. To the right is where Martinez will have Señora Anderson. I am certain he will have his man at the door. The cook, maid, and gardener live in the building to the left of the main house."

"How about the man at the door?" Pete said. "Does Martinez have more than one?"

"Unless something has changed, Martinez only has one. He brags about how he has the local police in his pocket. Since he is not involved in drugs, the cartels let him alone."

"His confidence is a weakness," Reid said. "Something we'll take advantage of." She checked the time. "We'll leave about 7:30. It's going to be a long wait until then. My stomach's growling, can you get us something to eat? We better move after you do. I don't want anyone getting suspicious of us staying too long."

Esteban pointed. "See the trucks behind the buildings? We can park behind them. I have taken a nap back there before starting my drive home. Your pickup will be fine where it is."

"That's handy," Reid said.

Pete looked out the window. "I'll say."

"Sure is, for that and something else I have in mind." She poked Pete's chest. "I'm gonna make sure you look as much like the captured man we want you to appear to be."

Esteban chuckled. "Señor, I'm glad I'm not you. As far as food, what would you like?"

"Grab whatever," Reid said.

"Me too," Pete said.

Esteban left the van. Fifteen minutes later, all three were eating from white paper bags and drinking from Styrofoam cups.

Pete chewed, swallowed, and licked his lips. "Not bad."

Reid sipped from a cup. "Some kind of meat with a sauce, Esteban?"

"La barbacoa de cabra. It's a specialty here."

Pete opened his sandwich and frowned. "'Cabra.' You mean goat."

"As authentic as it gets, isn't it, Detective? Shut up and eat so I can get you ready for the last part of our trip."

Meals done, Reid retrieved the duct tape from her truck. Esteban drove the van behind several eighteen wheelers parked at the rear of the restaurant, adjacent to their fueling stations. Most of the trucks were idling, their drivers likely sleeping in the rear of the oversized cabs in preparation for another long haul. Esteban parked and left the engine running. "I'll run the air conditioning while we wait. It's going to be hot in the compartment as it is."

"That's thoughtful of you." Reid held up the duct tape toward Pete. "Your turn."

"What the hell are you gonna do with that?"

"This comes after."

"After what?"

Reid sighed on the outside but grinned on the inside. She had told him once she could kick his ass. Now she was about to do it. "I told you before and I'll tell you again—for this to work, we need to make it look as authentic as possible. You tell me, how should you look for Martinez to believe Esteban taped you up and threw you in back of the van?"

"Me wetting my pants isn't enough?"

"You're not detecting, Detective. It'll take more than that and you know it. How's this for a start?" She smiled, patted his cheek, and ripped his shirt open. Buttons clattered against the van's metal walls.

Pete eyed his shirt. "Why do I think that's only the beginning?"

"Because it isn't," Reid said, opening the van's rear door. "Let's get out and get your dirtied up."

"Then?"

Reid shrugged. "We'll see."

On the driver's side, to keep hidden from the service station, she picked up a handful of the dirt from the dusty parking lot and rubbed it on Pete's face and shirt. "Not good enough." She opened the driver's door. "Esteban, do you have a wrench in here?" Esteban handed her a large adjustable wrench, and she closed the door.

Pete's eyes narrowed. "What're you gonna do with that thing?"

"Wouldn't you think for that older man in there to tape a big, strong you up, he would have to knock you out first?" She hefted the wrench. "I do."

"What good am I unconscious?"

"I just want to hit you hard enough so you'll bleed in your hair. After that I want you to roll around in the dirt and wet your pants. Then you can get in the van and I'll tape you up."

"You sure about this?"

"I can get Esteban to hit you."

"I don't want to be hit at all, dammit. Don't you have a pocketknife? You gave it to me to cut the tape on his wrists at my house when Martinez called. Nick my scalp enough to make it bleed."

Reid snapped her fingers. "Why didn't I think of that?" She opened the knife and tested the blade's edge. "Lean over." Pete did as she asked, and she made a half inch cut in his scalp that immediately oozed blood.

Pete touched the cut and winced. "Happy now?"

"Nope." Reid pointed the knife blade at the ground. "Drop and roll. Pretend you're on fire if it'll help." Pete shook his head but did so, dust boiling up around him.

A noise came from inside the van, and Reid raised her head. Shoulders bouncing with each chuckle, Esteban laughed.

Pete stood. "Damn if I thought I'd ride three hours into Mexico to roll around in the dirt and have an old Mexican bandit—ex-bandit I hope—laugh at me."

Reid placed her hands on her hips. "You do remember why we're doing this?"

"I know, I know." He turned around. "Do me the favor of not laughing while I pee, okay? This is embarrassing enough as it is." A few seconds passed. Pete didn't turn around.

Reid gave him a few more seconds, tapping the toe of her boot in the dirt. "I thought you had to go so bad."

"I can't go with you back there. I'll go in the van after you tape me up."

"Damn if that's so. You forget the rest of our plan already?"

Seconds later, Pete emitted a slight grunt.

"That's the way to man up." Reid opened the van's rear doors. "Climb in so I can tape you up. The sun's going down and we've gotta roll."

26

Pete sat in back of the van, ankles and wrists straining against the duct tape. Before getting inside, he had done as Reid had asked concerning his pants. Now, aside from being filthy and having blood running down his face, he smelled of urine. Warm, wet urine. At least she hadn't taped his mouth.

"You making it okay down there?"

"It's pretty tight." Reid's muffled voice came from the hidden compartment beneath him. "I'm glad I had you pee outside. It might have dripped on me."

"Happy to oblige. How's the heat?"

"We just left. Thing is, I need to stay in here until dark. Hell, I might even pee on myself."

"That's an amusing thought. Let's hope it doesn't come to that."

"Me too. I haven't had diaper rash since—well, since I was in diapers."

Pete swallowed. What was Connie going through? If she were pregnant, how would that affect her? Was she getting enough to eat and drink? Was she having morning sickness? Far as he knew, she was okay, because she had said so in the letters, but Martinez could make her write anything.

"Mighty quiet up there, Detective. Getting your mind settled for what we're about to do?"

"I'm worried about Connie."

"That's multiplied because she might be pregnant, right?"

"You think? I'm not crazy about being delivered helpless into Martinez's hands."

"Got to keep telling yourself it'll be okay."

The van turned. Pete braced himself to keep from shifting. Gravel crunched beneath the tires.

"We just turned onto the road that leads to Martinez's estate," Esteban said. "We'll be there soon."

"How long is soon?" Pete said.

"The road is a mile long. I cannot drive fast. Two or three minutes."

"What did he say?" Reid said.

"Hear that gravel?" Pete said. "We'll be there in a few minutes."

"I don't know if I can stand it that long." She coughed. "Dust is coming in here from somewhere."

"I guess human trafficker's guest standards aren't that high."

"What did you say?"

"I said you better stop coughing before we get there. How much tape is left?"

"Don't even think about it."

"Trying to stay positive. You did suggest that, you know."

"Sounds like my sense of humor is rubbing off on you."

"Don't you mean *strange* sense of humor? Here we are, hundreds of miles inside Mexico, trying to rescue my wife from a sorry son-of-a-bitch, and we're joking around."

"I saw some crime thriller novels on your bookshelf in your living room. Wouldn't you like to read one with a main character like me, who can find a little humor in a situation like this?"

Pete knocked on the van's floor. "Good point."

The van slowed. "We are here," Esteban said. The light grew dim. "I'm pulling into a shed to keep Señorita Reid cool while she waits. Be calm. I'm going to get Martinez. He won't react well to me bringing you here. I'll talk to him before we return." The van's door squeaked open, slammed shut, and Pete stretched out on the metal floor.

"We're here, Reid. Esteban's gone to get Martinez. This will be the last time I talk to you until later. Look, if it doesn't work out, thanks for trying."

"No try, Detective, do. Got that?"

"I still want you to know how much I appreciate everything."

"I know all that without you telling me. The only reason I'm helping is to get another steak dinner out of you. Oh yeah, and to meet the woman who puts up with you all the time. I've got a few shooting trophies at home. I might have to install a new nameplate on one and present it to her. She damn well deserves it."

Pete chuckled. "You're too much, you know that?"

Voices came from outside.

"Reid, they're—"

"Hush, I hear them."

The voices neared. They sounded calm so far, but Pete couldn't understand the rapid-fire Spanish, a verbal blur to his ear. The latch clicked on the van's rear double doors, and he finally got a look at the sorry excuse for a man who had kidnapped his wife.

Martinez stood beside Esteban, hands on narrow hips. He raised a cigarette to his thin lips and puffed until the tip glowed red. Smoke entered the van—stinking, nauseating smoke. Martinez scratched a chin gray with beard and said something to Esteban in Spanish. Pete wanted to scream at Martinez for what he had done to Connie, but he and Reid had decided it would be best to act beaten down and not say anything until Martinez spoke directly to him.

Another man appeared. He and Esteban pulled Pete from the van and drug him to a small building. Martinez walked beside him, laughing the entire way. They stopped, propped Pete up near a closed door, and Martinez faced him, his face inches away from Pete's. He smiled, breath stinking of cigarette smoke.

"Señor Anderson, I am generally a happy man, that is until people disappoint me." He glanced at Esteban. "My friend has disappointed me." He puffed the cigarette. "You have disappointed me." He dropped the spent butt. "As Esteban has made me see, I believe I can still salvage the situation." He nodded toward the door. "Your wife is inside. Esteban suggests—and I agree—that perhaps a night with her will make you understand the seriousness of our partnership, since my package to you was not enough to do so."

"All I want is to get out of this with my wife alive and go home. How many more killings will that take, dammit?"

Martinez smiled, yellowed teeth beneath a gray moustache hiding his upper lip. "It will take as many as I say, which will be enough to rid me of my competition in Laredo. Perhaps that will be enough, perhaps not. It is possible I may need assistance elsewhere."

"You think I'll keep killing as long as you say, even to the point of doing it somewhere else?"

Martinez spread his hands. "Look at yourself, Señor. I am not the one whose head is bloody ... who is covered in dirt ... who has had to relieve himself in his own pants like a child."

He nodded to the man standing by the door, moved away, and the man punched Pete in the gut. Air whooshed from his lungs as he doubled over, gasping for breath and trying not to throw up or faint. The man dragged him to the side. Martinez unlocked the door. The man threw Pete inside to the floor. "Pete? Pete!" A face appeared above him—Connie's face. Everything would be alright now. He was ... he was home.

* * *

Outside the heavy wooden door of Connie's room, at least two different voices spoke. Martinez's high-pitched accent took most of the conversation, but who was the other man speaking un-accented English? The lock rattled and the door opened. The guard threw Pete inside and slammed the door shut. Pete collapsed on the floor, gray tape around his wrists and ankles, eyes closed. She fell to her knees and lifted his head. A mix of blood and dirt stained his face. "Pete! What did they do to you?" She ripped the tape from his wrists. He moaned and opened his eyes.

"Connie? Where—?"

"Shh, you're okay. What did they do to you?"

He tried to sit up but winced and stayed on one elbow. "Hit me in the stomach. Knocked my breath out." He took several hacking coughs. "Did I pass out?"

"For a minute. If you're like me, Martinez's stinking cigarettes are enough to make anyone pass out." She took hold of his arm. "Let's get you in a chair so you can tell me what's going on."

She helped him up, eased him into a chair, and slid one over for herself. He tried to raise from his slump but winced again. "I hope that bastard didn't break a rib. Hurts like hell."

She unbuttoned the remaining buttons. "Looks like they drug you around by the shirt." She fingered his chest and stomach. "Your ribs are okay. Maybe it's how you fell when he threw you in."

199

"It's getting better. Dammit, here I am letting you treat me like an invalid, and I'm not asking about you. Are you alright? They do anything to you?"

"Considering I've been kidnapped, driven three hours into another country, been held for almost three weeks while my husband has been forced to kill for one of the worst excuses for a man I've ever met, I'm doing okay."

Pete placed his hand on her stomach. "I saw the pregnancy test in the bag on the counter. Do you know yet?"

"If morning sickness is a sign" —she smiled— "and it is, I'm pregnant."

Pete sank into her arms and sobbed while she held him. Now that they were together again, how would they get back home? She allowed him to finish. The strain of not knowing where she was or what was happening to her must have been nearly as bad as what she had been going through. "Pete?"

He lifted his head and wiped his eyes. "Sorry about that."

"Sorry for what, showing me how much you missed me? I'll show you how much I missed you when I get you home." She paused. "That's the question, isn't it? How are we getting out of here? If you're here all by yourself—"

Pete held a finger to his lips. "Help's coming after dark. Is there somewhere in here to talk without being overheard? I don't want to take any chances."

"Hold on." She rose, turned the air conditioner on full, and opened the bathroom door. "In here." Once they were in the bathroom, she left the door open. Between the noise of the AC and being away from the main door, they shouldn't be heard.

"Don't tell me the local Mexican authorities are involved," she said. "Some are more likely to help Martinez than us."

"I know better than that. I couldn't get any law enforcement involved even if I wanted to. Martinez said he would kill you if I did."

"Then what are we going to do?"

"Not what, who. If anyone is capable of getting us out of this mess, she is."

"Whoever she is, I hope *she* has some help."

"Believe it or not, she does. Believe it or not, it's inside help."

"That's crazy. Out of Martinez's men, who can we trust?"

"Sweetheart, you just need to *trust* me. As far as the woman" —he tugged his shirt— "this was her idea."

"How about the blood in your hair and the pee I smell? She must be quite the woman if that was her idea too."

"She is. Yes, all this—the whole rescue—was her idea. She even cut my head and ripped my shirt open."

"I can't wait to meet her."

Pete glanced at his watch. "You'll meet her pretty soon if everything works out."

"You mentioned something about help coming after dark. How is she going to get here? I hope she brings a gun or two."

"Don't worry, everything is planned."

27

Inside the hidden compartment, Reid waited. It had grown hot during the last part of the trip, but the cramped area was cooling. Cramped? What an understatement. There was barely enough room to move sideways, and the top, almost like a coffin lid, nearly touched her nose. Although the air was cooling, it was stuffy, and every time she blinked, her eyelids tried to stick together from the dust that had worked its way in during the drive on the gravel road. She touched her cheek and rubbed her fingertips together. Fine sandpapery particles coated her fingertips, plus her tongue and teeth. A bottle of ice-cold water would come in handy right about now, to rinse her mouth and clean her face and eyes.

Before climbing in, she had removed the remaining gun from the safe. It now rested on her chest, a solid reminder of why she was here. It would come in handy in case someone burst in and opened the lid of her metal coffin. That might be a welcome relief at this point.

She waited a few more minutes. How much time had passed since they had taken Pete and slammed the doors shut? Having neither a luminous dial nor a button for a light, her watch failed her. She should have brought her aluminum flashlight. With five D batteries inside, it made for a hell of an equalizer when it came to busting a bad guy's head.

How much longer should she wait? Raise the cover? See if it was dark? A tentative push revealed darkness in the van's interior, possibly because of the shed Esteban had mentioned.

She raised the cover all the way, holding the edge so it wouldn't fall over. Dim light shone through the windshield, too early for Martinez's bedtime. Lie back down and close the coffin lid? Not no, *hell* no. The cooler and the water in it. Had Pete and Esteban drunk the four bottles she had packed? She eased the cover over, leaning it against the van's inside wall, and crept to the front for a bottle of water from the cooler. She rinsed her mouth and spat. A small amount of grit remained. Repeating the process, she ran her tongue over her teeth and spat. Much better. She tilted the bottle to enjoy the ice-cold water down her parched throat. Had she ever been this thirsty? Like with when she had considered lying back down and closing the lid on the van's hidden metal coffin, not no, *hell* no. She wet a paper towel from a partial roll tucked under a seat and wiped her face, eyes, and arms, staining the paper towel brown, like on Pete's parents' dusty car.

As if her brain were the toy mouse her long dead cat used to smack back and forth along the kitchen floor, questions battered her mind. How long had it been since she had seen that car the first time, when the old man—Pete—had killed that pimp? How long had it been since her parents' house had been broken into, when she had returned to sit in the false comfort of her bed and had seen the vision in the mirror of her mother wiping the cuts on her back from those damned rusty springs? They seemed to penetrate her soul, her psyche, as horribly as the rape. She had lived with the scars, dealt with the rape, but what would she do if she ever found the excuse for a man that started it all? What an idiotic question. Would killing him end the nightmares? She doubted if she would ever be lucky enough to find out.

Reid willed the questions to a stop, blinked her now clean eyelids, and shook her head. PTSD again?

She glanced at her dim reflection in the rearview mirror. "Keep it together, you. It's almost time to kick a bad guy's ass."

The passenger door mirror reflected dim light from one of the outbuildings. A stout Mexican stood by the door. She checked the map Esteban had drawn. The man stood by the room where Connie was held.

Reid wedged the gun into her jeans and moved to the driver's side, losing the reflection of the man in the mirror. She couldn't see him in the driver's side mirror, so he shouldn't be able to see her. A slow pull on the driver's side door handle yielded a soft click. A slower push yielded a softer squeak. She climbed out, eased the door closed, and crept to the front of the van, keeping it between her and the man. No need in tempting fate. She closed her eyes and listened.

Faint men's voices from the main house, Esteban's and Martinez's. A rustling overhead in the shed's rafters. Birds? Mice? A coyote yipped in the distance.

A warm breeze died against her cheek as she opened her eyes. Continue to wait.

She sat in the dirt, leaned against the shed, and hugged her knees to her chest. The aroma of food, something with tomatoes, slipped between the darkened walls on another breeze, and her mouth watered. After she and Esteban secured Martinez and his man, maybe she would help herself. She shook her head. What a dumb idea. Getting the hell out of Mexico was priority. She covered a yawn. A shower and a bed. How long before she could enjoy such simple things again? Another yawn, and she rested her head on her knees. She would close her eyes for just a minute. Rest them from that damned ghost-grit sensation of dust.

* * *

On the porch of the main house, Esteban moved a few steps away from Martinez. The man smoked with a vengeance, blowing stinking clouds of foulness into the cooling night air.

The conversations concerning Pete, both before throwing him into the building and after, started with Martinez's rage and ended with simmering calm when Esteban had reassured him he would do whatever it took to continue the plan. During dinner, when they sat across from each other, Martinez sulked in silence between bites of beef empanada and sips of expensive American bourbon. Afterward, he told Esteban he wanted to talk to him, and Esteban followed him onto the porch.

Martinez blew another choking cloud of smoke his way and stubbed the cigarette out on the porch railing, marked with countless burns. "My friend, I have depended on you for many years, as you have depended on me. Tell me again why I should not kill the detective and his wife and start over with another man. This time I need more than your assurance—I need facts, evidence—something I can take within my teeth like a coyote pup snatching a young, squealing rabbit from its nest of brothers and sisters."

Esteban placed his hands on the rail and stared at the millions of stars beginning to glitter in the night sky. "I think the detective will never be caught, at least not soon. I tell you again, the only reason I captured him is because I saw him leaving his house. You haven't heard the rest of the story. After you sent the email, I drove there as you suggested. He was backing out of his driveway like a madman, tires squealing. Naturally, I followed. He drove to the country and pulled onto a dirt road. I waited about half a mile away with binoculars. After a while, when an old, dirty car came from the road, I remembered the news report from the last killing. Since the shooter was seen driving a similar car, it seemed the detective might be driving the car while shooting the men. It was quite an ingenious thing to do."

"The car would have been recognized sooner or later."

"I asked him about that after I captured him. He said he was going to change vehicles soon."

"Why would he tell you that?"

"I think to impress upon me—and you, since he knew I would tell you these things—the fact that he shouldn't be killed. Would you not do so yourself?"

"This is true. Will you return him tomorrow?"

"I think so. I also think we should not press him. Perhaps we should even pay him."

Martinez spat in the dirt. "Pay this gringo detective? I would rather throw money to a pig."

"You already pay the local policía, why not him? Also, we should not force him to kill more than the next three men. A man can only take so much before he breaks. After that, pay him and return his wife. Then we move on to the next town using another man. Or perhaps we hire a professional to do the killing. Maybe cartel. They seem to enjoy their work."

"I will consider it. You did not finish the story about how you caught him, or why."

"I apologize. It is my fault for not being vigilant. When he pulled from the dirt road in the dusty, green car, I followed him to his house. When he got out of the car, he had what looked like a gray wig in his hand. I wondered if the man was losing his senses. It was only while I was driving here that I managed to recall the news report again. It stated the man doing the shooting had gray hair and a beard. I parked a few houses down from his to wait. He surprised me from the back of my van. I can only suppose he left his back door and snuck through the yards of his neighbors. He jerked the door open and tried to pull me out. I held onto the steering wheel long enough to grab a wrench from the other seat."

Martinez rubbed his bearded chin. "So that is why his head is bloody. You were fortunate you had a wrench handy and he did not have a gun. Perhaps his mind was not clear as you said. Do you have any idea why he would attack you, or what would have made him suspicious of you?"

I do not know for sure. It is likely he noticed the van when I followed him into the country, then again as I waited on his street. Again, I apologize. I will do whatever I can to make it up to you."

Martinez lit another cigarette and dropped into in a nearby chair. "In all the years we have known each other, you have never failed me. Are you tired? I am." He stood and raised his watch so the light from the porch would shine on it. "It is late."

"Before I go to bed," Esteban said, "I need to check the van. According to the temperature gauge, it was running hot."

Martinez laughed. "I would do that if I were you. One does not want to be broken down along those empty stretches of road on the way back to Laredo."

He went inside. Esteban left for the building where the detective and his wife were held. He greeted Diego, the guard who sat beneath a dim light by the door, and added, "How are our prisoners?"

"What about you?" Diego said. "After we threw the gringo in with his wife, I could hear Martinez yelling at you in the house."

"We have come to an agreement. I will return the man to Laredo tomorrow. He may still be of use if he agrees to our terms."

"That is a good thing. As you and I know, Martinez does not like having his routine interrupted."

"I'll be working on the van before I go to bed. It should not take long."

Diego drew a pistol from a holster. "Gracias. I would not have wanted to mistake you for a coyote."

Esteban clapped the man on the back. "You and I both. Will you stay out here long? I cannot imagine Martinez not letting you sleep."

"I will go soon. Before I do, I turn on an alarm we had installed yesterday. If anyone opens the door, trust me, we will know."

Esteban raised his brows. "I didn't know about this. How do you turn it on?"

Diego rose from the chair and took a small remote from his pocket. "One push on this button is all it takes." He sat back down.

"That is interesting." Esteban yawned. "I better check on the van and go to bed. I have a long drive tomorrow."

While Esteban hurried to the shed, two shadows moved across the curtains of Martinez's room. Gabriella would be with him. Esteban clenched his fingers into fists. He wanted to rush into the room, kill Martinez, and get Gabriella away from here. Instead, for Diego's benefit, he opened the driver door of the van and pretended to fiddle with something. When complete darkness fell, he would get Señorita Reid and carry out their plan.

28

Reid jerked upright. Sleep? Had she been asleep? Then what had woken her? She stood and went to the van's fender. The driver's door stood open. Cursing under her breath, she drew the pistol and took a shooter's stance. A man climbed out and closed the door. She took aim, fingertip on the trigger.

"Señorita Reid?"

Heart pounding in her chest, she lowered the gun. "Esteban," she hissed, "back here."

He joined her at the front of the van. "Martinez is in bed. We should give him time to fall asleep. The guard also."

"He's not going to stand watch all night?"

"Martinez has an alarm."

"Where does the guard sleep?"

"In the building with the cook and gardener. If we're quiet, we should be able to get in the main house without waking anyone."

"What kind of lock does the door of the building where Pete and Connie are being held have?"

"It's not a padlock but a lock in the door itself. It would make too much noise to break it down."

"How do the others feel about Martinez?"

"Except for Diego—he is the guard—they tolerate him."

"So Diego is our only worry. I assume he's armed?"

"He showed me the gun. He seems ready to use it."

"His problem, not ours."

"Another problem is the alarm. Martinez had it installed yesterday."

"We'll worry about that when the time comes. Can we get to the main house through the back? I don't want to risk anyone seeing us in the lights from the windows on these buildings. You never know when someone might go the bathroom."

"Let us see if Diego has left yet." Esteban went to the end of the van, Reid right behind him. A shadow fell across the yard, coming closer. Esteban motioned her back. She hurried to the front of the van.

"Esteban, you still working?" an unfamiliar voice said. "Sounds like you are complaining about it too."

"I wanted to check the spare tire before I left. You can never be too safe."

"See you in the morning."

Reid peered around the van. The shadow moved away, getting longer with each step. Esteban motioned her forward, and she whispered, "How long does it take him to go to sleep?"

"I don't know."

"I don't like 'I don't know,' I like to know." She pulled off her boots and gave them to Esteban. "Stay here." She ran lightly on her toes across the dirt yard, gun in hand, and smashed it into the back of Diego's head. Stunned, he dropped to his knees. She finished him off with one more strike and waved to Esteban, who came running.

"How did you know he would not hear you?"

"Didn't you hear how he walked, like a bull stomping around an arena? I probably could have done that in my boots."

Esteban knelt to look at Diego. "We should tie him up."

"Let's drag him in front of the van and use duct tape. That includes his mouth."

"Good idea. I have always thought he talked too much."

Reid took hold of a leg. "Why, Esteban, I do believe you have a sense of humor."

"It has been hidden under years of doing Martinez's bidding."

"Maybe that'll change after tonight. Let's go."

They secured Diego, including several sticky wraps around his mouth. Reid slipped her boots back on and returned to the end of the van with Esteban, who said, "Should we get the remote for the alarm and turn it off?"

"Good idea. Throw his gun under the van and get the keys too."

"We could release the detective and his wife."

"They're safer where they are."

Esteban went to front of the van and returned with the alarm remote and keys for the lock. "I already turned the alarm off."

Reid faced the house, where a light in a single upstairs window illuminated white curtains. "Any chance Martinez sleeps with the light on?"

"Not usually. He knows I will be returning to the house to sleep. If he hears any noise, he will think it is me."

"Sounds good, let's go." They eased around behind the shed and made their way to the back of the main house, which also had a porch. The wooden boards creaked with their footsteps. Esteban turned the doorknob and a light flickered on inside. Reid moved to one side of the door, and so did he. He peeked through the door window, placed his finger to his lips, and motioned Reid to stay. Stepping inside, he left the door cracked open.

"Hola, Gabriella, it's good to see you. Are you not sleepy?"

Reid peeked inside. Esteban must want her to hear the conversation, with the view an added benefit. A stunning dark-haired young woman, barefooted and wearing a long, white nightgown, stood beside a refrigerator, glass in one hand, bandage on the other. This was Gabriella, the girl who had lost her fingertip to Martinez.

"I was thirsty, and a little hungry," she said.

"I noticed you were not at dinner."

"When Enrique is angry, he is silent. I do not want to be around him when he is either."

Esteban moved closer. "Do you ever want to be around him?" He picked up her bandaged hand. "Surely you do not."

Gabriella's head dropped. "Does it matter what I want?"

Esteban placed his fingers under her chin and lifted her head. "Do you trust me? If you do, you can have that choice."

"I have always trusted you, Esteban. You remind me of my grandfather. If he had been alive, I do not think he would have let my parents sell me to Enrique."

"Can you do as I ask?"

She nodded.

"Good." Esteban opened the door. Reid entered, and he gestured toward her. "This is a friend. I will tell you more later. Right now, I need you to stay here. Will you do that?"

Gabriella nodded again. Esteban faced Reid. "Follow me, but quietly. If Martinez's room had not been on the other side of the house, I would not have talked so much."

On tiptoe, Reid stayed on Esteban's heels, up a flight of stairs until they stopped at a door. He pulled the gun from his belt, she brought hers up, and he knocked. "Enrique, it is Esteban, may I come in?"

"Where is Gabriella, what is she doing down there? If she keeps eating at night, she will become fat like a cow."

"May I come in? The van is worse than I thought."

"Come in and get it over with. I am tired."

Esteban nodded to Reid and shoved the door in. Martinez jerked upright in the bed and reached for a nightstand drawer. Reid made two quick steps and drove the gun barrel into his temple. "Entirely too slow, old man. Back in the middle of the bed." She took a gun from the drawer and stuck it in her belt. Damn. On her last trip to Mexico, she couldn't get a gun. Now she had more than she needed. She stepped back and took a quick glance at Esteban. "How do we—"

"Esteban! Who is this woman? What are you doing? You point a gun at *me*, your lifelong friend? Do you forget how I saved your life as a boy?"

"*Saved* my life? Literally, that is the truth. Believe me, you took more than you saved. Get up."

"I will not. You will shoot this—this—American bitch and drag her body into the desert for the coyotes. Do it now, do you understand me?"

Esteban placed two shaking hands on the gun and aimed it at Martinez's head. "One of the things I most regret is what we did to that young girl that night in El Paso. You talked me into helping you. You talked those boys into raping her. You called her an 'American bitch' as we walked away. I should put a bullet into your head for every time she was violated."

In Reid's hand, the gun became an overwhelming weight. It fell to her side as she stumbled back a step. If what she was hearing was true. … She shook her head, trying to keep the reality of Esteban's words from taking her into unconsciousness. When the feeling passed, she raised the gun. "Esteban, what did the girl look like? Did she have red—"

"Shoot her and be done with it!" Martinez yelled. "We can make this right if you do what I say!"

Esteban's hands shook even harder. "Make it right? You took my life. You took who knows how many lives of the women you shipped like cattle to the United States. No more, do you hear me, no more!"

Martinez threw up his hands. Esteban pulled the trigger and the gun fired, but with a loud pop, not the explosive roar necessary to propel a bullet from the barrel. He racked the slide. An unfired round dropped to the floor. He aimed and pulled the trigger again, achieving the same pop, similar to a kernel of popcorn exploding in a microwave. After repeating the sequence two more times, he glared at Reid. "You gave me a gun that would not work?"

"I used Pete's pliers to remove the bullets when I cleaned your guns. I emptied the powder from the cartridges and pressed the bullets back in with the vice. I didn't know if I could trust you. I didn't see you being in any danger, not until now. Look at it from my point of view. Wouldn't you have done the same thing?"

"He needs to die."

"What we *need*, Esteban, is to get out of here. Don't forget Gabriella."

"Esteban, I warn you," Martinez said. "You know not what you do."

"Shut up you son of the devil, I know exactly what I do. I only wish I had learned it long ago." Glancing at Reid, Esteban nodded toward Martinez. "What are your plans for him?"

"Remember what we did to solve Diego's talking problem?"

"In here or out there?"

"I'm not going to carry him down those steps, are you?"

"I do not want to touch him."

Reid waved the gun at Martinez. "Move. We've got some place to be and you're holding us up. If you open your mouth, I'll personally make sure you meet your father—the devil himself."

Behind the van, they taped Martinez to match a snoring Diego, including his mouth, his ankles, and his hands behind his back. Gabriella packed her things, and Esteban settled her in the van. Esteban and Reid started for the building where Connie and Pete were held. Esteban stopped after a few steps. "When I was talking about the girl in El Paso, why did you ask about her hair?"

"I lived in El Paso when I was young. I remember my parents talking about a girl with red hair being raped. It wasn't in the news because her parents didn't want it reported. At least that's what my parents heard."

"Her hair was red and she was long legged, like you. Enrique had been watching her ride by on her bicycle and said he would catch her one night and let the boys in that area see what it was like to be a man. I wish to God I had not been a part of it." Esteban hung his head. "What can I do about it now?"

"Maybe it's time to forgive yourself. It's not like you weren't forced to do it."

"I wish I could apologize to the girl. I always wondered if life treated her better than she was treated that night."

"Seems I recall she's doing well."

"I am happy to know that. Now, let us get Señor Anderson and his wife and get away from here." He gave her the keys. They continued to the building and she knocked on the door.

"Hey, Detective, guess who?"

The door knob rattled. "Reid, is that—"

"Were you expecting pizza? I'm opening the door. Don't worry, all the bad guys are accounted for. Be quiet though, we don't want to wake anyone in the other house."

"Just open the damned door so I can hug you."

Reid turned the key, and a grinning Pete opened his arms. She placed a hand on his chest. "Whoa there, not until after you've had a shower." She stepped around Pete and offered her hand to Connie. "It's about time I met your wife. I'd hate to go through all this trouble and have her shoot *me*."

Connie pointed toward the door. "We need to go, introductions later."

Reid eyed Pete. "Decisive, I like her already. I agree, it's time to get the hell out of here."

Outside, Connie stopped and stared at Esteban. "What's he doing here? He's one of the men that kidnapped me."

"Connie," Reid said, "at this moment you have to believe me when I say you can trust him. We'll have time for answers later."

They piled into the van, Esteban and Gabriella in the front, Reid, Pete, and Connie in back. "Wait a minute," Reid said, "Martinez comes with us."

Esteban turned around and gave Reid the gun with the powderless rounds. "If you give me a gun that works, I can shoot him."

Pete faced Reid. "What's that supposed to mean? You checked his guns yourself."

"Tell you about it later." Reid stuck the gun in her belt and opened the rear doors. "Give me a hand, Pete. Martinez is going to have the pleasure of riding in that damned hidden compartment."

They wrestled a wide-eyed Martinez into the compartment and slammed the door shut while his muffled screams came from beneath the tape. Esteban faced Reid. "What about Diego?"

She pulled the Van's rear doors shut. "To hell with him."

29

On the return trip to the truck stop, everyone grew quiet. Pete sat on the van's floor, holding Connie's head in his lap and stroking her hair. Reid caught a glimpse of Gabriella in the mirror. The young woman alternated between biting her lower lip and glancing out the window beside her. Even Martinez was silent. Maybe the dust had clogged his nose to the point of killing him.

At the truck stop, Reid breathed a sigh of relief. In the lights, Dad's truck sat unharmed.

Esteban parked in back behind several eighteen-wheelers. Pete helped Connie up. "What are you going to do with Martinez? We can't take him back."

"Believe me," Reid said, "I know that."

"Then what—"

"Part of that depends on Esteban." She faced him. "What are your plans from here?"

The tired man blinked. "I have been thinking about that. Gabriella, do you want me to take you back to your parents?"

The young woman didn't hesitate. "I want to go to America with you."

"Then that compartment will be used one more time for something good instead of something evil." Esteban faced Reid. "Have you decided what to do with Martinez?"

"Pete and Connie and I are going to follow you in my truck. I want you to stop along the way, wherever we're the least likely to be seen."

217

"What then?"

"That's for me to worry about."

Esteban drove to Reid's truck. When Pete headed to the passenger's side door, Reid grabbed his arm. "I want you and Connie up front. When we stop, Martinez and I are going for a walk. If you see any headlights while I'm gone, leave and come back when the road is clear."

"Where will you be gone *to*, other than for a walk?"

"All you need to know is it concerns Martinez. Anyone need the bathroom before we go?"

Pete eyed his pants. "I'm good."

"I do," Connie said. "The baby's crowding my bladder, even at his or her young age."

Reid clapped Pete on the back. "Congrats, Daddy, great news."

"What will be 'great' is when we get home. Will you walk Connie inside? Between the dirt and the blood in my hair, not to mention the pee smell, I'll draw too much attention. Before you go, give me one of those guns and pull your shirt over the other one. You don't need to draw any more attention than you already do."

Reid and Connie visited the restroom and returned to the truck, where all three climbed in. Pete followed Esteban down the highway.

Mile after mile they followed the van's red tail lights. Eventually, the painted lines on the highway became a blur, but frequently, the light of the huge full moon illuminated the gray flash of a coyote speeding across the road, or an armadillo scurrying along the side, and the movement would bring Reid out of her weary semi-trance. The stars formed a washed-out sky, their light diminished because of the full moon's brightness.

The scene was similar to when Reid's dad and Bob sat out on the front porch, to enjoy their conversation while sipping Jack Daniels. She licked her lips, almost tasting the caramel-bitterness the one time her dad had offered her a taste. After swallowing the burning liquid, she ran inside to tell her mom, who immediately hurried outside to complain.

Reid closed her eyes.

* * *

"Reid, Reid. Is she asleep, Connie? Wake her—"

"I'm awake, I'm awake." Reid rubbed her eyes. "Is Esteban—"

"He's stopping." Pete eased the truck off the side of the road. "Don't know what you've got planned. I still have the gun you gave me at the truck stop."

"I'll be glad to get rid of the one in my waistband. Damn thing's about gnawed a hole in my side. Let me have that one, I'll get rid of it now. No need in forgetting before we get to the border." Reid unbuckled the seat belt and stuck the gun in her waistband. "Connie, can you let the seat up so I can get out?" Connie did so, and Reid entered the cool night air. Esteban waited by the rear of the van, Martinez beside him.

His pajama's, dirty from the ride in the compartment, wisps of gray hair waving in the breeze, the skinny old man looked as if he couldn't harm a Mexican bean beetle. Reid knew better. He had ruined many a life, hers included, and it was time to stop him from ruining any more. She cut the tape from around his ankles. "Ready for a walk?"

Martinez answered with incoherent mumbling beneath the tape on his mouth.

"Just a walk, that's all. I'll even take that tape off your mouth if you won't yell." Martinez nodded. She ripped the tape off, likely removing some of his beard and moustache in the process. That was the least of his problems.

He worked his jaw. "I have money, much money …"

"How much?"

"Millions in American dollars, at my house in two safes."

Let's hope it's waiting for you when you get back."

"You … you are not going to kill me?"

"After our walk, I'm leaving with my friends. By the time you make it back to the highway, we'll be across the border."

"I could walk back sooner than—"

"And some of your fellow countrymen—*and* women—think I'm estúpidos. I'll tape your ankles again before I leave. That means you'll have to crawl back to the road on your belly like a snake."

In the distance, a coyote yipped. Another answered. And another.

"Hear that? They sound hungry. Let's hope your knees don't bleed too much while you're making your way back across the rocks and cactus. You know, I've often wondered what a scorpion sting feels like. Maybe you can experience that and let me know. Hell, it might even happen before I get back to the road. If I hear you scream, I'll have a good idea. Oh, I forgot about rattlesnakes. Northern Mexico has Sonoran Sidewinders. Let's hope you don't meet up with one of those."

"But … but …"

Reid shrugged and took the gun from her belt. "Beats the hell out of the alternative, sí, señor?"

"Please, I beg you—Esteban, do not let her—"

Reid slapped him, a vicious right that rocked his head and stung her hand. At this point she didn't care if she broke it. "*You* have the gall to beg anyone anything?" She grabbed him by the arm and threw him in the dirt. "I can always tape your ankles and make you crawl. Make up your mind, I've had all of you I can take."

Martinez stood and stumbled into the desert. Reid faced Esteban. "I'll catch up to you back in Laredo." In the headlights of her truck, she could see Esteban swallow.

"I hope not like you just did with Martinez. You are a hard woman, Señorita Reíd, hard as stone."

She patted his shoulder. "Only when it's called for, my friend, only when it's called for."

Esteban returned to the van and drove down the highway.

Reid caught up to Martinez. The man shuffled along, dust rising in small clouds beneath his bare feet. "You're doing well, old man. Just remember, each step brings you to a place where you'll no longer have me on your conscience."

"Why should I have you on my conscience?" Martinez coughed. "We have never met before."

Reid said nothing.

About a quarter mile into their walk, the horn of her dad's truck echoed through the desert. She faced the road. As Pete left, a set of headlights glowed in the distance, a mile or more down the long stretch of road.

Esteban fell. "I cannot ... cannot go any farther." He sucked in huge, wheezing breaths.

"Take a break. Ever think about giving up smoking?"

"What are you talking about?" He wheezed again, followed with several hacking coughs.

"Too late now."

He spat in the sand. "You ... you are insane."

"You have no idea."

While Martinez continued to suck in air, Reid took in the sight of this pristine section of Mexican desert. The gorgeous moon, so huge and bright that its light cast shadows, lit the landscape as far as she could see. Scrub brush and the occasional cactus formed a shimmering green backdrop, wet with a rare south-of-the-border dew. A freshening wind kissed her cheek, bringing the scent of a skunk that had likely ruined a coyote's dinner plans.

She prodded Martinez with her boot. "Time to get this over with."

Martinez stumbled and fell another quarter mile. Reid told him to stop. He swayed back and forth, a dead man hanging from a rope in a gentle breeze, then dropped to his rear. She slid the gun in her belt, taped his ankles, and squatted on her heels in front of him.

"Señor—and I use that term as loosely as possible, because in no way, shape, or form are you *anything* resembling a gentleman—do you know why you're sitting in the middle of the desert with this, as you say, 'American bitch?'"

Martinez slowly raised his head. "I do not know." He licked his lips. "Nor do I care."

"Remember when Esteban mentioned the girl who was raped in El Paso?"

"How am I to remember a thing that happened so long ago?"

Reid bit her lower lip.

Tasted blood.

"I'll refresh your memory. You stopped a young girl on a bicycle, a young girl who had everything to live for. You took her innocence by holding your hand over her mouth and blowing your stinking cigarette smoke into her face. You held her there, smoking and laughing. You did that while she was raped over and over and over again on a filthy box spring that had leaned against a fence until the springs rusted and stuck out of the rotten fabric." She took hold of her hair. "My hair was red back then—as red as my shorts and underwear were when I finally made it home."

Martinez's eyes opened wide, so wide the moon reflected in them.

Reid stood. "Don't worry. I'll be a lot more merciful with you than you were with me."

Martinez started to roll over, but Reid jerked him upright, dropped to her knees behind him, and snaked her left arm around his thin neck. With his chin forced upward, all he could manage was an anguished groan. His oily hair stank of cigarettes. The bones in his shoulders pressed against her arms. How easy it would be to snap his neck, to hear the brittle crack as she twisted his head to one side. Like Esteban had said, she was a hard woman, as hard as any stone she had ever come up against. Men, women, nightmares, losing her parents, losing her job, none of it mattered. She would die before she broke against anyone or anything.

She clamped her hand over Martinez's mouth and pinched his nostrils shut. He kicked, bucked, dust flew up around them, all while a guttural moan from his throat vibrated against her forearm.

But his head never moved.

When his chest stopped heaving, she wrenched his head viciously to one side, and the vertebrae gave way with a sickening snap. She stood and he fell, a heap of filth ruining the Mexican desert.

She hurried back to the road, disassembling the guns and throwing pieces left and right. In the distance, her truck's headlights, with its recognizable fog lights, appeared. A coyote yipped. Another answered.

Reid smiled.

The desert would soon be pristine again.

***

A welcome change, the border crossing came and went without issue. After crossing the Rio Grande, Reid asked Connie to lower the window. Even with the long-haul truck belching black clouds of diesel exhaust ahead of them, America never smelled so sweet.

They pulled into Pete's driveway around three in the morning, took showers and collapsed into their respective beds. When the sun rose, Reid rolled over, checked the time, and closed her eyes.

Breakfast could wait.

30

Reid sprang upright in bed. The sheets, were they—?

Knock, knock, knock. "Reid, it's Connie. You alive in there?"

Reid focused her blurry eyes on the clock on the nightstand. Two o'clock? She had slept ten hours? "Barely. I had no idea it was so late."

"Us too, we haven't been up long. I left some of my clothes by the door if you need them. The jeans might be a bit short, the shirt a little baggy."

Reid checked the clothes she had brought from home. Everything was either dirty or wrinkled. She wasn't about to wear anything from the pile she had thrown in the floor last night. "Thanks. You know us ladies, we never have a thing to wear."

"Pete's cooking bacon and eggs. I don't know about you, but I'm starving. Pete's a pretty good cook, but you know that already." Connie's footsteps faded down the hall.

Reid returned to the bed and dropped to the mattress. So Pete had shared the fact that she had eaten here. What else might the good detective-slash-husband have told his wife? Footsteps returned. Connie again?

"Need help with the door? I can get Pete to open it like he did last time."

"I, uh … I think I can handle it."

"Thought I'd ask." Connie's giggles faded with her footsteps.

Reid jerked the door open, gathered the clothes, and closed it. As hard as Pete was to deal with, Connie might be worse. Reid dressed, raised her hair brush, and shrugged in the mirror. What a dumb thing to think about Connie being worse than Pete. At least she had a sense of humor.

Reid jerked on the doorknob and frowned. Had she shoved it closed that hard? After what she had been through last night, damn if she would let this door win. Once more she pulled, two handed, and it popped open. The aroma of bacon and coffee welcomed her into the hall. The Andersons sure knew how to make a girl feel welcome.

Connie was placing strips of bacon on a plate while Pete flipped eggs. He glanced over his shoulder at Reid. "Well, well, look who rose from the dead. Grab some coffee, breakfast will be ready in a second."

Reid poured a cup and took a seat. "You two sure are perky this morning."

Pete set a plate in front of her. "That'd be afternoon. Forgetting your *details?*"

"Detective, it's still not too late for me to kick your ass in your own house."

Connie took a seat. "Honey, you didn't tell me about that. Don't be holding out on me."

Pete smiled, this time the biggest Reid had ever seen. She sipped coffee. "Wow, is that good. Now, about what Pete's been telling you, Mrs. Detective. Care to fill me in?"

"We talked and talked while we waited for you to get us out of that building. What did you expect us to do?"

"After being apart three weeks, you could have thought of something." She looked over her shoulder at Pete at the stove. "Right, Detective?"

Pete brought the rest of the food and sat. "Wasn't quite the time or place. Besides, when I do it, I do it right. Connie's pregnant, remember?"

"Which means you'll have a little detective whining late at night in about eight months."

"Don't you mean crying?"

"Not if she or he takes after you." Reid faced Connie. "Did he tell you how he whined when he couldn't find his tourist visa at the—"

Pete cleared his throat. "You'll like my cooking a lot better if you don't let it get cold."

Connie sipped coffee and returned the cup to the saucer. "What do you call a girl detective, a detective-ess?"

"I have no idea." Reid faced Pete. "Do you?"

"I don't intend to find out. Daughter or son, I'd rather they do something else with their lives."

"Like what?" Connie said. "We didn't cover that last night."

"How about a name?" Reid sipped coffee.

Connie waved her fork at Reid. "Pete mentioned Pamela. How about that?"

"Your asshat husband can't keep anything to himself."

"What's wrong with Pamela?" Pete said.

"To be honest," Connie said, "I don't like it either."

"You and me both." Reid raised a forkful of eggs.

Connie sipped coffee and lowered the cup. "I like Reid myself."

"Me too," Pete said. "How about it, amazing-rescuer-of-my-wife? Let's make it unanimous."

"Come on, guys, you're joking, right?"

"Sounds like a yes to me, sweetheart." Pete raised his coffee cup high in the air. "Time for a toast."

As Connie tapped her cup to Pete's, Reid's cheeks grew warm, and Connie said, "To baby Reid Anderson—boy or a girl, the name works either way. No arguments from the namesake. For what you did for us—all three of us—we'll always be more grateful than you'll ever know." She faced Pete who nodded. Connie lowered the cup to the table and turned her chair toward Reid. Her smile was gone. What in the world was she thinking?

"I want you to stay a while if you can." She took Reid's hand in hers. "I'd like to get to know the woman who I'm naming my baby after. You've been through entirely too much to not need serious downtime too."

Reid swallowed. Connie had said "too much." What had Pete told her? "Pete, did you ...?"

"I hope you don't mind, Reid. I told her what happened to you back in El Paso, when you were a teenager. Remember what I said about Connie wanting to change jobs so she could help returning Vets? Maybe she could help you too, or at least be a sympathetic ear."

Connie gently squeezed Reid's hands. "Please think about. We'd love to have you."

Dark eyes, laughing eyes, searched Reid's, and she swallowed again. As the weight of the last week lifted from her shoulders—a thousand-pound concrete block of fear she had never desired—tears filled her eyes. Now, to have that fear replaced with gratitude for these two people who were offering their home and friendship, she finally had something real to cry for.

Connie held her, rocked her, stroked her hair, and Reid sobbed almost as terribly as when her parents had died. What was it about being held by this woman, this almost perfect stranger? Was it that she knew about the rape, that the shared burden had lightened Reid's soul already? Or could it be that she already felt like a friend? Or were Reid's tears part of something else, something like feeling completely welcome without wanting to get up and run away? Back when she was eighteen, her shrink had mentioned this concerning her nightmares, that possibly they were about her trying to get away from some hidden part of her psyche. She had immediately scoffed at the notion. Back then her parents were alive, so what did she have to run from?

The nightmares, naturally.

And now the urge to run was gone.

Another thing weighed on her mind, something she couldn't quite comprehend. As Connie held her, and the tears continued, that thing hit her as unexpectedly as being jerked off a bicycle while riding back home from soccer practice.

She had never wanted to kill, but when her own life had been threatened, there was only one choice—to end the life of the person who not only threatened her, but threatened others. Six, no, seven men now lay dead. Some might say *because* of her. Those men made the choices that had led to their deaths, likely victimizing untold numbers of women along the way, likely victimizing more if they hadn't run into Reid. She had to be hard, hard as stone like Esteban had said, since so many refused the responsibility. She wasn't about to collapse into a quivering, useless heap when a challenge presented itself, especially if accepting that challenge kept others safe along the way. Yes, she would stay. To be here with Pete and Connie while they planned for the birth of their first child sounded like the ideal thing to do. For a while, at least.

She sat up and wiped her eyes. "Sorry about that, Connie, didn't mean to get you all wet."

"You know as well as I do you don't have anything to be sorry about. You're the toughest woman I've ever known. Pete even broke down when he saw me last night. Tough or not, every woman needs a good cry now and then." Connie turned back to the table and raised her fork. "Let's eat, I hate cold eggs."

"Me too," Pete said. "All this crying stuff has almost taken away my appetite."

Connie pointed the fork at him. "Just because I've been gone doesn't mean you're going to get away with comments like that. Besides, you've got two women to deal with now."

"Didn't catch that, did you? She never said if she would stay or not."

"Maybe she needs a reason other than keeping you straight."

"I'll call work and tell them I'll be back Monday. That way our guest and you can have some time to yourselves."

Connie faced Reid. "I do have another reason." Reid waited for her to continue, but it seemed Connie wanted her to ask. Reid didn't mind a bit.

"What might that be, mommy-to-be?"

"Pete told me how well you can shoot. Can you can teach me? I thought about it before." She glared at Pete. "But you know how men can be when they're trying to teach a woman something they think they're an expert at. Anyway, after being taken out of my own home so easily, I'd like to know how to stop that from happening again."

"That I can do. For a minute I thought you were going to ask me to help paint the baby's room."

"Thanks for offering," Pete said. "Since I'm going back to work, that's a great idea."

Reid laughed. "I walked right into that one, didn't I?"

"You sure did," Connie said. "Let's visit the local home improvement store this week for paint samples. I need a few days to clean the house first."

Reid glanced at Pete. "Your husband's a fine cook, but he isn't much of a housekeeper. I'll give you a hand with that and the painting too."

"Great." As if Connie's hand were a pistol, she aimed her finger at Pete. "Then we can visit the gun range Saturday and you can show me how to outshoot that cowboy over there."

* * *

At the gun range, Reid showed Connie the basics, including the thumbs forward grip, stance, and how to load a magazine. Connie shot a few groups. While they were re-loading magazines, an aged voice came from behind them. "Howdy, ladies. Which one of you is Annie, as in Annie Oakley?"

As Pete smiled, big and broad, Reid crossed her arms. "Not amusing, Detective, not amusing at all."

"Can't a guy have a little fun?"

"I have to get used to it. What're you doing here?"

Still facing the target, Connie removed her ear muffs. "What was—Hey, look who snuck in. What's up?"

"I was about to ask him that myself," Reid said. "If he starts acting like a know-it-all, I'll shoot another target like I did last time. That shut him up."

Pete kissed Connie and winked at Reid. "Want one?"

Reid opened her mouth, but her mind went blank. Since a snappy comeback wasn't forthcoming, she simply closed her mouth and glared at Pete.

Connie laughed. "Now look who's speechless."

Pete laughed too, shoulders bouncing. "I'm glad we asked her to stay. I wouldn't have missed that for anything."

Reid checked the time. "With that out of the way, how about dinner, my treat? That is, if you can point me in the direction of the nearest steak house."

"I know the perfect place," Connie said. "We can stop by the grocery and pick up whatever we need and cook at home."

"You might as well get your good-for-nothing husband to do some work since he left such a mess while you were gone. He also promised me a steak dinner."

"Another reason I'm glad you stayed." Connie tousled Pete's hair. "Someone to help me give Detective Anderson here a hard time."

* * *

While Connie made the salads, Reid joined Pete by the smoking grill, where she handed him a cold beer. "Thought you could use one of these, seeing as you're out here working so hard."

Pete took the beer and sat. "Tough job, but somebody's gotta do it."

Reid sat and took a swallow of the beer she had brought for herself. Such a simple pleasure, sitting in the shade, having a beer with a new friend, not even thinking about how to get him in bed.

Funny thing, except for Pete, she hadn't even thought about sex since this whole insane episode of her trip had started. Could it be that men, or at least her supposed need for men, was part of her need for running, except running *to* something rather than running away from something? If so, it might be part of the entire rape, PTSD cycle too, and that might be gone as well. She hoped so, because that might keep her out of places like that bar, especially at so late an hour when the less than desirable element preferred to be out and about.

Pete nudged her foot, which wore a new pair of strappy sandals. "Mighty deep in thought there, Pamela."

"You know better."

"It got you out of your trance, which was what I was trying to do."

"Maybe I've overstayed my welcome. You've learned what buttons to push."

"Stay as long as you like." He laughed. "I'll even fix the door."

"Which leads me to this question … are you as nearsighted as you said you were or not?"

"What makes you ask that now?"

"You haven't been wearing glasses lately. If not, did you enjoy seeing me in the middle of your hall, naked as the day I was born? Forget that. How about the day you watched me in your tub?"

Pete smiled that familiar slight smile around the corners of his mouth. "That's a good question. A better one is did you *want* me to enjoy seeing you naked?"

Reid's mouth fell open, and Pete laughed. "Speaking of enjoying things, I'm really enjoying seeing that expression."

She smirked, tipped the bottle to drink, and so did Pete. He checked the steaks, flipped the sizzling rib eyes, and returned to the chair. "When we were coming back from our trip down south, there were a lot of things I had questions about."

"You didn't ask then, meaning you want answers now."

"To start, since Esteban turned out to be someone we could trust—hard as that is to believe since he had a major hand in Connie's kidnapping—the plan went perfectly. Saying that, what made you bring Martinez with us when Esteban offered to kill him before we left?"

"I've been wondering when you were gonna ask about that."

"And?"

Reid didn't want to answer, at least not honestly. Sure, Pete and Connie already knew Esteban had kidnapped her, but they also knew he lived close by and had helped them. Since that was the case, it would serve no purpose to tell them he had a hand in the rape in El Paso.

"It's like this, Pete—he needed to feel a little of the suffering he had inflicted on others over the years. A bullet to the head was too good for that."

"Connie and I figured you'd shot him when I left because of that other driver. You didn't do that?"

"I clamped my hand over his mouth and nose until he stopped breathing. Then I snapped his scrawny neck."

"Damn. Remind me to never get on your bad side. That's one of the hardest ways to kill someone I ever heard of."

"It wasn't hard."

"I didn't mean that way. Don't get me wrong, I'm not trying to criticize you. I mean as in 'without feeling.'"

"Don't you think he deserved it?"

"For you to kill him like that sounds like it was a lot more personal than because of Connie." Pete slid forward in the chair. "Wait a minute, Connie said Martinez smoked and laughed like some insane version of the bad guy in a horror movie. You said the same thing about the guy that grabbed your bike that night you were—" Pete's eyes widened. "You killed Martinez by holding your hand over his mouth like he did you? Esteban said they worked together in the past, so that means he was the guy that dragged you off your bike before you could scream? Damn, Reid, how can you let him get away with that?"

"*Now* you criticize me?" Reid's face grew hot. No need to deny it now, or Pete might go back to Esteban's and beat the truth out of him. "You heard Esteban say he was sorry for being involved with Martinez. When we confronted Martinez, Esteban said helping him that night was one of the things he regretted the most. That's when I knew the man who grabbed my bike was Martinez. Esteban even tried to shoot him after he said he regretted it."

"What do you mean he 'tried?' That's right, when we were deciding what to do about Diego, Esteban mentioned his gun not working. So what—"

"Remember when I cleaned his guns? I pulled the bullets from the casings and dumped the powder. I pressed the bullets back in with your vice."

"Why do that if you trusted him?"

"My parents didn't raise a fool, that's why."

Reid paused to consider her previous thought about how Connie and Pete, especially Pete, might handle knowing Esteban's connection to the rape. "Believe it or not, I've forgiven Esteban. You know as well as I do, we wouldn't have gotten Connie out of there without his help."

Pete had rested his elbows on his knees while listening. He sat up and slid back in the chair. "If you can do that, I'm glad for you. Still, he didn't have to take her to begin with."

"He made the right choice in the end, which is what's important to me. I'm not telling you what to do, only what I'm doing. It's not like I expect you to let him remodel your house. I expect you to keep that to yourself too. Connie doesn't need to know anything about it."

"Makes sense. No need to add to her stress."

Reid said nothing. Apparently, Pete had forgotten about the two men she had told Esteban she had killed in Mexico. Good thing. No need in reliving that mess."

She sniffed. Smoke was pouring from the grill. "As far as unforgivable offenses, we're going to have a problem if you let our dinner burn."

Pete jumped from the chair, raised the grill lid, and flipped the steaks. "There's no moo left in these. Can you handle that?"

"What are friends for? If not to eat each other's nearly burnt cooking."

31

Three weekends later, coffee in hand, Reid stepped onto the deck. After lightning had flashed and thunder had boomed most of the night, wind and rain slashing the house in torrents, Sunday morning had dawned fresh and clean. Connie joined her, and they sipped coffee while discussing the baby's room, including furniture to match the new coat of yellow paint.

Reid swallowed the last of the lukewarm coffee and placed the mug on the table. "As nice as this is, I can't stay forever."

"I wasn't hoping you'd stay forever." Connie patted her tummy. "Only long enough to see your protégé when she's born."

"How do you know she's a she? You can't count on that old Mexican wives' tale. How can hanging your wedding ring over your belly and watching which way it swings be accurate?"

Maybe it's all in the hair you use to hang it from. Maybe I should try it with yours instead of mine."

Reid yanked a hair that had about a quarter inch of red near the root. "Even if your ring moves in a circle like it did with your hair, I still say it doesn't mean anything."

"Oh, ye of little faith." Connie tied her ring to Reid's hair and held it over her tummy. "Let's see what happens."

At first the ring twirled as if the hair was twisted, and Reid held her breath. When Connie did the same thing with her own hair, the magic seemed real. Reid, who'd never put much stock in superstition, remained silent, content to let the mother-to-be have her fun. This time it was the same. Almost. The ring began moving, slowly, surely, until the motion became a straight line above Connie's tummy.

Reid pointed at the ring. "See? Now it says you're having a boy. How can that be a logical way to tell the sex of a baby? You'll have to wait until you're far enough along until the ultrasound can—"

The ring slowed, almost stopped, and began moving again, tracing an almost perfect circle in the air.

Connie grinned. "You were saying?"

"I'm not saying anything. We'll have to wait and see."

Connie returned the ring to her finger. "How can you do that if you leave?"

"It's getting to be that time. You—Pete too—have been great. I don't remember being this content. At least not since before … you know."

"Since before what happened when you were a teenager, you mean."

"I need to get home. To do what I'm not sure."

Connie placed her hand on Reid's. "I meant what I said about you staying until the baby's born."

"I can't depend on your kindness forever, but it's been easy to get used to. I'll keep in touch. I'm still thinking about heading to the mountains of Virginia and the east coast of North Carolina. I'll stop by on the way if I do."

"You're not going soon, are you? The weather stays warm here through the winter, definitely not in the Virginia mountains."

"I'll wait until late summer next year. I might hit the coast first and do the mountains another time. Maybe I'll catch the leaves at their peak."

"Sounds like a plan." Connie fingered her ring. "Have you been wondering when we might tell Pete's mom about being a grandmother?"

"It crossed my mind. The way Pete described her illness, it hasn't progressed to the point of her not being able to communicate."

"We're going later this morning. Are you up for a two-hour drive?"

"Piece of cake after our last adventure."

"Really? We weren't sure you would. You know, the family thing, a place like that. Even though it's an assisted living facility, it can be a depressing place to visit."

"I'd like to meet the woman who made that beautiful quilt with the butterflies and dragonflies and hummingbirds."

"When did you see that? Pete usually keeps it in a chest at the end of our bed."

"I was cool the first night I came here. He gave it to me to cover up."

"In jeans? We don't keep the AC that low."

"I was uh …"

"Yes?"

"I wasn't wearing jeans, I was wearing a dress."

"A skimpy dress I bet, if you got so cold you needed to cover up. Did the dress—*and* your plan to seduce my husband—work?"

Reid held up her hands. "No, Connie, I swear, he was the perfect gentleman the entire time I stayed here. He is definitely a one-woman man."

"Not through any fault of you not trying, right?"

"How about this?" Reid lowered her hands. "I'll bring the dress back when I visit. Maybe you can have better luck with it than I did. Teal should go with your hair as well as it did with mine."

"Ooh, I like teal, sounds sexy. Tell you what, you bring it back and I'll stop giving you a hard time. I realize you thought he was available." Connie offered her hand. "Deal?"

Reid spread her arms for a hug. "I think we can do better than that."

* * *

Inside the assisted living facility in San Antonio, Reid wrinkled her nose. The air possessed that same medicinal—kind of like rubbing alcohol—smell she associated with hospitals. Pete stopped at a desk to inform the receptionist about visiting his mother, and Reid followed him and Connie through a maze of white halls.

In wheel chairs, wrinkled and white-haired men and women rolled hesitantly. Most turned the large circular handle attached to the wheel with fingers twisted and swollen by arthritis, but a few eased along, using their feet to pull themselves forward in a slow-motion crawl. Others gripped a hand rail to shuffle by, as if they were worn out soldiers on their final march.

Pete rounded a corner and stopped to face Reid. "I want to show you something before we see Mom. She might be there now."

"Sounds intriguing, lead the way." She followed Pete to a room where more people in wheel chairs sat, circled around a large glass case. The residents were watching, some pointing, many smiling, because inside the case fluttered at least a dozen multicolored finches. With yellow feathers, white, white with dark collars around their necks, including several with so many colors they resembled a parrot, the palm-sized birds zoomed back and forth. They either landed on perches or disappeared inside birdhouses that resembled small, enclosed hanging baskets, but with a hole in the middle for the finches to enter.

Reid moved closer, and the finches perched near the glass zipped inside one of the houses to peek out. She counted six tiny pairs of black eyes peering at her, heads twisting side to side as if they were asking each other when she was going to leave.

Pete and Connie joined her at the case, where Connie glanced her way. "Aren't they cute? If I had to be in here, I think I'd spend most of my time watching them too."

"They look like flying pieces of hard candy." Reid pointed. "Especially those yellow—"

"Aren't they pretty?" Someone touched her arm. "I'm a little late getting here today."

"Hi, Mom," Pete said. "Thought we might find you here."

"Whoever you are, I'm not your mother. Doesn't matter. Why don't you and these two young girls come to my room so we can chat? My boy's forgotten me. I can always see the birds."

"Why not?" Reid said. "That's what we came for."

In the room, Reid waited in a corner while Pete and Connie talked with Mrs. Anderson, whose short round form sat on the bed and whose dark hair streaked with gray was up in a bun. The woman's voice squeaked as if it needed oiling, like the hinges on the building where Pete kept the dusty old car. She still managed a running conversation, asking Pete and Connie what they were up to.

"... but I wish that boy of mine would come see me. He said he would when he brought me here." Mrs. Anderson hung her head and shook it slowly.

"He'll come soon," Connie said, patting Mrs. Anderson's hand. "Try not to get upset, okay? I'm sure he's been busy."

Reid stepped from the corner to stand between Pete and his mom. "Ma'am, what's your son look like?"

"He's … who are you, young lady? My, but you're a pretty young thing. Have you started college yet?"

"I haven't graduated high school yet." Reid faced Pete and mouthed, "Your mom made my day." She faced Mrs. Anderson again. "What do you think I should take in college if I go?"

Mrs. Anderson studied her, dark eyes flicking back and forth, long but thin eyelashes batting, lips pursing until she smiled. "What about a model? I hear they make a lot of money."

Reid wanted to laugh but didn't. "I'll keep that in mind. As far as your son, could you tell me his name and what he looks like? Maybe I can find him for you." While she held his mom's attention, Reid motioned Pete to leave the room.

Mrs. Anderson touched a fingertip to her chin. "He's tall … a bit taller than you. My, I bet you drive those high school boys wild with those long legs of yours. When I was your age, I could do the same thing with my boobs." She glanced down. "Now all they do is sit in my lap."

Reid hid a grin while Connie giggled. Pete's mom was funnier than all three of them put together.

After the almost uncontrollable urge to laugh had passed, Reid said, "Something else? Does he have dark hair?"

"He does. He's tall too. Did I tell you that?"

"I'll check the halls. Connie will keep you company. We're both graduating this year."

Mrs. Anderson eyed Connie. "Oh my, the good Lord sure is making girls pretty these days."

"I think so too," Connie said. "As far as how the good Lord makes us, you're beautiful too. Beauty like yours, on the inside, never fades." She pulled a chair over. "Let's get to know each other while Reid finds your son."

Mrs. Anderson raised her eyes to Reid. "Did I tell you his name's Pete? Tell him I'll tan his behind if he doesn't hurry up and come see his mother."

"Don't worry, I'll tell him."

Outside the room, Pete was leaning against the wall. "When I was little, she threatened to tan my behind then too. Never did though."

"I like your mom. I wonder if she'll do anything else to make me glad I came on this visit?"

"She's quite a character, even when she doesn't know who I am."

"Let's get back in. I want to see how it goes when I introduce you." Reid returned to the room with Pete. "Look who I found outside the door. He heard us talking and didn't want to barge in."

Pete shook his mom's foot. "Hi, Mom. Sorry about not visiting before now. Things have been hectic back at home."

"It's about time you got here, young man. Give your mother a hug and a kiss and pull up a chair and tell me how you've been. I see you brought Connie too. It's so good to see you both."

Pete did as she asked. Reid opened the door. "You three enjoy your visit. I'll step out for a while."

"You most certainly will not, young lady. Since you found him for me, you need to stick around and keep him in line. Lord knows I had a hard time doing that when he was a boy." Mrs. Anderson patted the bed. "Sit right here while we chat."

"I agree, Reid" Connie said. "We need all the help we can get when it comes to Pete."

"'Reid?'" Mrs. Andersons's faint gray eyebrows rose. "That's a different name for a girl, isn't it?"

"Beats the heck out of my other name."

"Which is?"

Reid stuck out her tongue and shook her head. "Pamela."

"What's wrong with that name?"

"Nothing, I guess. I prefer Reid."

Connie patted Mrs. Andrew's hand again. "Do you like her name? That's what we picked for our baby girl."

Mrs. Anderson's eyes and mouth opened wide, and she clapped her hands. "Me? A grandmother? That's wonderful!" She stood from the bed and opened her arms. "Come here you two. This news is worthy of a big hug."

While she, Pete, and Connie held each other, she glanced back at Reid. "Come on up here and get some of this, young lady. If you hadn't found him for me, who knows where he would be by now."

"I don't think there's room."

Pete took an arm from around his mom. "You heard the lady, get up here."

As Reid joined the group hug, unexpected tears stung her eyes. This was family, something she had missed terribly since she had lost her parents.

Mrs. Anderson lowered her arms. "My old wings are getting tired." She eased onto the bed. "When's the baby—" Her forehead wrinkled. "You asked if I could get used to *her* name. How do you know the baby's a she when you're not even showing?"

"Remember that test you showed me right after Pete and I got married?" Connie said. "The one with the hair and the ring? That's how."

"Except when we did it this morning, Reid said, "it went both ways."

Mrs. Anderson pursed her lips. "My, isn't that interesting."

"How so?" Pete said.

"You'll find out."

"A woman of mystery," Reid said. "I like your mom, Pete."

"I like you too," Mrs. Anderson said. "Pete, look up on that shelf. There's a hanky I just finished. I want Reid to have it."

"There's quite a few up here, Mom. How about I give them to you and you pick it out?"

"That's fine."

Pete brought her about a dozen handkerchiefs, each with various needlepoint patterns stitched into the white fabric. She turned the corners up, searching for the one she wanted. "I hope I didn't misplace it. No, here it is." She held the handkerchief up. "I hope you like hummingbirds and butterflies and dragonflies. I made a quilt like that a long time ago and always loved it." She lay the multicolored stitching on Reid's lap.

"This is beautiful, Mrs. Anderson, thank you so much."

"Hold on, I might have one more you'll like." She searched through the rest of the handkerchiefs, took another one out, and placed it on Reid's lap too. The stitching perfectly matched the glass case with the finches. It included a pair in midflight, three on perches, and one group peering from one of the basket-like houses. The six pairs of black eyes seemed to search for some unknown something, focused at what looked like a finch-sized hole in the glass near the center.

Reid touched the spot. "Is this supposed to be a hole in the glass?"

Mrs. Anderson nodded. "Ahh, you noticed my tiny detail. I should have given you this one to start with."

"Why's that?"

"See those birds in their house? They're looking at that hole. It represents a new life with new challenges. Those particular birds are so used to sitting in their glass case and being taken care of, they're not sure if they want a new life or not." Mrs.

Anderson softly smiled. "Now you, I can tell what you want. You're a young lady who's starting out fresh. I can see the sparkle of new horizons in your eyes."

Reid swallowed, but the lump in her throat wouldn't disappear. This woman, who had been diagnosed with a such a terrible disease, had described exactly how she now felt since so many difficult parts of her life had come to an end.

"I'll always cherish these gifts, Mrs. Anderson. I'll remember what you said too. Thank you so much."

"Why thank you, Reid. Thank you for finding this rascal son of mine too. Maybe when those grandkids come along, they—along with Connie—will keep a tight leash on him."

"Grand*kid*," Pete said. "Not 'kids.' Don't worry, Connie does a fine job of, as you say, 'keeping a tight leash on me.'"

"I'm just an old woman on vacation," Mrs. Anderson said. "What do I know. I say she needs all the help she can get."

* * *

On the way home, Reid patted Pete's shoulder. "Did Connie tell you I'm leaving in the morning?"

His reflection in the rear-view mirror frowned. "I don't know why."

"Like your mom said, it's time for the sparkle of new horizons."

"I guess." His reflection grinned. "Connie and I could always hire you to clean house and babysit."

Connie slapped his shoulder. "And have you make her dress in a French maid's outfit? I don't think so."

Quiet resumed. Reid settled back into the seat. One question remained, and that was what to do with the money she had taken from Esteban.

* * *

That night, while she packed, she took the bag of money from a back corner of the closet. She had thought about the 130,000 dollars over the past several days, but couldn't think of what to do with all of it. Part of her recoiled at spending any of it, since it could be considered "dirty" money, made through prostitution and from the suffering of those women. The practical part said she could use it, at least some of it. Then there was the part that kept telling her she deserved it, because she had suffered so much at the hands of Martinez herself. In the end, she came up with a compromise, including what she had thought about when she took it that day, which would have to wait until she returned home.

* * *

After breakfast the next morning, and after packing everything in her dad's truck, she returned to the guest room for the money. Pete and Connie waited in the living room. Reid joined them on the sofa.

"Is that the money you took from Esteban that day?" Pete said. "I forgot about it in all the craziness of questioning him and trying to get to Monterrey."

Reid dropped the bag on the coffee table. "You forgot 130,000 dollars? I suppose being forced to pee on yourself might do that."

"Yeah, right. Let's hope that never happens again." He slipped his arm around Connie. "Mostly it was because I wanted something worth a lot more than 130,000 dollars back home."

"Aww, how sweet," Connie said. "I mostly wanted to get home so you could take a shower. Next time you go out on an international rescue, how about wearing an adult diaper? At least you can throw it away after you go potty."

Reid laughed. "Are you sure you don't want to take her back to Mexico, Pete?"

"He knows I'm teasing," Connie said. "Any idea what you're going to do with the money?"

"I wanted to ask you both if you think it would be wrong to use it. The practical side of me knows it can come in handy. It might come in handy for you too, with the baby on the way."

"It's dirty money," Connie said.

"I could take it back to Esteban."

"Why should he benefit from Martinez's crimes?" Pete said.

Reid took a bundle of hundred-dollar bills from the bag. "There's no easy answer."

Connie placed her hand on Reid's. "When I said that about 'dirty money,' I meant for me, not you. I'm not about to judge you after your ordeal as a teenager. I doubt you'll ever find the men who did that—I'd hate to be them if you did. Use it any way you see fit."

Reid put the bundle of money back in the bag. "How about taking half and donating it to the women's shelters in Laredo?"

"Great idea," Pete said. "I'll have to check how that works with the government. They can be pretty strict about where donations originate, especially with that amount."

"They don't need to know where it came from. The charity reports it, not you. Send them an amount anonymously every few months or so and feel good that Martinez's dirty money is doing good work."

"Good idea. Connie tells me you're continuing your trip late next summer. You can stop by and help with the 3 a.m. feedings."

"Not if Connie breastfeeds."

"Here I was, thinking you knew so much about so many things. Ever heard of breast pumps?"

"You know how I am about a good night's sleep. I might change a diaper or two, or feed her during the day."

"How is the baby now a 'her'?" Connie said. "You said you didn't believe in that ring trick."

"A figure of speech." Reid dumped half the money out on the coffee table and stood. "It's about that time."

Connie stood and opened her arms. "And time for another group hug."

32

On the way home, Reid drove to Esteban's home improvement shop. She wanted to see how Gabriella's injured finger was healing and how she was adjusting to living in America.

Reid parked in front of the shop that shimmered in the morning sun with a new coat of white paint. She started toward the door but stopped. The van gleamed with a recent wax job, and a new set of tires shone shiny-black against the pavement. If Esteban had ended the business of being a criminal, the home improvement trade must be paying off.

The office was empty. Behind the door to the back, a circular saw's high-pitched whine slowed to a low-pitched whine as it bit into a piece of wood, like when her dad had used his circular saw. Several new samples of granite countertops leaned against a wall. The saw slowed further, as if it were a dying siren on an old police car on an older TV show, then stopped. "Anyone home? Esteban? Gabriella?"

Brushing sawdust from his arms, Esteban entered from the door to the back room. "Ahh, Señorita Reid." He removed earplugs. "I thought I heard someone. It's good to see you. Did you see my new paint and my new countertops I am now installing?"

"New tires on the van too. Is business picking up?"

"After I added new services it did. I have time now, since I do not have to ... well, you know."

"You must be doing well. It takes a lot of money to get a business going. Either that or you had more money hidden around here."

"What you took was all. Keep it if you still have it, or give it to someone in need, whatever you care to do. I have all the money I could ever want. If you will accept it, so will you."

Reid paused. After figuring out a use for the money packed in the Gold Wing, other than the thing at home, she was about to have more money to worry with? "How much exactly is all the money a person could want?"

"Let's sit and I'll tell you. Would you like something to drink? Gabriella made a fresh pitcher of agua fresca this morning." Esteban stuck his head in the door he had just come from. "Gabriella! Bring two glasses of agua fresca and come say hello to Señorita Reid."

Esteban sat at his desk while Reid took a chair across from him. "Is her finger healing well?"

"I had her apply for asylum so she could see a doctor. I told them she was my niece, that she had been kidnapped and tortured by the one of the cartels. When they saw what Martinez did to her finger, they did not hesitate. Her injury is healing well."

"I don't normally approve of lying, Esteban. In this case, I understand. You're doing a fine thing helping Gabriella."

"Thank you." He rubbed his chin. "But I wish I could have done so fine a thing long ago, by not helping Martinez with what he did to that young girl in El Paso. I meant what I said about that being my biggest regret. It was not—" Esteban lowered his eyes. "I cannot put into words how bad a thing it was. I had nightmares about it for years afterward. Even now, if I try, I can see her trying to get away."

"Then don't try. If she knew you like I know you, I think there's a chance she would forgive you. Since I gave you a worthless gun that night, I guess it didn't seem like I trusted you. Being cautious is in my DNA—it takes me a while to trust anyone."

"Are you saying you trust me now?"

"You did well that night, as well as anyone could've asked. Pete's not likely to thank you himself, but I'm thanking you now."

"No, Señorita Reid, thank *you*. I will always be grateful for how you helped me. As far as the money, why don't—"

The same door opened, and Gabriella bounced in. She wore a pink T-shirt with an American female Pop artist on the front, new jeans with holes ripped in them from the factory, and pink sneakers. "Uncle, did you say— Señorita Reid, it is so good to see you!"

"It's good to see you too, Gabriella. Wow, you look like a properly dressed young American woman already. Are you happy in America?"

"I am. If not for you and Esteban, who knows where I might be. Martinez might have grown tired of me by now. Whenever that happened, he either sold the girls or killed them. That is what the gardener told me."

"How about we not talk about Martinez. He'll never harm you or anyone else again."

"I will be glad to do that. Uncle, I was in the back and did not hear what you said. Did you need something?"

"I'm good," Reid said. "I need to hit the road."

"Thank you again, Señorita Reid."

Gabriella left, and Reid faced Esteban. "I think I may have figured out how you got the money you mentioned earlier. Go ahead and tell me. I'm dying to know if I'm right."

"You are one of most intelligent women I've ever had the pleasure of meeting, Señorita Reid. You already know, don't you?"

"You found those safes at Martinez's house and opened them, right?"

"It was much more difficult to find them than I thought it would be."

"Because they were hidden?"

"It wasn't hard to find them because they were hidden. It was hard to find them because of the ashes."

Reid tilted her head to one side. "What ashes?"

"The ashes that were all that was left of Martinez's house."

Reid slid forward in the chair. "Go ahead, this I gotta hear."

"A few days after all of us returned from Monterrey, I started thinking about Martinez's money. I drove back the following weekend. The cook and the maid and the gardener were standing outside, watching the main house burn. I asked what had happened. The gardener laughed and said they were celebrating because they would no longer have to work for a— Well, I won't say what he said. They were so happy, they joined arms and danced in a circle. They even grabbed my arm and pulled me along with them."

"Sounds like quite a party. What happened to Diego?"

"They cut the tape off and he left. He probably went to find work with the one of the cartels."

"The others set the house on fire?"

"Exactly. They left after it collapsed. I stayed overnight because it would be too hot to search for the safes. Even then it didn't cool off until the following night."

"How did you open them?"

"With a crowbar from one of the sheds."

"If you have all the money you'll ever need, why keep working?"

"Do you remember what I told you about my work?"

"Something about how you enjoy making things new again?"

"*Old* things new again. Now, since you have helped me and Gabriella, that is how we feel, like new again."

Esteban moved the chair and rug aside, opened the same safe Reid had opened the last time she was here, and took out a bag that resembled the one she had taken. "Now, for the money. "He placed it on the desk. "Come and see, Señorita Reid, this is for you."

Reid opened the cloth bag—to stare at more bundles of U.S. currency than she could easily count. "This looks like it's more than what I took from the safe before. There has to be at least one, two, three…" She continued counting. "There's fifty bundles here—500,000 dollars. Are you telling me Martinez *did* have a million dollars, and you're giving me *half?*"

"Oh, no, the rest is in the compartment in the van. It was so much, I had no place to put it. I have a larger safe coming for the back of the shop. I also need it for my business."

"What do you mean it was 'so much?'"

"There are five more bags like this in the van."

"What? That's … that's three million dollars!"

"And half is yours. May you use it in good health."

Reid dropped to the chair. What the hell was she supposed to do with a million and a half dollars?

Esteban laughed. "You look the same way I felt when I saw how much it was—white as if all the blood had left my face. I knew Martinez had a lot of money, but not that much."

"I don't—" Reid rubbed her forehead. "I don't know what to say."

"You don't have to say anything, Señorita Reid. "Do what you will with it. You could always use it to help others like I'm helping Gabriella. I plan to give some to the places in the city where women go to get away from their bad husbands."

"You mean shelters," Reid said. At this rate, including what Pete and Connie would donate, Laredo would have one of the nicest women's shelters in Webb County, maybe even in all of Texas.

On the way home, she considered what to do with the money. The options were endless, varied, and some thrilled her, like renting a house on the beach on the Outer Banks late next summer. There, as Pete's mom had said, she could have all the sparkling horizons she could ever dream of. She still wanted to help people. With so much cash on hand, those options were endless as well.

***

On the outskirts of Del Rio, the same billboard advertising Harry's Burgers loomed, so Reid stopped for lunch. The red booths, the red stools that would spin by the counter, the sizzle of a fresh hamburger patty hitting the grill, the wet crash of fries splashing into hot oil—everything was the same.

Menu in hand, Katrina stepped from the back.

And the waitress, darn it, was the same.

"Booth or bar, ma'am?"

Reid pursed her lips. Again with the ma'am?

After an outstanding meal that included fresh peach pie, minus any conflict with Katrina, thanks to Reid's black hair, she left the busy waitress a sizeable tip, hit the road, and nine hours later, pulled into her parents' driveway.

Bob as usual—she would have it no other way—met her at the fence door, April the poodle by his side. He welcomed Reid with a hug.

"You sure been gone a while, Pammy. I started to call a few times but figured you'd be alright. You have yourself some kinda big adventure out on the road?" Bob stood on tiptoe and brushed her hair aside on the top of her head. "What in the world did you do to your hair? You goin' two-toned?"

Reid gave his shoulder a slight shove. "Come on, Bob, don't you think black hair with red roots is sexy?"

"I, uh …" Bob blushed. "Don't be asking a man who feels like your second dad a question like that. It ain't proper."

Reid kissed his freshly shaven cheek. "Is that proper?" She wrinkled her nose. "Is that aftershave I smell? Have you found a nice cowgirl at the grocery, or at church?"

Bob rubbed his cheek. "None of those ladies had enough spirit for this old coot. I did find a bonafide cowgal at the VFW dance a couple of weeks ago. I was just headed out to pick her up and go for a bite. Care to join us?"

"I'm tired as can be, maybe another time. While I'm thinking about it, I want to invite you to a cookout. I'm inviting Carletta and Armando too. Invite your 'cowgal,' we'll have a great night. I have something I want to talk over with you. Carletta and Armando too."

"Sounds serious. Should I be worried?"

"The topic affects all of you, but it's nothing to worry about. In fact, it's a good thing."

"I've always been one for good things, like sippin' whisky on the porch with your dad. Any chance it could be something like that?"

"Hey, you never know, right?"

"So, you're handing me a mystery to wait for. I can do that. Let me know when and I'll give you a hand. It'll be like old times … well, without your mom and dad."

"You know as well as I do, they'll be right there with us, don't you?"

Bob kissed her cheek. "That I do, Pammy, that I do."

Reid unpacked and called Carletta about the cookout. Carletta said she looked forward to it, including how she might even allow Armando to have something other than "food for goats," since he was doing so well with his dieting.

* * *

The last day of May the following year, while the sun set behind North Franklin Peak, Reid stopped in the driveway beside the Honda Gold Wing, having finished a twenty-five-mile run.

Over the past year, she had cleaned the house, cleaned her guns, and returned to her exercise routine. Her calves ached at first, but within a week, her muscles cramped less at night and tired less with each run. Within a month, two miles became five. Within another month, five miles became ten. No doubt about it, hard work paid off, rewarding her with the grand total of a twenty-five-mile run and her best time ever.

Her phone vibrated in her pocket. It was Pete. "How's it going, Detective? Isn't Connie about to pop yet?"

"That's why I called."

"And?"

"*And* I wonder if I should keep you in suspense a little longer?"

"Since you two have been making me wait all these months to know the baby's sex, don't you think it's time you told me?"

Pete laughed. "It's gonna be a surprise, that's for sure."

"The ring trick was right, it's a girl?"

"Remember how Connie used your hair that time?"

"It went both—" Reid almost dropped the phone. "Twins? Connie had twins?"

"A boy and a girl. I'd say that ring trick was accurate."

"I don't know why we didn't think of that to start with."

"Mom did. Remember what she said when we told her?"

"That's right, she said grand*kids*, not grand*kid*. You still naming the girl after me?"

"Pamela, you mean?"

"Not funny, Detective."

"Yes, Reid, we're naming her Reid. We haven't decided on a boy's name yet. None of the names we were considering seem to fit, know what I mean? We have until Connie comes home."

"Only a day or so. Not much time."

"Tell me about it."

Reid could almost see him frowning.

After more discussion concerning the two baby's weight and length, Reid said good bye and gave the Honda's padded seat a rub. She pulled the clutch lever and ran her fingers over the freshly waxed surfaces, cool from sitting in the late afternoon shade. Could her faithful ride wait three more months? Since she still had things to do, it would have to. After that, she and the Honda would be ready to roll.

33

Labor Day weekend, after a traffic-filled drive along the Interstate 10 section of the El Paso to Laredo trip, Reid pulled into Pete and Connie's driveway. She beeped the Gold Wing's horn and killed the purring engine, giving her reliable companion a well-deserved rest.

Pete stepped out onto the porch. "What the—? You didn't tell us you bought a trailer. What are you hauling in that thing, skimpy dresses?"

"You wish. How are Mommy and the babies?"

Pete opened the door. "Come on in and see."

On the sofa, Connie sat with one dark haired baby nursing in her arms. The other slept in one of two matching bassinets by the coffee table.

"Whoa," Reid said, they're huge."

"They aren't that big." Connie looked up from the baby. "They're only three months old."

Reid laughed. "I meant your breasts."

"I'll be glad when they're back to normal. I don't understand why so many women want big breasts. Makes my back hurt."

Reid glanced at her own chest. "I can't see those on me either." She sat beside Connie. "The teal dress I brought won't fit you anytime soon."

"How about never. Since I'm nowhere near as tall as you. I can get it hemmed if I can get back into shape one day."

Reid aimed a thumb at Pete, who was sitting in a chair by the TV. "I bet that guy doesn't mind your new figure."

Pete winked. "No complaints here."

Reid stood to peek at the baby in the bassinette. "Who's who and what did you name the boy? I can't tell them apart."

The baby in the bassinette whimpered, and Pete picked him—or her—up. "This little lady is Reid."

Reid studied the baby Connie held, who had finished nursing and was now being burped. "And this," Connie said, "is Clancy."

"Isn't Clancy Irish? I thought you might have picked something more traditional, like … I don't know, something other than Clancy."

"See how hard picking a name is?" Pete sat with Reid in his arms.

Connie offered Clancy to Reid. "I need to run to the bathroom. Be right back."

Reid held Clancy in the crook of her elbow. As his dark brown eyes peered at her, he pursed his lips, blew a bubble, and frowned as he passed gas.

"Alright, Son," Pete said, "way to go."

Reid held Clancy up so she could look into his eyes. "Don't you listen to a thing that man says. No matter what he tells you, girls don't like it when a boy has gas around them, got that?" Clancy made a face resembling a stressed smile, blinked, and let Reid know that since he was all boy, he intended to ignore her advice.

"See there," Pete said, "got him trained already."

Connie returned. "Let me have that little man and see if he's still hungry." While she situated Clancy at her other breast, Pete placed the baby girl in Reid's arms. As she held her, Reid's namesake yawned and closed her eyes.

Reid kissed the feather-soft forehead. "The perfect little lady." She faced Connie. "What made you give Clancy his name?"

"After Pete called to tell you I delivered, we checked the internet for boy's names having something to do with the color red. I guess you already know your name is one of those. We wanted another name that had the same connection, so we picked Clancy."

"What's that connection?"

"It has the same 'red' meaning." Pete grinned. "It also has a connection to you."

"You gonna make me ask? What are you grinning about anyway?"

"It means 'red-haired warrior.' I see your red hair is back to being one of your most outstanding features, like it was when we met."

"I had the ends trimmed before I left home. Last of the black."

Connie placed the now sleeping Clancy in his bassinette. "Kind of short, isn't it?"

"Shoulder length works. I don't have to worry about keeping it tucked into my jacket to avoid tangles. No bangs though, thank goodness."

"I like your new jacket," Pete said. "Black and silver, pretty snazzy."

"A lot cooler too. It's vented so the air can flow in and out while I ride."

"Last time we talked," Connie said, "you mentioned how you had gotten your runs up to around twenty miles. What else have you been doing to keep busy?"

"Pete saw my new trailer—that was one. Another thing is getting my house ready for my new renters."

Connie's eyebrows rose. "Where are you going to live?"

"Yeah," Pete said, "that's a pretty big step. You plan to travel around on your bike forever?"

"No, Detective, not forever. Remember when I said I was going to North Carolina? That's my next stop. If I like the Outer Banks like I think I will, I'll rent a house on the beach for a couple of weeks. Then I'll get something a little—no, make that a lot—more reasonable. Roanoke Island, what the locals call Manteo, should have something in my price range."

"We have nice beaches in Texas. Why go all the way to the east coast?"

"To be honest, everything I've read about the area so far makes me feel connected to it. It's built up, but there are plenty of places that are nothing more than national seashore. Kind of wild and free, you know?"

"Sounds great," Connie said. "Just listening to you talk about it makes me want to see it too. How long will you stay there?"

"I'm taking life as it comes. I might get a job as a waitress, a life guard, who knows."

"What about the renters you mentioned?" Pete said.

"Remember Juan, the man I went to see in Chihuahua City? Him and his wife and their three-year-old son. His sister-in-law and his niece, Margarita, live there too. His sister-in-law has a baby, so it's a full house."

"Margarita worked at the hotel, right? How did you get everyone to America?"

"Remember Carletta, the lady who kept me when I was a kid? Armando—he's her husband—has a construction business. I asked him to sponsor Juan by giving him a job. It's not all that easy to get a work visa."

"That's a nice thing you're doing," Pete said. "What does the family think of America?"

"Juan and Bob hit it off right away. Juan promised to show him how to make homemade Mexican beer. The ladies like all the conveniences. Margarita wants to go to college to be a nurse."

"Sounds good. I was watching the news the other day. I saw where El Paso is expanding their women's shelter. Did Esteban's money have anything to do with that?"

"You didn't think I would let Laredo outdo my home town, did you? On your local news a few months ago, I saw where Laredo's women's shelter was doing the same thing."

"You must have missed the story about them getting new kitchen equipment. They announced that about a week after we sent in our donation of some of Esteban's money. They announced the expansion a few weeks later. We thought you might have donated the other half."

Reid wasn't about to bring up Esteban's name. His donation probably financed the expansion. "Wasn't me. I doubt sixty-five thousand dollars would build an expansion. Maybe you inspired another generous person who had reason to help women in need."

"If that's the case," Connie said, "how could the El Paso shelter expand?"

Reid suppressed a grin. "Another generous benefactor?"

"Regardless," Pete said, "as long as women are being helped to get back on their feet, that's what matters."

Reid stood and peeked at the two sleeping babies. Both sets of pink lips worked in and out as if they were still nursing. "You definitely have two cuties here. How are they at 3 a.m.?"

"Sounds like an offer to stay and help," Pete said.

"About a week. I want to get to North Carolina before bikini weather ends."

"If my body was bikini-ready," Connie said, "I might join you. Think Pete could handle the kids by himself?"

"Not unless he grows breasts."

Connie stuck out her tongue. "Yuck. I just got a visual in my head of Pete in a bikini and—"

"*And* you don't have to say another word."

Pete stood. "Before you" —he cleared his throat— "*ladies* abuse me anymore, I'm grabbing a beer. As far as me handling the kids, they would be a piece of cake compared to you two."

* * *

The following weekend, after enjoying seven days of diaper changing, feedings with bottled breast milk, and one night that consisted of two hours of holding a pillow over her head while the babies cried for who knew what reason, Reid stood by the Honda, ready to say her goodbyes.

Pete held Clancy while Connie held Reid. Reid kissed the baby's soft cheeks and smoothed their fine hairs down on their heads that smelled of baby shampoo, then tickled their feet while they kicked and spread their toes. "I'm going to miss you two." She swallowed." Your mom and dad too. I feel like I have another family, like Bob, Carletta, and Armando, but here in Laredo."

"You *are* family," Pete said. "But you have to take me for a ride on your bike to prove it."

Reid faced Connie. "He's been telling you a lot about when I stayed here. Did he tell you he asked me to take him on a ride back when I thought he had invited me over for something other than getting me to help rescue you?"

"He did?" Connie punched Pete's arm. "Must have slipped his mind. So far, everything he's told me, you instigated whatever it was. Like the night of the teal dress."

Reid laughed. "Sounds like a horror movie."

"If he had taken the bite—I mean bait—it would have been."

"Are you telling me the detective is a biter, or was that a slip?"

"Slip or not," Pete said, "I'd be a dead man either way."

"As far as the bike ride," Reid said, "I don't have another helmet." She paused. "I better get out of here before I cry. I haven't done that since about this time last year." She faced Connie. "Thank you for having me stay after our trip to Mexico. Those days with you and Pete are some I'll never forget. That was the most at peace I've been with myself in a long time."

Connie placed baby Reid in Pete's arms. "After that too, I hope."

"Like Pete's mom said, I'm ready to see those new horizons. How about a hug?"

Reid and Connie separated. Connie took the squirming babies from Pete. "I think these two are ready for brunch. Reid, you be safe out on the road. If anyone gets in your way, you know what to do."

Reid eyed Pete. "Even though I have my Glock on my hip, I won't be shooting them, will I, Detective?"

Pete raised an eyebrow. "Let's hope not. That can get a person involved in who knows what kind of drama."

Connie took the babies inside. Pete took a step closer to Reid. "Do I have to tell you how much I appreciate everything you did for us, when you could have just ridden away?"

"Glad to do it. I'm also glad to put an end to Martinez."

"Don't even say his name. The only memory I want to have of him is that he's a pile of bones in a Mexican desert."

"Amen to that," Reid said, meaning it. "Before I go, I have one last request."

"Don't tell me you want a kiss?"

Reid shook her head. "And to think there was a time when I thought you probably didn't have much of an ego. No, I want you to confess to seeing me naked in your hall when my towel fell off."

"Flesh-colored blur, honest."

"I wasn't a flesh-colored blur in your tub that day, was I?"

"Do you fault me for enjoying the site of a beautiful woman in my own bathroom?"

"I bet you haven't told Connie about that. What about the towel thing, you lie to me or not?"

"This from the woman who told my own mother how she liked her because she's a woman of mystery?"

"Don't go dragging your mother into this. When we drove up the other day to introduce her to her grandkids, she told Connie and me that only applied to women, not men."

"When did she say that?"

"When you went back to the car for the diaper bag. Tell the truth now, what did you see?"

Pete shrugged and handed her a pair of glasses from his pocket. She set them on her nose but only saw a blur. "There's nothing wrong with my eyes, meaning your glasses don't tell me a thing."

"If they did, the mystery would have been solved. Like you told Einstein the bartender that day, sometimes it's a lot more fun to *not* know than it is to know."

Reid hugged Pete. "Just like you'll never know how good it would've been if you hadn't turned me down that night in your guest room."

* * *

A couple of miles later, on Highway 59 East, as the wind fresh with the morning slipped under her face shield, Reid downshifted and pulled the rumbling Gold Wing onto the side of the road. Driving toward the sparkle of new horizons over the Outer Banks was a fine thing, but not with the rising sun in her eyes.

Sunglasses on, she twisted the throttle and pulled out onto the deserted highway.

She could almost smell the salt air.

Please enjoy the first chapter of Reid Stone: Red Rage, due out later in 2022.

Ellen drove by the bar. The lot was full, so she parked on the side of Beach Road and got out of her car. From her left, a steady wind tinged with the smell of salt blew off the Atlantic. Nags Head, North Carolina, her favorite place in the world, especially for a weekend break from college.

What sounded like live music—a thudding bass line with an electric guitar riff—thrummed through the bar's walls. Time for a drink. If a nice guy bought her one, all the better. Just to make sure, she checked her reflection in the passenger window of her car, made possible by a nearby streetlight. Lipstick applied, mascara touched up, brunette hair in a ponytail, snug jeans, modest cleavage peeking from her yellow blouse—each combined to guarantee at least a drink or two. If she started a new relationship after breaking up with that jerk of a boyfriend she had caught cheating on her last weekend, so much the better.

As she left for the bar door, her cell rang in the purse slung over her shoulder. The screen said it was her roommate from college. Away on a thirty-day trip to Europe, Ellen's parents lived in nearby Manteo, and her friend was there with a migraine. She swiped the phone's screen. "What's up, Lynn? Is your headache better and you want me drive back for you?"

"I just threw up. Does that sound like I want you to drive back for me?"

"Then why are you calling?"

"I know you're not over Tim, so be careful. You're way too trusting for bars filled with guys on vacation looking for girls."

Lynn, ever the worrying dorm mom. Ellen smirked. "Maybe I'll bring one home for you."

"And I'll throw up on him. Watch how much you drink. I'm not there to drive."

"Will do, Mom. Catch you later." Ellen ended the call and killed the power on the phone to stop Lynn from bugging her.

Outside the bar doors, she walked through a cloud of cigarette smoke from two guys. The guys watched her. One licked his lips.

Inside, the music blared from the band on a corner stage. Spotting an empty seat at the bar, Ellen hurried to it. The bartender, a young woman about her age, took her order of white wine. It came a moment later, and Ellen sipped.

She didn't care much for loud and crowded scenes but needed a change from being the downhome girl her parents approved of. Well, not *too* much of a change. Like Lynn had suggested, most of these guys were probably looking for a one-night stand, and Ellen preferred something more meaningful, especially before sex.

In front of the stage, a few couples danced. Tables filled the rest of the room. Booths lined the walls. Both were filled with all manner of customers. Most were young. Most were men. Most were probably on the hunt. But maybe, just maybe, there was a nice one mixed in with the crowd.

Conversations lashed back and forth: some about work, some about play, some about relationships, some about the music: a mix of rock and head banger.

And then there were the smells: aftershave, cologne, antiperspirant or the lack of it, evidenced by the hint of underarm order when a scruffy looking guy walked by.

Ellen sipped wine. Enjoying the vanilla finish, she noticed the smokers returning. One of the guys, a thin specimen with the fringe of dark beard lining his chin and upper lip, was shaking his head as if something were bothering him. The guy beside him, a jock type with huge biceps, patted the first guy's shoulder, possibly offering a sympathetic ear.

In Ellen's experience, someone was always going through a hard time. In the case of people her age, it usually had something to do with relationships. Her parents were great role models. Married for twenty-five years—the reason for their trip to Europe—they personified love. Lunch dates, walks on the beach at night—

something Ellen loved—and weekend strolls on Manteo's waterfront kept their love burning brightly.

She sipped wine again. Why couldn't a great guy like her dad come along and, as cliché as it sounded, sweep her off her feet?

The guy with the problem crossed the crowded floor and sat a few seats down from Ellen. The other guy joined him, patting his back this time. Whatever was bothering the first guy was really getting to him. They were well dressed, maybe professionals. Slacks, dress shirts, and loafers completed their attire. Almost twins but not. Almost planned but not. Were they brothers? Could be. Or maybe they worked together.

The bartender came over and took the guy's orders, returned with beers and a bowl of potato chips. Both crunched and drank, drank and crunched.

Bothered Guy rubbed his eyes like sand was in them. If he had lost a love, Ellen knew how he felt. She watched until she couldn't stand it, then sat beside him. "I'm sorry to ask, but are you okay?"

He wiped his eyes with a napkin. "I guess I look like a big wuss."

"Feeling sad enough to cry doesn't make someone a wuss. Can I ask what's wrong?"

"See there?" the other guy asked this guy. "There's plenty of nice girls around. You just have to know where to find them."

The comment struck Ellen as sarcastic. "I don't want to offend anyone, but nice girls *do* go to bars."

Bothered Guy faced her. "I'm Jamie. This musclehead next to me is Phil. I'm sorry if my crying is a pain."

Ellen told him her name. He rubbed his eyes again. Phil came over to Ellen. "He just lost his girlfriend. Would you believe her name was Ellen too?"

"I know the feeling," Ellen said. "I'm trying to get over a bad relationship myself."

Phil leaned close to Ellen's ear. "It wasn't a bad relationship," he whispered. "They were supposed to meet in Nags Head this weekend. He was gonna ask her to marry him, but she was killed in a car accident on the way here. When it happened, he called and asked if I could come and help him through it."

Ellen covered her mouth. "I'm—" She lowered her hand to Jamie's arm. "I'm so sorry, I didn't know."

Blinking, he faced her. "It's okay. I just— It's just— I mean, how often do we get to find our soulmates and lose them right at what's supposed to be our happiest time?" He started to touch Ellen's hand but didn't. "You remind me so much of her. The same eyes. The same cute nose. The same lips. She just got a job as a nurse. We met six months ago. I'm graduating next year with a business degree." He tugged his collar. "Phil and I work part time at a restaurant near school. That's why our clothes are alike. I was in a hurry to get her. He was too, after I called him. He's a great friend."

"Yep," Phil said, patting Jamie's back. "We're hard-workin' guys, slingin' food to the masses."

"Forget him," Jaime said, adding a smile that let Ellen know he was joking. A cute smile at that.

She touched his arm again. "Can I ask what Ellen was like? I love the beach and walking on it, especially at night. The way those ghost crabs run around still makes me squeal like a kid."

Jamie's eyes lit up. "Really? Ellen did that too." He shared a soft smile. "Wow, you made my night. I didn't think I'd be smiling again so soon."

"Good," Ellen said, returning the smile. "I'm glad I could help."

Phil nodded. "Cool. What if we took a walk on the beach in honor of Allie's memory? I'll pick up a twelve pack and some more chips and we can do it up right."

Ellen caught the name difference. Maybe Allie was Ellen's nickname? For some reason her inner radar went off at all the coincidences between her and Ellen. Regardless, what harm would a quick walk on the beach do? She told Jamie and Phil to meet her at the beach access parking lot about a quarter mile below Jennette's Pier. The pier's lights made stargazing a pain, not that the full moon would help. Regardless, when they were done walking, it would only be a short drive to Manteo and home.

Minutes later they arrived. True to Phil's word, he brought a twelve pack of beer and two huge bags of chips. Having skipped supper to keep trim, Ellen looked forward to both. With any luck,

Jamie would turn out to be the next man of her dreams—one who wasn't a jerk like her last boyfriend.

He turned a flashlight on, shined it at her feet, and waved her over. "I can't thank you enough for doing this."

Phil twisted the cap off a beer bottle and gave it to Ellen. "There ya go, ice cold." He opened the two bags of chips and gave her one. She took a handful, munched and swallowed, and drank the cold beer.

Overhead, the full moon illuminated the line of sand dunes to her left. On either side of the beach access parking lot, oceanfront rentals, lights on in most every window, dotted the landscape.

Ellen took Jamie's hand and led him to the steps over the dune. What a perfect night to take a walk on the beach with a nice guy.

About the Author

After a steady diet of Lee Child's *Jack Reacher* series, J. D. James, author J. Willis Sanders' alter ego, decided to give writing a thriller novel a shot with *Reid Stone: Hard as Stone.*

With comments from beta readers, such as "She's the woman every woman wants to be" and "When are you gonna write about that redheaded woman again?" J. D. knew *Reid Stone* was a character worthy of her own series.

Living in southern Virginia, J. D. often asks the question: what trouble can Reid Stone get into next, and what criminal can she remove from the human food chain?

To follow the author's work and to sign up to his newsletter, visit: https://jwillissanders.wixsite.com/writer